OF FIRE AND STONE

BOOK III OF
THE CARROWKEEL SERIES

NINA ORAM

Text Copyright © 2020 Nina Oram
Cover Art © 2020 Bede Rogerson
Map © 2020 Brian Rayner

First published by Luna Press Publishing, Edinburgh, 2020

www.lunapresspublishing.com

ISBN-13: 978-1-911143-88-8

For my nieces and nephews and their children:
Alannah, Amiee, Oscar, Monty and Mason.
Thanks to everyone for their love and support, but
especial thanks to Francesca and Luna, Bill & Denise,
Shell & Roy, Sam & Bri, Kathryn, Clare, Mum
and of course, Joe.

Contents

Chapter One	1
Chapter Two	3
Chapter Three	14
Chapter Four	22
Chapter Five	30
Chapter Six	43
Chapter Seven	49
Chapter Eight	57
Chapter Nine	65
Chapter Ten	74
Chapter Eleven	83
Chapter Twelve	95
Chapter Thirteen	101
Chapter Fourteen	111
Chapter Fifteen	119
Chapter Sixteen	128
Chapter Seventeen	134
Chapter Eighteen	144
Chapter Nineteen	152
Chapter Twenty	161
Chapter Twenty-One	173
Chapter Twenty-Two	183
Chapter Twenty-Three	193
Chapter Twenty-Five	200
Chapter Twenty-Six	206

Connacht

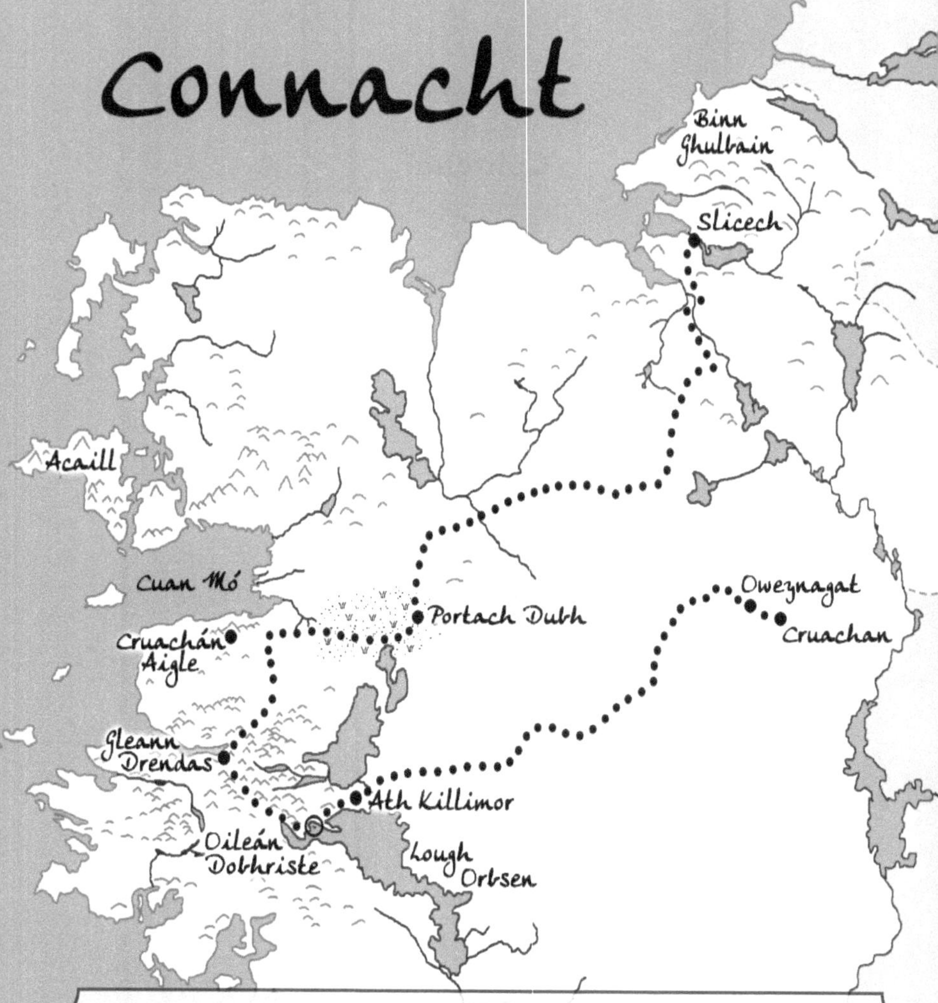

LEGEND:

Binn Ghulbain - BenBulben (Mountain)

Slicech - Sligo

Acaill - Achill

Cuan Mo - Clew Bay

Cruachan Aigle - Ancient name for Croagh Patrick. (Mountain)

Gleann Drendas - Drendas' Valley, fictional valley located on site of Leenane village

Oilean Dobhriste - Sacred Isle (fictional)

Ath Kilimor - fictional.

Lough Orbsen - Ancient name for Lough Corrib

Oweynagat - Cave of the Cats.

Cruachan - Ancient Celtic city, remains now known as Rathcroghan

Chapter One

For Malachy, everything spun crazily. Bathed in green light, his whole body tingled. Remembering Seamus' words in the tomb, he thought of Jasmine, his mind clinging to her as if she were the last thing in the world. He turned and turned, his stomach churning, until he forgot everything else in the jumbled, chaotic spinning. Abruptly, it stopped; a light flashed, its brilliance half-blinding him, and then he was through and out the other side, falling through wind and rain. He hit the ground, his body sprawling, the scent of wet earth and grass in his nostrils. He rolled over and, feeling the rain on his face, opened his eyes. Stars twinkled, the sheer volume of their number lighting up the sky and the ground around him. He staggered to his feet, breathing heavily, and pulled his cloak tight, lifting the hood over his head. Trees lined three sides; he guessed he was on the edge of a forest, although it was hard to tell, even with the light from the stars.

"Jasmine! Seamus!"

No answer. Straining to hear over the wind and rain and the rustling trees, he called again. The wind blew harder, tore through the trees with a whistling, unearthly howl, as if to mock his efforts. He groaned. How stupid was he? He probably wasn't even in the right time, and, even if he was, Seamus and Jasmine could be anywhere. Who knew how much time had passed since they arrived? He might never find them. He might be stuck here forever.

He shivered. Despite the wind, the rain seemed to be easing, which was just as well, as it was already beginning to soak through the thick wool of his cloak. But it didn't solve the problem of what to do next. He looked around him. Reason said he should find some shelter inside the forest and wait for the night to pass, but that meant getting even further behind Seamus and Jasmine. The other option was to turn away from the forest and look for some kind of settlement and hope to find Jasmine and Seamus there. He frowned, undecided, and then abruptly the weather decided for him. The clouds parted and a large, low moon appeared, illuminating the ground all around him. He was right; he was stood on the edge of a forest, the ground sloping down towards what looked like a river, shining silver in the moonlight. If this was still Sligo, or rather where Sligo was going to be, the river had to be the Garavogue, and where there was a river, there had to be – something, but hopefully it would be people living beside fresh, running water. For a moment, he imagined a fire, warmth and Jasmine's face smiling at him. Then, fixing his eyes on the ground, he began to walk towards it.

Wide, the river flowed silently, its smooth, dark surface capturing the moon and reflecting it back. Following its flow, Malachy walked along a riverbank flattened into a rough path. A path meant people, possibly living somewhere nearby. Encouraged, he walked faster, and soon dark shapes appeared, tall with round, peaked tops. He grinned to himself. The sky was becoming lighter, turning from dark blue to a dark grey, as dawn approached. He was almost there. Ahead, a thick, high fence, made from roughly chopped wood, encircled round houses, their roofs made of some kind of thatch. The path turned away from the river and moved towards the village. It circled the fence and he followed it to what he hoped would be the entrance. A tree lay to his right, its trunk over a metre thick and its canopy high and wide. He passed under it. Something flashed towards him; he glimpsed an arm, a torso, and then his legs were kicked from underneath him and he fell hard to the ground. Winded, struggling to breathe, he watched helplessly as a man leant over him. Fingers grabbed his hair, twisting as their owner tilted back his head and pressed a knife, the blade shining in the half-light, to his throat.

Chapter Two

Just two days before, Jasmine and Seamus had stepped into the light and Malachy, Grainne and the abbey in Sligo had disappeared. Spinning furiously, their bodies flung backwards by the velocity, their tightly clutched hands were the only thing keeping them together. Light danced across her face, down her arm and across to Seamus and back again, giving them both a strange, greenish glow. Iomlan was singing inside her with the throbbing power of a whole orchestra. Filling her head, it echoed through every part of her and lost and entranced, even Malachy was forgotten. The same was happening to Seamus; she could feel it even if she'd hadn't been able to see it in his face. His features alive with rapture, one brief, glorious taste of the sublime. It strengthened him, reinvigorated his mind and body after Cormac's attack. And then, all too quickly, it was over. A brief flash of blinding light and they were through and out the other side, tumbling as they hit the ground. The singing stopped, but she could still hear it; thin, ghostly, like an echo or the dying notes of an organ lifting up to the rafters.

A warm breeze floated across her face. She opened her eyes and could see nothing but a blur. She felt dislocated. Her body, shocked and disorientated, was reduced to a heartbeat, like a baby born into the harsh, noisy world. And then her eyes cleared, and even the echo stopped as the world came rushing back.

Men, too many to count, their feet and hair flying, ran towards them, carrying weapons: swords, spears, axes and long knives. They shouted as they ran, bellowed at the top of their lungs, the noise deafening, primeval. Jasmine froze, unable to process what was happening. Her mind registered blue sky, a forest to her left and right and a distant figure dressed in a long black cloak. Then the men were on top of them, weapons swinging. Seamus reacted instantly. Abandoning all concern for his opponents, he threw them backwards, turned them, twisting, arms flaying, into one another. Weapons clanged; metal sliding and scraping. Blades, spikes and spears pierced flesh and dug into limbs, sending blood splattering and filling the air with shrieks of pain. More came, leaping over the fallen and charging, but Seamus was ready. His Iomlan flashed, sending them tumbling. Jasmine's ears rang, everything happening around her with dizzying speed, but now new men were behind them, their numbers creeping from the forest. One, axe swinging, leapt towards Seamus, but, finally reacting, Jasmine knocked him away. Iomlan burst out of her, surging over the men like water released from a dam, sending them flying. The man with the axe jumped to his feet, aimed his blade towards Seamus' neck, but she grabbed at it with Iomlan, and pulling it down and around, drove it hard into his thigh. With a loud scream, he dropped the axe and fell to the ground, blood pumping. Behind him, came a second wave. Turning to meet them, Jasmine gave a shout of her own, as loud and wild as the power coursing through her. Joining Seamus, she stood unflinching against the human tide, feeling her body tremble with excitement.

*

The fight ended as quickly as it started. The men who were able were beginning to back away, retreating into the trees. Of Ellyllon there was no sign. Blood pounded in her ears, Iomlan swirled and swirled, eager for more. Her head singing with elation, the urge to send Iomlan after them, to cut them down and punish them was too strong. She focussed.

"Jasmine!" Seamus' shout cut through the red mist in her brain.

Panting, her chest heaving, she forced Iomlan down. One hand pressing his stomach, Seamus gazed at her and suddenly he looked old, shattered; his body drooping with tiredness and his eyes stricken.

Fool; old and weak.

Jasmine pushed the thought away. It wasn't hers. Sneering, dripping with contempt, it couldn't be. Afraid, she stretched out her hand towards him, telling herself it was him that needed reassurance. The air behind him stirred; Ellyllon appeared, his hand poised and his arm thrusting.

She threw Iomlan at him, already knowing she was too late. Ellyllon's body arched in pain and she heard him hiss. His arm was still thrusting, only Seamus wasn't there; he was moving, spinning around to face him. Ellyllon jerked, his body spasming. He cried out as he was pulled forward and back, as if caught between two forces, Jasmine's from the front and an unknown attacker from behind. Another spasm and his attacker stepped out from behind a tree. Slight, he was dressed in a tunic so long it could have been a robe, his long black hair braided and tied intricately to his head. Piercing blue eyes shone out of a long black beard and moustache. In his right hand he held a sword.

"Daire!" Ellyllon hissed, giving him a look of pure hatred.

His body flopped forward. He glared at Jasmine and then, abruptly, disappeared.

"Come," the man called Daire said, beckoning with his hand. "Quickly. He will bring others."

He spoke Irish. Sort of. Seamus and Jasmine looked at one another.

"Come!" He beckoned again, looking about him, as if anticipating a second attack. Seamus moved first, then Jasmine. Confident now that they would follow, Daire sheathed his sword and turning, slipped between two trees.

*

Staying just ahead, Daire led them through the forest. Weaving between trees, they scrambled through the undergrowth, not so much as following a path as creating one. The forest creaked and rustled around them, a myriad of sounds that had Jasmine glancing back, half-expecting to see what was left of Ellyllon's men come creeping towards them. But there was no one there; no glimpse of an arm or the side of a face as the men flitted from tree to tree. Daire and Seamus were getting ahead of her; she was losing them. She sped up, had almost caught up with them, when she stumbled over a tree root. She grabbed a branch, steadying herself as Daire and then Seamus skirted a holly bush. She followed them past the holly and stepped into a clearing. In the centre a second man sat astride a horse, holding the reins of three others. His face calm, he watched them approach.

"Ferdia." Daire announced him, with a wide sweep of his arm.

Wide and tall, Ferdia was the physical opposite of Daire. He reminded Jasmine of Brennan, only without the muscles, the broad cheeks and flat nose, and Viking blond hair. Cut roughly and a shade lighter and shorter than Daire's, his dark brown hair was twisted into a single plait. His beard and moustache shared the same rough cut. A sword and scabbard hung from one side of a wide leather belt. Thrust deep in the other was a small horn made of bone.

The two men clasped hands and looked deep into each other's eyes.

"We will ride," Daire said, breaking away first. He took the reins and, dividing them, held out two pairs to Seamus. "Mount."

Without a word, Seamus took them, passing one set on to Jasmine. Daire mounted, watching while they did the same.

"Do not speak." Putting his finger to his lips, Daire gave them a meaningful look before nodding to Ferdia.

Riding in single file, they followed Ferdia as he led them through the forest. No one spoke. Seamus was protecting them, stopping Ellyllon from following. Jasmine could feel the gentle rhythm of his Iomlan, but if the two men sensed it, they showed no sign. Daire, of course, had Iomlan, but she couldn't sense anything from Ferdia; if he had any power, it was well-hidden. But who were they and what did they want? They'd been waiting for them, that much was obvious, and just like Ellyllon had known to expect them. *Wait a minute.* The horse beneath her kept going, its head and neck plodding. How did they know they were coming?

Above the trees, the sky darkened and rain began to fall, the drops bouncing through leaves and branches and dripping softly down. Ferdia said something and he and Daire stopped. Turning in the saddle, they watched and waited for Seamus and then Jasmine to join them.

"With rain, night comes early," Daire explained. "We will sleep here, Seamus and Jasmine."

Jasmine's mouth dropped. "How do you know our names? Or where to find us?"

He grinned. "I was sent to find you. The prophecy speaks of the Three and Ellyllon spoke your names: Seamus, Jasmine and Malachy." His grin faded. "Where is the third?"

Jasmine swallowed and looked away.

"Malachy didn't come," Seamus replied, his voice casual. Shifting in his saddle, he gave Daire a shrewd look. "You know Ellyllon and he definitely knows you. Why are you helping us? What do you want?"

"I will tell you, but you are my charges and first you must sit, eat and rest."

He dismounted and, after a moment's hesitation, Seamus followed. Jasmine looked at Ferdia, and when he didn't move, she threw her leg over her saddle and slipped to the forest floor.

*

While Daire started a fire with a few sticks, Ferdia prowled the forest floor, looking for firewood. Sitting down next to Seamus, Jasmine watched Ferdia flit between the trees. It was on the tip of her tongue to offer him help, but Seamus looked so tired, his face drawn and pale, that she was reluctant to leave him. Whatever strength travelling inside the portal had given him, the fight and their flight through the forest had taken away again. The fire lit, Daire sat back.

"Ellyllon came to my village half a moon ago, in the time of shadows."

"He means dusk," Seamus murmured quietly to Jasmine.

"It is the time of the demon, the dark Gods," Daire continued, seeming not to notice. "Sat in the light of the fire, we drank to Lugh's health and the ground before us was empty. I lowered my cup and a dark, hooded figure stood before us. He lowered his hood, showed us his black, empty eyes and even our bravest warriors were fearful. He lifted his hands and the men fell back. Seeing them, he smiled. Eyes, gleaming in a face as white as death, fixed on our Chieftain, Garach, and he began to speak."

Daire gestured as he talked, telling his story as much through his hands, the expression on his face, as he did with words. He was a natural storyteller, Jasmine realised.

"He spoke long into the night and, as the sun rose, word was sent to the chieftains to the east and west. I am Daire, son of Drendas and druid to the village of Slicech and the tribe of Garach, my word valued above all others, until he came. He spoke and they could not help but heed, for I sensed the power in his words, his voice. He spoke of a time beyond the life of these forests, of a time when all men will hold a power greater than magic, the power to fly like a bird, or swim like a fish, to hold unimaginable riches in one hand or to live far beyond their allotted time. Lastly, he spoke of his need for aid and a future that would not come to pass without the warriors of Erin."

He paused. Ferdia was back, carrying a huge armful of wood. Bending over, he let the load drop next to the fire, then, kneeling down, began to build up the fire. Daire watched him, but his eyes were unfocussed, unseeing. Jasmine glanced at Seamus, but his whole attention was on Daire. After a moment, he shook himself and stirred.

"They believed him?" Seamus asked, leaning forward.

"Yes, for he told them their names would ring out in the glory of their deeds, never to be forgotten. What warrior could resist?"

"And you?"

Daire smiled, his face tight. "I am no warrior. I follow the teachings of Drendas and the path of the Goddess. His words had no power over me. He spoke of man holding power over the earth, the sea and the sky. It cannot be so; there must be harmony between all things. Druid lore and the Goddess demand it. He lies, twists the truth as a new baby feeds; without end."

Seamus nodded and Jasmine, watching and listening, remembered Seamus telling her something similar. His version of the world was more sophisticated, using science instead of faith, but the central tenet, an almost spiritual belief in life and the natural world, was the same.

"Not all druids follow the Gods. One, Cathbad, from Connacht's nothern lands, follows a darker path. He has become Ellyllon's second, his advisor and a bridge between him and the clans. I vowed my allegiance, for I could see no other vow would be tolerated," Daire continued. "I had no wish to flee, and I thought to learn more of what he planned."

"And did yer?" Seamus asked eagerly.

He shook his head. "Only of his wish to unite the druids and their chieftains under his word, his lore. And, soon, three would come to challenge him."

"So, you were waiting for us?!"

"I hoped to ally myself with you." He paused, giving Seamus a strange look, "The Druid, Drendas, foretold the coming of the Three just as he foretold the coming of Ellyllon. He told me I should find you and bring you to him."

"Who is this druid, Drendas?"

"He is the wisest and the most powerful druid in all of Connacht. He is my father."

"Did he say why he wanted you to bring us to him?"

"No. He said only that you would come and that I should bring you to him."

Seamus watched Ferdia settle himself. "Your father has got a lot right, to be fair, but he's wrong about the Three. Malachy's not coming. He chose to stay. Without Iomlan, he's no way to follow us." He paused, waiting for Daire to argue, and when he didn't, he turned to Jasmine. "But I don't understand why Ellyllon would want to align himself with Irish druids? How would it help him get his revenge?"

Jasmine looked away, trying to think.

"He doesn't have power of his own. Maybe he wants to use theirs?" she offered.

"Of course, that's it!" Seamus cried. "Well done, Jasmine!"

She flushed with pleasure. Ferdia caught her eye and gave her an encouraging smile. Embarrassed, she grinned back.

"Out and out war between the tribes and druids of Ireland and Britain," Seamus was saying excitedly, "would destroy the Druid hierarchy."

Jasmine's face fell. "But won't that change history?"

"It will. And with the British druids gone, or, like their Irish cousins, loyal to Ellyllon, I've no doubt he'll turn his attention to Europe. He'll change everything, the whole of history, with himself reigning supreme.

He'll be like a god, with total power."

Total power. Exactly what Ellyllon wanted, what he craved. Only he still wouldn't have Iomlan, still wouldn't feel it coming from within.

"Seamus, I think he wants more than power." She stopped, realising suddenly that she hadn't told him about Ellyllon, the things he'd said to her inside the abbey. There hadn't been time.

He looked at her, as if struck by her tone. "Go on."

She shifted uncomfortably, conscious of Daire and Ferdia staring. "I think he wants to have Iomlan again. Inside the abbey, Ellyllon talked to me, and I realised, for the first time, er, he misses Iomlan."

"Misses Iomlan?"

"You were right all along; he doesn't have power, well, not much. He said the druids hadn't managed to take it all; he was too powerful. I don't understand how it works, but he doesn't have Iomlan like you and me. He misses it, craves it, how it feels, y'know, inside. Like losing part of yourself. He didn't use Cormac just to set a trap for us, he used his power too, only he got Cormac to divert it, to flow it through him, just so he could, er, feel it."

She took a breath, conscious that she'd rattled it out. For a few minutes, no one spoke. Ferdia's fire crackled in the silence.

"I never thought – but why wouldn't he miss it?" Seamus wondered softly, almost to himself. "It was part of him. John still feels it, so why wouldn't Ellyllon?"

John. She'd almost forgotten he'd had Iomlan. He seemed so far away, was so far away, her mum too. The two of them part of another life, another reality. One with another, impossibly young, Jasmine.

Daire lent forward. "Iomlan?"

"Yes, it's what we call the druid's power. I thought – why, don't you?"

"No, magic has no need for a name, it is. You believe Ellyllon has no magic?"

"From what Jasmine is saying, no, not like us. He was once a druid, but in punishment for his crimes, his magic was taken from him. He has some power, but it is – limited. To live he feeds off our young, when the magic is still new."

Daire frowned as he struggled to follow Seamus' meaning. "But this is a corruption of our ways. How can a druid be made so?"

"I don't know. But as long as he feeds, we can't kill him. And the more he speaks, the more will follow him."

The fire flared as the flames caught the larger sticks. While they'd talked the forest had darkened as dusk approached. Ferdia scrambled to his feet and went over to the horses.

Daire's eyes glittered. "You must speak with my father. He will know how to stop him."

He glanced across at Ferdia who was carrying a sack back to them.

"Yes," Ferdia agreed, speaking for the first time. "Drendas will know."

"Where he is? Is he far?"

"To the southwest," Daire replied. "At the sea mouth below Mweelrea."

"Mweelrea's in Connemara. Sea mouth – you're talking about Leenane!"

"Leenane? I know not of such a place."

"It doesn't matter, I know where ya mean. It'll take too long to get there. We haven't time; we have to stop Ellyllon before he masses his army."

"But as we speak, druids ride to him, bringing with them their clan's fiercest warriors. Others will follow, for they do not know he hides his true nature. I would speak with them, but I fear they would not listen. But they would listen to my father, and only on his word will they stand with us."

"So what are you suggesting? We amass an army of druids of our own?"

Daire stared at him. "Can you best them alone? For I could not."

"The enemy of my enemy is my friend," Ferdia interjected. "We must unite against him, else old friends become enemies."

Seamus sighed heavily and glanced at Jasmine again, his question unspoken.

"What else can we do?" she asked helplessly. "They're right; we can't fight Ellyllon and all the Irish druids together. And without Daire's help, he might've killed you."

"Ah, it's not that easy to kill this old luthramon. But yer right. Ellyllon bet on us following him, so he knows we won't stop. Maybe that druid army of his isn't just for the Druid Council."

"Ellyllon's influence is as the minnow; to attack my father would turn the druids against him, but as his influence grows—"

He let it hang. Looking from one to the other of them, he waited, expectant.

"We'll go with you and talk to your father."

Daire smiled and nodded. "It is as he foretold. Come, we must eat, rest, for tomorrow we ride."

After they'd eaten, Seamus nudged her and indicated with his head and the two of them got to their feet and wandered over to the horses. Ferdia and Daire watched them go, but neither said anything.

"We need to talk," Seamus murmured as he led her to a spot behind the horses. "It's about Drendas."

He glanced over her shoulder and moving in close, continued. "We know nothing about him and only have Daire's word that he'll help us against Ellyllon."

She took that in. "You think it's a trap?"

"No, I don't think so, or I'm not sure." Seamus rubbed at his face irritably. "I just can't help but think this is all too convenient. Daire appearing just in time to save me, and he just happens to be with the first tribe Ellyllon meets, and his father just happens to be the only druid who will stand against Ellyllon."

Jasmine frowned. When he put it like that…

"Even if Drendas is standing against Ellyllon, how do we know we can trust him? He might be the same as Ellyllon, or something even worse?" He sighed. "I don't think we have a choice. If there's even the smallest chance that what Daire is saying is true, then we have to get to his father. All I'm saying is keep ya wits about ya; don't trust anyone." He grinned suddenly. "Except me, of course."

"What about Malachy? Do you believe what Daire said, about the Three?"

"No, of course not. Drendas obviously fancies himself as a bit of soothsayer and he's got his son well-trained. It is odd though. I didn't think of it before, but you, me and Malachy, we are three, and three is a potent number in Celtic beliefs. In a lot of beliefs, to be fair."

"So, you do believe it!"

"No, I didn't say that!" He snapped, but almost immediately regretted it. "I'm sorry, Jasmine, I shouldn't take it out on you. But I don't like it. Every time I think we're getting ahead, I find out Ellyllon's been pulling the strings all along." He shook his head. "I'm wore out. I'm too old for all this killing, but I can't think of what else to do."

"It's OK, neither can I." She wanted to say she understood, that he almost died, that he was still weak, recovering, but she couldn't seem to find the words.

Seamus smiled ruefully. "Daire's right; we need rest. Both of us. A good night's sleep and we'll feel better in the morning."

"Yeah." Impulsively, she threw her arms around him.

For a moment, he froze, as if caught by surprise that it should be her comforting him, and then, pressing his face tight to hers, he hugged her back.

*

Later that night, curled up in her cloak, Jasmine tried to sleep, but it just wouldn't come. Seamus, snoring gently beside her, had gone out like a light, his body and mind exhausted. Dark; the moon and stars lost behind thick cloud, the only light came from the low fire. Maybe it was just her imagination, but in the stillness of the night, the noises of this forest seemed louder. Every sound magnified: the creak of a tree, the wind through the leaves, the soft pad of footsteps or snuffle of a nose as an animal came creeping. Keeping watch, Daire used his Iomlan to hide them, his protection allowing Seamus to relax and to sleep. Jasmine turned over. He probably needed days of rest, not just one night. At least with Daire he got that one night; without him, he wouldn't even have had that. Of course she could've done it just as well, but she doubted that Seamus would've let himself go like that if it were her doing it. After everything, he still didn't trust in her or her ability.

The end of a tree root was poking into her side. Uncomfortable, she shifted until she found a better spot. She couldn't deny he felt responsible for her. It seemed like years ago, but hadn't he promised John he'd protect her? She thought of Ellyllon's horde, the shout they'd made as they'd descended on them and the battle that had ensued. But how could he have known then what they'd face? He couldn't protect her from everything any more than she could protect him.

Turning again, she pulled her cloak even tighter around her. Images flashed through her head, details of the battle she hadn't even realised she'd seen. Blood, broken bodies and faces twisted in fear and pain. Seeing them should repulse her, make her feel sick to her stomach, but she felt nothing apart from a cold dispassion. Maybe it wasn't just her physical body Seamus should be worried about; it was her soul, for he'd seen what she was going to do. Without him, his intervention, she'd have mown down the retreating men and murdered them as they lay helpless on the ground. *Bloodlust.* The word sprang into her mind, and she couldn't deny that it fitted. Caught up in the heat of battle, it was as if she'd wanted to kill and keep on killing. Like she was enjoying it. Having Iomlan had obviously changed her, but what if it were still changing her? Ellyllon believed it was still growing inside her, even though it wasn't supposed to do that. Maybe there was something wrong with her, her connection to Iomlan? Or maybe she wasn't strong enough? Unless… she went cold. If Ellyllon was right, and Iomlan was still growing, maybe it was becoming too strong for her?

And if that was the case, how far could it grow, without the balance tipping away from her, or cancelling her out all together? Iomlan had already twice taken control of her. In the end, when it had finally stopped growing, who would control who?

Chapter Three

Ferdia and Daire woke them at dawn. Jasmine's head was thick from lack of sleep, but Seamus seemed a lot better. He'd lost the haggard look, although his eyes were still tired, and he chatted brightly to Daire and Ferdia over breakfast. Jasmine tried to listen, but she couldn't stop thinking of last night and the thoughts that had run through her head.

"Jasmine, time to go."

A hand touched her shoulder and she looked up. Seamus was bent over her.

"Are you alright?" he asked then, concerned.

She shook herself. "Yeah, just didn't sleep very well."

"That's all it is?"

"Yeah, course." He had enough to deal with. She tried to reassure him with a smile, but he didn't look reassured, so she tried another tack. "I was thinking of Malachy."

His shoulders relaxed. "Don't be worrying about him, he's fine." He glanced at Daire and Ferdia moving towards the horses. "He'll be with Grainne and Brennan, still trying to learn how to hold that sword."

She laughed, part of her knowing it would be expected. "Yeah, you're right."

Smiling back, he patted her shoulder. "Come on, we'd best not keep them waiting."

Pleased she'd managed to reassure him, she pushed the thoughts of last night away. It was just the shock of the battle coming out in midnight terrors. Understandable, and not really surprising, she told herself as they joined Daire and Ferdia next to the horses.

"Ferdia will lead you south," Daire said quickly.

Seamus' eyes narrowed. "And where will you be?"

"I will be here."

"But Ellyllon saw you help us!" Jasmine exclaimed. "It isn't safe."

"There are those in the tribe who are still loyal to me; I will be well. But I must wait for the third."

Jasmine and Seamus looked at one another; for a moment, she couldn't understand what Daire meant, and then it clicked.

"Malachy? You're waiting for Malachy?"

"I told you last night, Malachy's not coming," Seamus protested. "He chose to stay."

"And I gave my father my vow. When the Three came, I would bring them to him."

"But—" Seamus stopped, seemed perplexed by Daire's serene, unwavering certainty.

"He will come. But I will wait three days, no more," Daire continued, looking between them. "Cathbad knows Drendas is my father. He and Ellyllon will try to stop you reaching him. Watch for them, and the druids and chieftains that follow him. Ferdia will guide you. Listen to him and you will reach my father, for there is no better guide, no better hunter. Now, go, quickly." Waiting for Seamus and Jasmine to mount, he turned to Ferdia, "Ride safe, my love."

Embracing, they kissed long and tenderly.

"May the Goddess protect you." Ferdia touched his cheek and they parted.

Ferdia glanced at Jasmine and, conscious that she was staring, she blushed and looked away. The two of them mounted their horses.

"Dagda ride with you." With a wave, Daire turned his horse and, slipping between the trees, disappeared.

*

With Ferdia leading, they headed south again, following a narrow, earthen road through the trees. The land, almost completely covered with forest, was even wilder, its vegetation thick and untouched. They saw and heard no one. In scattered settlements, the Celtic tribes seemed almost lost inside the country's vast forest. There were only the trees, their branches stretching upwards, their soft, green canopies rustling gently, soothing and comforting as a mother's murmur. Her eyes half-closing, Jasmine listened to it and felt strangely at home. Gone were the harsh, brittle metals of the modern world, the bewitching light of technology. Beneath the green, the warm scent of earth and moss all around her, this was where she belonged...

She crept forward, moving stealthily, her hands parting fern and hogweed as she stepped. Inside the clearing, a doe, its light brown hide speckled with white, lifted its head and stiffened. She stopped, but it was too late; with one jump, the doe was away, bouncing effortlessly through the trees. Quick as a flash, she focussed,

…Jasmine stirred. Her horse had slowed and Seamus and Ferdia were some way ahead. Kicking her heels, she urged her horse faster, catching them up. Seamus turned as she approached but, to her relief, didn't say anything. Slotting in between them, she turned the image of the doe in her mind. There was a quality to the image; it felt like a memory, but it couldn't be. It wasn't hers and it couldn't be Iomlan's. Iomlan wasn't sentient; it couldn't have memories. Was this another sign of Iomlan's growing dominance?

Stop it, she told herself quickly. *It's not helping.*

"A stream lies to the east. There the horses will drink and rest," Ferdia said suddenly.

A few minutes later, he left the road and led them to the edge of a small stream. Leaving the horses to drink, they sat together under a huge oak tree and rested. Not for long; fifteen minutes and already Ferdia was up and moving towards his horse.

Regaining the road, they travelled for a half a mile or so then turned to the west, heading first towards Clew Bay then on to Connemara. There was no road, just the vague outline of a rough path, but still Ferdia led them expertly through the forest.

"How long have you known Daire?" Seamus asked Ferdia.

"Since I was a boy. My mother served Drendas."

"So you know Drendas well?"

Ferdia nodded. "I was raised in his house. My mother was from Ulster, daughter of Condere. My father was a warrior in the tribe of Noisiu. Killed before they wedded, I was birthed into dishonour. Daire's mother died birthing and Drendas offered my mother sanctuary if she would care for him and the infant. It was an honour. It saved my mother's shame, for Noisiu and my grandfather feared to insult a druid."

Seamus frowned. "So you were brought up brothers?"

Ferdia shook his head. "No, never brothers. My mother is of noble birth, but Daire is the son of a mighty druid. I would not have spoken of my love had not Daire spoken of his."

"And Drendas approved?"

"Yes." Ferdia glanced at Jasmine. "He told Daire he had chosen well, for my heart is strong. Stronger even than my arm." He flexed it, as if to show Seamus exactly how strong it was.

Seamus' lips twitched. "And your mother?"

"She died of the fever. Not even Drendas' art could save her."

"I'm sorry for your loss." Seamus sobered instantly. Ferdia shrugged. "She sits with Dagda, bathed in his light."

"Ah, that's good," Seamus replied awkwardly.

*

The afternoon lengthened. "Jasmine?" Seamus said suddenly, reining in his horse.

She pulled up alongside him. He looked wrecked, with dark shadows under his eyes. One hand rubbed at his stomach, as if trying to ease its pain.

"I'm wore out. I don't seem to have any energy. Could you take over, keep us hidden?"

"Yeah, of course. Are – are you alright?"

"I'm grand." He smiled, blatantly lying.

Watching him, she focussed, spreading Iomlan over them like a net. His body still recuperating from the wound that had almost killed him, he would obviously be weakened for some time. Her instinct was right. Didn't he have enough to worry about without her sharing her childish fancies? She had to focus and stay strong; it was down to her now. With Seamus' strength depleted, they were going to need all the power she had.

They rode for another hour. Keeping a close eye on Seamus, Jasmine noticed his body was beginning to droop and his head nodding listlessly.

"We will rest," Ferdia said, and she knew he'd seen it too. "I know of a place nearby."

Lifting his head, Seamus nodded. They passed a thick, dense patch of willow. Following Ferdia, they turned left. Around them the forest thinned as the ground began to rise. Low in the sky, the sun played peekaboo through the branches. They hit a ridge and the trees opened up, showing them a high, rocky outcrop. They rode over to it.

"We rest here tonight," Ferdia said, dismounting.

"What? I thought we were just taking a break," Seamus protested, staying where he was. "We'll lose too much time. We should keep going."

Ferdia's jaw tightened. "I gave my word I would guide you. We rest here tonight."

Tethering his horse to a branch, he moved away. Seamus looked at Jasmine.

"I'm really tired, Seamus. Can't we do as he says?" she lied smoothly.

"I suppose so."

Awkwardly, he dismounted, Jasmine following.

"I'll tether them," she offered quickly, grabbing the reins off him. "You sit down."

For a moment, she thought he was going to argue and then he nodded. Limping slightly, he went over to where Ferdia was preparing the ground for a fire and flopped down. Jasmine tethered the horses. When she'd finished, Ferdia rejoined her.

"Jasmine," he said in a low voice, his eyes on Seamus. "Is he well?"

"Yes, no. I mean, before we came, he was injured, but I healed him."

Ferdia' eyes narrowed. "How was he hurt?"

"It's hard to explain. I guess — like he was stabbed. I mean, he was stabbed and lost a lot of blood."

"Blood?" His forehead smoothed. "He needs fresh meat. You make the fire and I will hunt."

With Ferdia gone, Jasmine gathered wood for the fire. Returning with an armful, she knelt down in front of Seamus. Sat against a fallen tree, he was asleep with his head thrown back. Being as quiet as she could, Jasmine placed the wood on the ground and began slowly building the fire. She'd almost finished when Seamus awoke with a start.

"Jasmine!" Sitting up, he blinked.

"How are you feeling?"

He dragged his hand through his hair. "Better."

He didn't look it.

"Where's Ferdia?"

"He's gone hunting."

"Hunting? For what?"

"Meat."

"Meat?"

"Yeah." She sighed. "There's something I need to tell you."

"Is it something to do with the scars on my stomach?"

It was her turn to start. She hadn't thought about scars.

"Yeah," she repeated and then slowly, choosing her words carefully, told him what happened.

*

"Why didn't you tell me before?" Seamus asked after she'd finished.

"Why didn't you ask?"

"There's not been the time."

She pulled a face.

"Point taken." He glanced down at his stomach. "I can't believe Cormac thought it would work."

"I think he believed Ellyllon because he wanted to. On the way to Sligo, I saw another side to him. All he cared about was power. He'd do anything, hurt anyone, to get it. He showed that by what he did to you."

"Is that why you aged him?"

"I suppose. Do you remember what you said to me in my bedroom, about Ellyllon? I thought it would be the same. If I left Cormac, he would be free to do anything he wanted, and I couldn't let that happen. I couldn't kill him, so I had to do something." She shrugged, "It sounds bad. I know it was horrible, but it felt right."

"And now?"

"It still feels right. I mean, I don't know what else I could've done."

"No, neither do I."

They sat in silence for a moment. He didn't say it, but she could hear the 'but'. He didn't agree with her. He was like Malachy; there were worse things than death.

He leant forward. "But I should say thank you. You stopped Cormac and healed me. You saved my life."

Surprised, she flushed with pleasure. "Oh, it wasn't just me. Grainne did most of it."

He grinned. "What did she do?"

"She kicked him. It doesn't sound much, but she was kickass."

"She is kickass, whatever that means." His grin faded. "How did you know how to heal me?"

She studied the ground. "I sort of figured it out. I, er, tried to heal the skin first, but it didn't work. Then I realised I had to heal it from the inside out."

"That was very clever of you. To heal is one of the most difficult things to do."

There was something in his voice. She looked at him, but there was no artifice in his face.

"Seamus, do you think Daire's right and Malachy did decide to follow us? I mean, he couldn't, could he? He couldn't open the portal."

"No, he couldn't." He frowned. "Not unless he changed his mind and followed us before the portal closed."

"But he couldn't, we'd've seen—" She stopped, remembering the way time differed. Her heart sank.

"I doubt it; the portal would've stayed open for a few minutes. Who knows when he'd arrive?"

"What do we do?"

"Hope Drendas is wrong." He sighed. "At least, if Daire stays and Malachy does come, he'll find him before Ellyllon does. But I hope to Christ he doesn't." He rubbed at his stomach. "I don't believe he will come. After the way I spoke to him, he shouldn't want to come anywhere near me, but that was the idea."

Seamus turned suddenly. Ferdia was back, stepping so quietly, Jasmine hadn't heard him.

"Jasmine, you have not lit the fire," he said bluntly, lifting up his hand and showing them the bodies of two dead rabbits. "Light it and I will skin these."

*

They ate rabbit roasted on a wooden spit. Seamus and Ferdia tore eagerly at the flesh, picked the meat from the bones, their fingers and lips thick with grease. Trying not to watch them, Jasmine played with hers. Strong, dark; the meat was mostly on the bone and she didn't have the stomach for it. It didn't help that she kept imagining them romping in the sunshine, their noses twitching as they nudged playfully at one another.

After eating, Jasmine left Seamus and Ferdia and wandered over to her horse. It nuzzled against her shoulder and she stroked its neck, tickled it behind the ears. Piebald, with rough thick hair and sturdy legs, it was a native horse, reminding her of the ponies you saw at the traveller festivals on TV. She pressed her cheek in close. This horse was much more affectionate than the last one; she could almost let herself get attached, even give it a name. She wished she was more like Malachy; he was so natural with them. "Jasmine?"

She whirled. It was Ferdia.

"You are sad."

His directness took her aback.

"I'm OK. Just missing Malachy."

"Malachy?"

"The third."

"Ah." He nodded wisely.

In the silence, she found herself wondering exactly how much of their conversation he'd heard.

"Malachy, he is your lover, your husband?"

She laughed, a sudden loud bark that had Seamus looking over at them. "No, not my husband. I suppose, you could say boyfriend or – lover. Well, maybe not now, but sort of. I wish."

Ferdia, she realised, didn't see the joke. To him, she'd likely be an old married woman by now, with a couple of kids hanging off her.

"Daire is my husband." He gave her a look. He was making a point, but she couldn't for the life of her think what it was. "Drendas blessed our union as a father and as druid. Many would not." He gave her another look.

That was it. Catching his meaning, she flushed. "You think, I'm – I don't agree?"

He'd seen her staring and misread her awkwardness.

"No, no." She stopped, conscious of the burn of her cheeks. "I wasn't – I mean, I er, I was just surprised. I didn't mean to stare. I thought, here, now, it wouldn't be OK. It'll be more traditional. Y'know, just men and women." Rubbing at her forehead, she wished she hadn't got into this. "I thought, we think, it's OK where we come from, although, of course, not everyone. There's some real homophobes out there."

Ferdia was staring at her as if she'd lost her mind. She couldn't blame him. She wasn't making much sense to herself, let alone to him.

"I'm not like that," she said finally. "I was just surprised. But who cares, as long as you're both happy. How can love be wrong?"

"Love is never wrong." Ferdia smiled, and she knew then it was alright.

*

They returned to the fire. Seamus was already asleep and they talked softly, so as not to disturb him. It wasn't long before Ferdia suggested they settle for the night. Dawn would come all too quickly and they needed to be ready to leave. He offered to keep first watch, but she refused, knowing that Iomlan was needed to shield them. They agreed Seamus would take over later, but for now he needed all the sleep he could get. She watched Ferdia snuggle down. She had no intention of waking Seamus until the early hours. An hour or two would do her. Give her enough to stop her falling asleep in the saddle. She could catch up the rest when they got to Drendas. Putting more wood on the fire, she sat back and let herself think of Malachy, imagining them together, doing normal, couply things, like Daire and Ferdia.

Chapter Four

"Get up," the man said in Irish. "Slow."

His hair was dark and his face all but covered by a long beard and moustache. His free hand tugged at Malachy's hair as if its owner was going to use it to lift him up. Malachy got the message and slowly, awkwardly, clambered to his feet, the knife moving with him. Sweating, he tried not to look down at the blade an inch from his skin.

"Good," the man whispered as soon as he was upright.

Without warning, he yanked hard on Malachy's hair, pulling his head backwards. For the briefest of moments, he studied his face and then he let go.

"What are you called?"

Malachy clamped his lips together, refusing to answer, and the knife moved closer. He shrank away, lifting and stretching to avoid the blade, but still it came. The fingers flexed, and the blade caressed his neck in the softest, lightest of kisses.

"What are you called?" the man repeated, his blue eyes furious.

"Malachy," he croaked.

Again, the knife fell back. The man grabbed the edge of his cloak near his neck and twisted.

"Walk. Don't speak." Keeping hold of his cloak, he pushed him forward in the direction he wanted him to go, away from the village and back towards the river.

*

They hadn't gone far when a shout came from behind them, followed by another.

"Don't stop," the man growled, his lips close to Malachy's ear.

Letting him go, he dug his elbow hard into Malachy's back, pushing him on.

"Finbar!"

The shout was much closer; whoever it was, they were catching them up.

"Stop!" the man ordered Malachy suddenly, tugging at his cloak to illustrate his words. Malachy did as he was told.

"Look down." He gave the cloak another yank. "Down. And don't speak."

His mind whirling, Malachy did as the voice said. Footsteps, moving fast, came towards them and the sound of men breathing. He couldn't help himself; he looked up.

"Down!" the voice hissed.

The knife was back, pressed to the side of his throat.

"Finbar, you didn't answer!" a new voice accused, sharp with annoyance.

"Did you call?" Malachy's captor's voice sounded different; older, more distracted.

"Old fool!" another voice muttered.

More movement. Two pairs of feet appeared to Malachy's right.

"What have you here?" The first voice's tone was suddenly casual, playful almost, but Malachy heard the suspicion.

"No one," Finbar said plaintively. "Ilech, he's mine. I found him. He's from the tribe of Aesar. I'm going to slit his throat and throw him into the river to float back to them."

The man called Ilech gave a laugh of delight.

"Aesar?! That pig! He sends a — what?" Malachy felt him lean towards him, his head lowered as if trying to see his face and kept his own carefully down. "A warrior? No, a boy, worse than a boy, with his skin so soft and hairless, to spy on us?" He straightened, his voice hardening, asserting his authority. "To slit his throat would be a waste of my arm and my blade. Come, maybe Garach will let you slit his throat after — if there is anything left."

"No, he's mine!" Finbar cried, sounding almost like a petulant child as he pulled Malachy away in a half-circle.

"Finbar, you one eyed eejit!" Ilech replied caustically. "See how he's dressed. He is no pup from the tribe of Aesar. He is the one the dark one seeks."

Malachy felt Finbar's grip on him lessen, felt the knife move away, then saw it out of the corner of his eye, swinging out and around, disappearing behind him.

Ilech was continuing. "Give him to me. I will be honoured and so too our tribe and the name of Garach."

"No, I will not!" Finbar shouted, "He's mine!"

He gave Malachy a violent push, sending him sprawling. Another shout and Malachy looked back just in time to see him jump at Ilech, his knife swinging in a wide arc. It caught him across the throat, cutting deep and sending a trail of blood through the air. The body toppled as, whirling, Finbar reached for the second man. Shocked as he was, the second man's instincts took over. Skipping out of reach, he turned and fled.

"He will rouse the village. We must leave!" Finbar cried, stepping over the body without a second look.

Malachy got to his feet.

"Now!" he growled, grabbing Malachy's arm and pushing him ahead of him.

Malachy dragged his eyes from the body on the ground, at the blood still pumping. It made him feel sick. "Who are you?"

Finbar ignored him. "The river – go. Run!"

He pushed Malachy again, and before he knew what he was doing Malachy was running along the path, hearing him close behind. They reached the river. Malachy stopped, but only for a second, as Finbar nudged him sideways, steering him left, downstream. They continued for a few minutes. Then, yelling at Malachy to stop, Finbar made his way to a large bed of tall reeds lying at the side of the river. Malachy watched as he dove into them, his hands reaching out, feeling, searching for something, then looked back. A line of lights, flame torches flickering at shoulder height, was making its way out of the village, moving rapidly as if the carriers were running. He heard them shout. They were coming for them.

"Help me!" Finbar shouted, looking back.

Malachy didn't need telling twice. Leaping forward, he paused briefly as his feet sank into water. By the time he reached Finbar the water was up to his knees. Bending, he reached down and felt the side of a small boat.

"Pull it!" Finbar ordered and the two of them began to heave the boat out, giving it all they had to get it free of the reeds and once more onto the water. The shouting was getting closer, Malachy turned and saw the first of the lights almost to the river.

"Shit!" He worked harder, panting with the effort, then suddenly the boat was free.

"Get in. Quickly!" Finbar cried, waiting as Malachy heaved himself up and over the side.

The boat rocked but remained upright. Another push and he joined Malachy inside. With agonising slowness, the boat began to drift out, towards the centre of the river. From behind them came a roar as the men saw them. Sitting ducks; to Malachy's horror Finbar stood up, his hand outstretched, pointing to the water at the back of the boat. It lurched suddenly and for a moment Malachy thought Finbar was going to fall, but somehow, he kept his balance. A spear whistled through the air, hit the water behind them with a loud splash, followed by a wall of arrows. Finbar waved his hand again and they fell away harmlessly. More men were coming, leaping into the water as if to swim after them, but it was too late. The boat was speeding away now, leaving the tribe far behind them.

*

Malachy observed the riverbank and the lights from the torches recede, then looked at Finbar. He was watching him in silence.

"Will they follow us?"

Finbar nodded, his face grim. He lowered his hand, and the boat slowed.

"We must row." He sat, joining Malachy. Reaching into the bottom of the boat, he pulled out a crafted oar. "Here." Giving it to Malachy, he reached down for a second.

They shifted slightly, getting into a better position on either side of the boat. Keeping an eye on each other's stroke they began slowly, easily to row. Silence. Made of a light lattice of wood, the boat skimmed the water, the only sound the dip and thrust of the oars. The riverbank slipped away.

"You don't have one eye," Malachy said after a few minutes.

Finbar laughed. "No, and I'm not Finbar."

"What happened to him? To the real Finbar?"

"Dead. Killed, not by me." The man who was not Finbar cocked his head and waited.

"So who are you?" Malachy obliged.

"I am called Daire."

They continued to row. The boat began to veer towards the bank, the outline of the reeds coming closer.

"Stop," Daire ordered. He rowed alone for a moment and the reeds moved away. "Again."

Malachy resumed. "Are you a druid?"

"Yes. I belonged to the village of Slicech, before Ellyllon came."

"Ellyllon! Ellyllon was there?"

"Not this day, but the tribe of Garach follow him."

"Is that why you're helping me? As revenge?" A thought occurred to him, "You wanted to know my name. How do you know about me? Who I am? Or where to find me?"

"You are one of the Three. Ellyllon spoke your name, as did Seamus."

"Seamus?! You met them? Are they OK?" Malachy cried, stopping rowing.

"They are well. They travel with Ferdia to my father, Drendas, the wisest of druid. Your coming was foretold. A few in the tribe are still loyal to me, but the others would cut my throat."

"That's why you used the knife. You had to be sure."

Daire nodded, and with one hand indicated Malachy's oar. The two began rowing again. "Ellyllon is cunning, and he knows of my treachery."

"And us, where are we going?"

"To my father. We will meet Seamus and Jasmine there."

There was another silence. They passed a huge clump of reeds, growing out from the side towards them, the long tall leaves looking eerie in the half-moonlight. Beyond them the countryside, unseen in the darkness, floated by. Malachy found himself thinking of Jasmine, wondering where she was, what she was doing, if she was alright.

*

Jasmine woke. It was bright, and dawn had long since passed. She sat up. Seamus had fallen asleep, and of Ferdia there was no sign. They weren't protected. Instantly, she sent Iomlan out, searching, probing. She gasped. Someone with Iomlan was out there and they were close. An image flashed through her mind, of a druid sending the warriors before him. Weapons raised, slowly, silently, they crept through the forest towards them.

*

"Seamus!" she shouted, scrambling to her feet.

"Wh-what?"

"They've found us!" Grabbing his arm, she began pulling him upwards, even as she threw Iomlan over them, like a net.

"Who is it? Ellyllon?"

"No, I think it's a druid. Come on!"

She tried to pull him towards the horses, but he refused to move.

"Where's Ferdia?"

"I don't know! We have to get out of here."

What was the matter with him? Why couldn't he see? She tugged his arm, but still he resisted.

"Wait a minute," he said, pulling away. "We can't go blindly charging through the forest. Who knows what we'd run into? Now, do you know exactly where the druid is?"

"I'm not sure. That way, I think." She pointed. "But they know exactly where we are. We have to go."

But Seamus was already focussing. She waited, shifting impatiently, the seconds feeling like minutes. The men could be out there, hidden among the green, watching them. She stared at the foliage, but it was impossible to see.

"He's there, but he's dissembling. I can't pinpoint him. I think he's somewhere west, or maybe north. Where the bloody hell is Ferdia?"

"Here." He stepped out from behind a tree.

"Where have you been?!"

"Two men wait to the east." He nodded, almost imperceptibly. "Scouts. I heard them speak. They are waiting for the warriors of Aurith. Loyal to Ellyllon; he rides from the north."

"Then who's the druid coming from the east?" Seamus asked, then quickly shook his head, "It's must be the one Daire told us about. Cathbad. He's followed us and now, he's trying to scare us, to drive us into a trap – Ferdia, what lies south?"

"Portach Dubh. Bog. The way is soft and treacherous and is said dark creatures live there."

"But there is a way through?"

Reluctantly, Ferdia nodded.

"Then we'll go south."

*

Pulling their horses behind them, they squeezed their way through the undergrowth. At the back, Jasmine's shoulders itched, awaiting the shout of a warrior, the sound of a charge, but nothing came. She was still protecting them, but ultimately, it would do them no good. They'd find the remains of their camp and for these men, surely, it would be easy to track them. With the broken and trampled undergrowth, she'd probably be able to track them herself, even without Iomlan. Seamus obviously believed that Cathbad, knowing the legends of the bog, was using it like a wall, pushing them into a corner and preparing to pounce. She hoped he was right. Hoped that going into the bog, the place of Ferdia's dark creatures, wasn't the worst thing they could do.

The trees thinned, the ground opening up to a host of white flowering hogweed, like a sea of light, airy cauliflower heads. Instantly Ferdia stopped and, swinging his leg upwards, clambered on top of his horse. Seamus followed and then Jasmine, the three of them urging their horses forward. A few minutes, and holding up his hand, Ferdia stopped again.

"Wait." Slipping off his horse, he began to look all around him. Then, with a loud exclamation, he parted and flattened a clump of hogweed.

Placed low to the ground was a narrow stone. Whorls of lichen all but hid the two symbols etched at the very top. Squatting down in front of it, Ferdia slowly rubbed his fingers across it.

"What is it?" Jasmine whispered.

"I'm not sure, but it looks like some kind of Ogham Stone," Seamus murmured back.

"What's it say?"

"I don't know, but it doesn't look like the usual Ogham writing."

Ferdia straightened. "The path lies to the west."

"Won't the local tribes know this path as well?"

"Probably," Seamus admitted.

"Then what are we doing? They could be there waiting for us."

Ferdia climbed back onto his horse. "We must be quiet. Come."

"Probably," Seamus repeated. "But don't worry. I have a plan."

Moving horizontally, they slowly approached the edge of the forest. Ferdia stopped and he and Seamus shared a look before they both dismounted. Jasmine followed, wincing at the noise she made. They inched forwarded and crouching low, peered out through the leaves. She held her breath. Bog lay ahead, the ground flat as far as the eye could see, with patches of green, brown and black mingling. Carefully, Ferdia lowered a small branch.

"There," he whispered, pointing.

Four men were stood on the patch of ground between the forest and the bog. Hands on hips, they were talking, boredom etched into the line of their bodies. They'd obviously been there for some time. Jasmine squinted. At their feet, lay something grey. Another stone, the marker for the start of the path. One of them yawned and stretched, the movement jiggling his sword. Catching the sunlight, the blade gleamed.

"There will be others," Ferdia said darkly.

"Yes," Seamus whispered, nodding. "Hiding in the trees. And more coming behind us."

He smiled at the horror on Jasmine's face. "I know what ya thinking; we should've gone west and tried to slip pass them. But then they'd be on our heels the whole way. This way, we'll put some distance between us." His smile faded. "If me plan works, that is."

Moving back, he straightened and waited for them to do the same. They bent their heads together.

"Jasmine, you're still protecting us?" She nodded. "Good. When I give the word, I want you to step out of the forest and, leading your horse, walk towards the men. Can ya do that for me?"

Not trusting herself to speak, she nodded.

"Seamus–?" Ferdia's eyes were wide.

"She's the only one who can do it. They won't harm her, they daren't. Ellyllon wants her alive. We just need a small fire."

The ground was dry, the floor of the forest like a tinderbox. It didn't take much, a few small twigs, some dry, dead foliage. Crouching, Seamus and Ferdia worked fast. Jasmine felt the tiniest surge in Seamus' Iomlan and the fire took. They straightened.

"Now, when I say, step out and walk towards them." Seamus said urgently, "Go slow, don't rush and don't look back, whatever you hear. When you get close enough, use Iomlan to incapacitate them. But don't take any chances. Give them a good blast. They might not want to kill you, but if you attack them, they will fight back. Now, are ya ready?"

She nodded and, positioning herself next to a gap in the trees, she looked at Seamus and waited. *Almost, almost.* Already, the fire was beginning to build, sending small puffs of smoke into the air. She wiped her palms against her tunic. Her mouth felt dry and she swallowed noisily, trying to lubricate it.

"Go!" Seamus hissed.

Swallowing again, she stepped through the trees. Totally exposed, she turned towards the men. Immediately one saw her. He shouted, lifting up his arm and pointing as the others turned. Three hands went to swords, unsheathing the blades and holding them out in front of them. The fourth warrior unslung a bow from his shoulder and, grabbing an arrow, pointed it towards her. He pulled back his arm and the bowstring tightened. Her breath caught.

Chapter Five

Nothing happened. The archer waited, his arm flexed and his bowstring taut. Seamus was right; they had no intention of killing her, although the threat was obviously there. She breathed out and, with the arrow still trained on her, began slowly to walk towards them. Behind her, Seamus' fire crackled. She could smell the smoke, the bitter scent of burning grass and plant, feel the pressure of Seamus' Iomlan as he gently pushed the fire her way. The men were looking at one another, exchanging doubtful glances. She knew they'd seen the smoke, and could guess what they were thinking. A fire was very bad. The land was too dry; it wouldn't take much for it to get completely out of control, and none of them wished to be burnt alive. She heard one of the men speak but couldn't quite make it out. Another answered, his tone high. They were starting to panic. Around her, the smoke was getting stronger. It stung her eyes and caught at the back of her throat, making her cough. Her back itched. She imagined it coming behind her, moving swiftly as it devoured everything in its path, and had to fight not to look back. She really hoped Seamus knew what he was doing. One of the men stepped forward, making sure to leave a space so as to obstruct the archer's view.

"Stop!" he shouted. "Stop."

She ignored him. She wasn't far, maybe forty yards away.

"Stop, or he fires."

Another few steps. She imagined more than saw the archer's fingers tighten. She let Iomlan build. Out of nowhere, she felt a new Iomlan. Powerful, it came from somewhere behind, but now Seamus was there. The two collided as the archer released his bow. It hurtled towards her, but she knocked it sideways, sending it harmlessly away into the trees. Already he was preparing to fire again, but from behind her came a loud roar, a furious whoosh. And a blast of heat, burning like a furnace, tore across her back and threw her to the ground.

*

Her ears ringing, she sat up. Two of the men were still on the ground, the archer and the one that had called to her, the other two disappearing between the trees. Her eyes stinging from the smoke, all around her was chaos. Over the roar of the fire, the crackle of burning wood and scrub, she could hear men shouting and a lone voice screaming and couldn't help herself. She looked back. Charging towards her was Ferdia, pulling two horses after him. Neighing loudly, their eyes wide and ears flat, she thought they would bolt, but somehow he kept control of them. Behind him and to his right, a wall of flame reached up to the heavens; black smoke billowed as the forest burned.

"Jasmine, the path!" Ferdia bellowed.

She scrambled to her feet and immediately began to cough. Ferdia was almost on top of her, the fire matching his pace. Through the smoke she glimpsed Seamus and his horse behind him, then she was running too. Ahead, the archer jumped to his feet. Iomlan swirled, preparing to attack, but with one quick look, he was gone, running down the side of the forest, his bow and arrow forgotten. More men appeared, coughing as they staggered out from between the trees, dodging flying wood, burning sticks and bits of branches as they sought desperately to escape the fire. Reacting without thinking, Jasmine blasted them with everything she had, and threw them, their bodies jerking, back in towards the flames. The grass caught where the wood landed. If she'd had time to stop, she would've realised that was how it had spread so quickly, but now there was nothing she could do but keep going. She reached the path and whirled, letting Ferdia run past her.

"Go, I'll follow!"

Struggling against the reins, he didn't argue. Seamus came next, gasping for breath, his face red with exertion. Off to their left an arrow appeared, coming through the smoke. She knocked it away, but another came, then another.

"I'll protect you!"

She knocked them away as Seamus and his horse went past. It must be more of Aurith's warriors, circling the forest and coming in from the west. Iomlan knew exactly what to do. Following its lead, she gathered her power to her, waiting for it to build before sending it out in a long, even stream towards the base of the fire. Immediately, the spread intensified, as if Iomlan were a wind, fanning the flames. It roared towards Aurith's men, as ferocious as any beast. The arrows stopped; she knew they were retreating, but the blood was throbbing through her veins, her head singing with the power running through her and the wild, raging fire. She didn't hesitate. Shifting Iomlan's position, the fire shifted with it, turning and following the men's trajectory. They would be running now, their lungs cramping as they tried to flee. Driven by Iomlan, the fire chased them, eating up and devouring the ground between them until there was nowhere left to go. Iomlan faded, but still she waited. Most of them died before the fire caught, asphyxiating on the smoke. She saw the end of the fire in her mind's eye, the ground scorched, what was left of the trees black and smoking. The ground would remain like that until the first shoots appeared, but of the men, there would be no trace. It was enough. Satisfied, Jasmine lowered her head and, turning her back on the conflagration, walked slowly away.

*

Once they were far enough away from the forest, Seamus and Ferdia stopped to wait for her. She joined them feeling strangely calm, serene almost. Seamus was staring at her, at her face blackened from the smoke and framed by the inferno behind, as if he didn't know her. She saw disgust in his face, horror that had turned his red face pale, and something else she couldn't identify.

"Can you stop it?" asked Ferdia.

"No," Seamus replied, still staring at her. "It would take too much time, too much power. I didn't mean to let it get so big, but I didn't count on Cathbad."

"Does Cathbad live?"

Seamus nodded. "I think so, yes."

"We must go before he gathers his wits."

Seamus stirred, as if waking from a sleep. "Yes."

Without another word, they mounted and, in single file, set off across the bog.

*

Riding last, the look on Seamus' face gnawed at her. He knew exactly what she'd done and couldn't hide his disgust. But there was something more; a strange light in his eyes. It reminded her of Malachy's face when he'd seen what she'd done to Cormac. And then, it hit her. It was fear. Seamus was afraid of her. For one terrible moment, she was almost pleased, then she thought of what Ellyllon had said and her stomach dropped. He was actually afraid of her. She looked back, at the fire still raging, the huge clouds of smoke. How many men had died in there? She'd thought after the village it couldn't get much worse, but how wrong she'd been. At least that had been unintentional, but now? The worse thing was she hadn't meant it at first; she'd just been following

Iomlan, but something had taken over. She hadn't just wanted to stop them from attacking them, she'd wanted to punish them for following Ellyllon. If she were a judge, she was one from the past, with a soft, black cloth and a cold, merciless eye, passing sentence on the poor and the desperate with the long drop of the hangman's rope. What was wrong with her?

Ferdia was talking, telling Seamus how Lugh had created the bog after razing the forest to the ground in a fit of pique. Hunched miserably in her saddle, Jasmine ignored him, but then Seamus interrupted him, his voice tetchy.

"What are the dark creatures that are supposed to live here?"

Jasmine looked up.

"Fairy kind. Dark, lowly brethren to the gods. Their magic is not like the druid; they seek only to feed."

"Of course, what else would they do?" Seamus snorted, "Go on."

"They snare travellers. Baffle them with a low, grey mist, then entice with a bright, shining light. Stepping off the path, the traveller flounders in the soft, sucking wet, and claws, green as the river reed, clutch at their ankles and pull them down."

"And these creatures, they don't attack people on the path?" Seamus asked, examining the ground to his left.

Ferdia shook his head. "They can only hope to make us stray."

"So, if no one sees them until it's too late, then no one has actually seen them. Convenient."

Ferdia looked back, confused by the unfamiliar word. If he noticed Seamus' tone, he didn't say anything. Jasmine winced. This was her fault. Unconsciously, Seamus was picking on him, taking his feelings about her out on him.

"I'm sorry, Ferdia," Seamus said, seeming suddenly to realise. "That was uncalled for."

Another look, but this time Ferdia simply shook his head as if exasperated by Seamus' eccentricity, or perhaps, his childlike naivety.

*

Despite Ferdia's dark creatures, they crossed the bog without incident. The markers worked perfectly, although sometimes Ferdia had to stop and dismount to find them in the long grass, but she guessed he knew the way pretty well and was just being cautious. In a few places, you could see glimpses of rough wooden slats built as part of an old, decaying walkway. This technology amazed her, for she couldn't imagine how they'd done it without some sort of machinery. But then, why should she be so surprised? If modern human beings could be so ingenious, why wouldn't their ancestors be? She studied Seamus' back, the shape of his head. This was getting serious; she should talk to him, tell him what was happening to her. But what was happening to her? It could be as Ellyllon said, and it was Iomlan growing inside her. But Ellyllon lied like most people breathed. Why should she believe him? What if it was just her? The corruption Seamus had warned her about right at the very beginning?

*

It was late when they left the bog and returned to the forest, the sky almost dark.

"We will sleep here tonight," Ferdia announced. "The horses must rest, as must we."

"I doubt Cathbad will rest." Seamus looked up at the sky, "We'll have no moonlight, there's too much cloud. Without the need to hide, he can use Iomlan to light his way."

"Even druid must rest," Ferdia disagreed. "And Aurith's people come from the mountains. They are fierce, strong and quick to temper, but you have killed many of his warriors, and he has many enemies. And Aurith is no fool."

"So?" Seamus shifted impatiently.

Ferdia smiled. "Cathbad is dark, treacherous and cunning, but he is not the dark one and cannot tame men to be his lambs. It will take time to persuade Aurith and the other chieftains, for they have witnessed your power."

"You Ferdia, are cleverer than you look."

Ferdia's smile widened. "Daire would wish me less so!"

Dismounting, he led them through a thicket to a tiny stream beyond. Together, he and Jasmine sorted the horses, leaving Seamus to sit and rest.

"He's better," Ferdia said, glancing back at him.

"Yes, but I think he's tired after today, using Iomlan."

"With Drendas, he will rest, sleep and grow strong."

"I can watch again tonight."

"And when will you rest, Jasmine?" Ferdia frowned.

She smiled. "When we reach Drendas."

Ferdia was too practical to argue. He knew just as well as her there was no choice. Reaching into his pack, he pulled out his wooden cup and handed it to her. "The water in the stream is good. Give him some."

She did as he said, filling the cup with water from the stream before taking it over to where Seamus was sitting with his eyes closed, his back against the tree. Even if she didn't know exactly what was happening, she should still tell Seamus and try to warn him. What if she lost control completely? She could hurt him, or Ferdia. Pausing, she glanced back and saw Ferdia busy with one of the horses, his back to her. But it was so difficult to know where to start. Her first thought was that it had begun when she'd attacked Cormac, but even if he was lying, Ellyllon had known something was happening before that. She remembered the dark room, her body frozen, unable to move, with Ellyllon's face looming over her. He'd known when he'd set his trap for them, known even before he'd gone through the rift. So when had it started? She studied Seamus' face. He looked so tired, it didn't seem fair, but she had to tell him.

"Seamus, water."

"Hmm?" He opened his eyes. "Thanks."

He took the cup and drank. Her heart went out to him, but she had to tell him. Go on, tell him. She opened her mouth to speak, but nothing came out.

"Jasmine?" He was staring at her over the rim of the cup.

She licked her lips. "Seamus, I–"

"I will hunt," Ferdia called. "Jasmine, will you gather wood?"

"Jasmine?" Seamus lowered the cup and leaned forward.

She couldn't do it. "Nothing." She looked away. "Coming, Ferdia."

Annoyed with herself, but also secretly relieved, Jasmine went in search of wood. Struggling with the thoughts that pushed her first one way and then the other, she went further than she meant to, as if by walking she could leave everything behind: herself, her power, Seamus even. By the time she returned, Ferdia was already back, plucking the feathers from the brightly coloured cock pheasant lying limp in his left hand.

"I was getting worried; you were so long," Seamus commented.

Said casually enough, he couldn't hide the tension in his voice.

"I didn't realise." she mugged, as if overcome by her silliness.

It was definitely too late to try and talk to Seamus; it would have to wait until tomorrow. *You're only putting it off*, she told herself sternly, *you're going to have to do it sometime.*

Tomorrow, she answered herself quickly. *I'll do it tomorrow, over breakfast.*

*

Later, with the pheasant ate and fresh water drunk from the stream, they settled for the night. Despite Seamus' protests, she took the first watch, promising to call him a few hours before dawn, even though she had no intention of doing so. She knew she'd never sleep; she was too wound up and didn't feel the slightest bit tired. Instead, after carefully spreading Iomlan's net of protection, she'd sat back and stared into the fire, listening to the sounds of the forest in the dark, moonless night.

*

"Jasmine? Jasmine?"

She looked up. In the half-light of dawn, Seamus and Ferdia were staring down at her.

"I'm sorry, what?"

Seamus sighed. "You fell asleep. You should've woken me. You watched all last night."

She sat up. "Oh, no!"

"It's alright. We're protected. I don't think you were asleep long, for I don't sense anyone."

Relieved, she sat back.

Ferdia passed her some more oatcakes and cheese. She placed them on her lap. Somehow, she just didn't fancy them. Seamus and Ferdia were exchanging looks. She stifled a yawn. Last night, it had been her and Ferdia worrying about Seamus, but now she was the object of concern. Ferdia placed his hand on Seamus' arm and she saw his lips form the words, as he whispered.

"She will rest when we get to Drendas."

Drendas, a voice inside her whispered eagerly. *Drendas*.

*

In the end, Seamus had refused to move until she'd drank and eaten something. She had to admit, it did help. Upping her blood sugar level, it cleared her head, making her feel more like her usual self. Setting off, they rode as fast as they could through the trees, each of them eager to reach the end of their journey.

*

The morning passed, and mountains, heralding the start of Connemara, rose high above the tree tops, their peaks blue-grey in the afternoon sunshine. Under its glare, the horses' heads nodded, in unison, like the slow ticking of a clock. Jasmine lifted her head and straightened against their soporific effect. To their right lay Croagh Patrick, its distinctive, triangular peak dominating the low land around it. She studied the eastern slope, screwing her eyes up against the sun. Longer, with the peak behind it, from this angle it made her think of a half-eroded Egyptian sphynx. Made of quartzite, the bare slopes shone in the sunlight. Croagh Patrick, only now it had an older name: Cruachan Aigle, from the god Crom. It was his mountain before the time of the Celts, before even Tuatha de Danann, when Saint Patrick, the man and legend was yet to be born and the pagan snakes of Ireland were still free from the scourge of Christianity. She turned back, her head floating. How did she know that? Scourge. It was a strange word; archaic, biblical almost. It didn't really sound like her. Maybe she'd read it somewhere? Her head felt light, as if she'd caught too much sun. She wiped the hair off her forehead. She was wandering, her brain fuzzy from lack of sleep. It would be easy to panic, to see it as yet another symptom of something wrong, but Seamus was right; one good night and she'd be as right as rain.

*

They moved south, deeper into Connemara, and the soil became increasingly rocky, the quality too poor to hold the trees. The last ones lay ahead, a small, thin tract of forest, framing Seamus and Ferdia as they rode. Chatting, they kept their voices carefully low, as if worried Cathbad could follow the sound. Or maybe they were talking about her. Sharing their concerns about the freak riding behind them. Anger stirred, but she pushed it down. *Come on, Jasmine*, she told herself, *keep it together*.

Seamus and Ferdia passed the last few trees and less than a minute later she joined them out in the open countryside. The sky was thick with big, white, fluffy clouds, their edges tinged with traces of pale grey, the ground beneath it a wide, flat valley cut by a river flowing through its centre. A rough stone path mimicking its meanderings, the two converging with the mountains into a point at the valley's far end.

Jasmine rubbed at her forehead. It was so hot, the sun beating down hard on the top of her head. She tried to stay alert, but the thoughts kept creeping. Three quarters of the way across the valley and the path and the river crossed one another, the path moving through the river at its shallowest point verging off to the right. Single file, they rode down the low bank and into the water. Crystal clear and shallow, it skimmed the top of the riverbed, making the stones sparkle. Hooves splashed through water, spraying it upwards, wetting the soles of their feet. Out the other side, the river bent again, going left this time, following the path but not quite going far enough to catch it, so they stayed where they were, just to its right. The valley ahead narrowed, its sides steepening as the mountains around it rose. Green grass gave way to brown, the grey of granite, the gently curving slopes chiselled by nature into something more jagged. Its rocky outcrops and peak, and high sheer drops, were littered with boulders. They loomed overhead, half in shadow, and Jasmine found herself watching them nervously.

*

The end of the valley was in sight.

"Drendas' home lies beyond," Ferdia explained, pointing. "His power will protect us."

Someone whispered her name. Low, it came from just behind her left ear. She spun, but there was nobody behind her; the path was clear.

"Jasmine."

The hairs on the back of her neck lifted and she saw Seamus' head jerk. Ellyllon. She knew it was him before she saw him, standing on the edge of an outcrop halfway up the next mountain. His body and face were obscured by his long, black cloak; beside him, a second figure wore a brown cloak with the hood pulled back. Tall, with yellow-blond hair that looked almost gold in the sunlight, his face was almost as pale as Ellyllon's. Across one shoulder curled a long plait, the hair around the opposite ear cut close with a sharp knife. Cathbad.

"Seamus, look!" she cried, looking wildly around for a chieftain and his warriors, but there was no sign of them.

"Ride for the ridge!" Seamus bellowed.

Kicking their heels and shouting, they forced their horses into a run. Too late, Cathbad raised his arms. Jasmine flinched, instinctively ducking her head, but nothing happened. And then came a low rumble and with agonising slowness, the large boulder a metre below Cathbad began to move. It rocked forward, for a moment poised, then fell. It rolled down the mountain, bouncing and falling and bringing others with it as gravity propelled it on, faster and faster. Cathbad raised his hands again, this time sending rocks down the mountain opposite. Without thinking, Jasmine send a pulse of Iomlan upwards. It caught Cathbad in the chest and he stumbled backwards, but now they were among the boulders, their horses skidding as they dodged flying stone and rock. Thrown sideways, she almost fell, but somehow kept her seat. More rocks fell, covering the path ahead of them and narrowing the only way out. Already Cathbad was back on his feet; she threw another pulse at him, but this time he was ready and deflected it with ease. A rock hurtled towards Seamus, crashing to the ground, but at the last moment he swerved and it rolled harmlessly away. An arrow buzzed, missing him by inches. A second arrow buzzed, but by a miracle, fell short.

"There!" Ferdia shouted, pointing.

It was the archer from the forest. He'd already released a third arrow and was preparing for a fourth. Seamus' Iomlan caught the third and knocked it away as Jasmine sent hers towards the archer, but it hit an invisible wall and bounced uselessly away. Cathbad! Following an instinct not her own, Jasmine gathered Iomlan to her then and, quick as a flash, split it into two. One pulse hurtled towards Cathbad and the other towards the archer. Cathbad shouted, a curse, more in anger than pain, and with the barrier gone, Iomlan caught the archer just under the chin. His head snapped back, the bow and arrow falling from his grasp. Slowly, his body began to topple. He fell, his arms and legs flailing as his body hit the side of the mountain and bounced. There was no time to watch. One by one, they thundered through the gap and out the other side.

*

They'd reached the end of the valley. The path turned a corner, skirted the lower slope of a mountain then rose again, as the river, still to their left, fell sharply away. Hooves thundered and the horses turned, their legs scrambling. Jasmine risked a glance backwards. Stood alone on the outcrop, Ellyllon was turned towards her. Even at this distance, she could feel the intensity of his gaze and knew suddenly that whatever happened, he'd never stop trying to use her. In his head, she was his, her power his due. Still rising, they turned another corner, then hit the top of the ridge and Ellyllon disappeared from view. Ahead lay a huge lake. Dark water, more black than blue, was framed on all sides by mountains. More peaks, grey and indistinct with distance, lay behind them. And then, they were charging downwards, following the slope towards the lake. They'd done it.

*

Halfway down the slope they stopped, breathing heavily. There was no sign of Ellyllon or Cathbad. Ferdia and Daire were right, neither of them would risk a confrontation with Drendas.

"Are you OK?" Jasmine asked Seamus.

He nodded, still breathless.

"They will not follow," Ferdia confirmed. "For this is the home of Drendas. And there, his house." He pointed.

Jasmine followed his finger. What she'd first though was a lake was actually a fjord. Shaped like a sock, it curved to the right before opening out into a wide, dark blue channel that went all the way to the sea. A beach nestled in the heel, its white sand gleaming in the sunlight, so bright it hurt your eyes to look at it. The path turned away from it, back towards the east. And there, behind the beach, lay a small round, wooden house, nestled into the side of the mountain, as if seeking protection. There was nothing, bar a few scraggy looking trees, pummelled sideways by the wind and rain, but water, grass, gorse and stone.

"It looks empty," Seamus commented.

Ferdia shook his head. "Drendas lives simply. His sheep roam free amongst the mountains, but they come when he calls."

He led them down the rest of the slope and across the grass towards the house. On the edge of the beach, he pulled on the reins and stopped his horse. "I will go first. Wait for me."

"I thought he was expecting us?" Seamus' eyebrows lifted.

"His ways are known only to him. I will go first."

"OK then." Seamus gave Jasmine a look, disbelief mixed with exasperation.

They watched Ferdia ride over to the house. Dismounting in one easy movement, he disappeared inside. Jasmine looked at Seamus.

"We'd better wait. My arse is sore; why don't we go for a quick walk, take a look around?"

Dismounting, they left the horses and wandered across the sand towards the water. Soft white slipped away from them, slowing them down.

"Now, would ya look at that?" Seamus spread his hands wide as he walked.

"Yeah." She had to admit it was breathtaking.

So quiet, so still, as if they were on a desert island or the only people left in the world, it couldn't feel any more remote. Jasmine lowered her head and watched her feet in the sand. If ever there was a time to tell Seamus, it was now.

"How did you know how to do that?" Stopping, he turned back to look at her.

Confused, it took her a moment. "What?"

"Split Iomlan in two like that?"

"Oh, I dunno. It just came to me."

"Like turning the fire on the men in the forest?"

So, he knew after all, and had got tired of waiting for her to say something. She stared at the sand, the tiny grains of white. Of course he knew. For a moment, neither of them spoke, and then she sighed.

"I have to tell you something."

"Yes?"

"It's, er, about Iomlan."

"What about it?"

A shell lay near to her left foot. Upturned, white tinged with orange gleamed. Stooping, she picked it up and turned it over. Conical orange ridges spread from the top downwards. Seamus waited.

Slowly, turning the shell over and over, she traced the ridges with her thumb. "On the way to Sligo, we stayed in a house, overnight. Ellyllon – he told me something."

The shell, like the sand, had been worn by the sea, its ridges and sharp edges smoothed and eased, like an ageing tyrant mellowed by time.

"What did he tell you?" Seamus' voice was heartbreakingly gentle. It made her want to cry. She didn't deserve such gentleness, not after what she'd done. With an effort she swallowed it down. "That, um, Iomlan, is, um, is still, um – growing inside me."

She looked up. The sun framed his face, obscuring his features. Even with Iomlan she couldn't tell what he was feeling.

"Go on."

"I thought he was lying, trying to unnerve me, I know it's not possible, but then all these things started happening and now I'm starting to think that maybe it's true."

"Jasmine, what things?"

She ignored him. "That's why he wanted to bring me through the portal with him. It's nothing to do with me, it's my Iomlan he wants." She shook her head. "I can feel it, Seamus, feel it changing me. I can't, I don't know how, to stop it. What if it's taking me over?!"

"What is?"

"Iomlan."

There was a pause.

"Ah, Jasmine, you know Iomlan doesn't work like that," Seamus said eventually. "It isn't sentient." He leant forward, and she saw the concern in his face. "I knew something was wrong, but I kept telling myself we had to make it here. I'm not as strong as I should be, I can't protect us, but Drendas can. But I was wrong. I should have asked you." He sighed. "But we're here now and I want you to tell me what's been happening. And don't leave anything out, no matter how tempting."

"OK." She opened her mouth to speak.

Her stomach crawled. Sudden, violent, it was as if it were full of spiders crawling around and around. Someone was using Iomlan, and they were close, too close. Cathbad! Ferdia was wrong and he'd followed them. She whirled, but there was no one there; the beach, the grass and fjord were empty.

"Seamus, where is he?"

Squinting, he scanned the horizon. "I don't know. I can't see him."

"Seamus!"

Behind him, something round, luminous broke the surface of the water. Moving slowly, it came towards them, growing as more and more of it appeared out of the water. The light was now too bright to look at. Jasmine fell back, shielding her eyes, and the shell fell softly to the sand.

Chapter Six

The light flickered and died and Jasmine lowered her hands. At the edge of the water stood a man. Dressed in a long tunic that reached down to his ankles, he was the epitome of what she thought a druid should look like. Old, his hair, beard and moustache white and flowing, in his hand he carried a long stick. At waist height, the gnarled length had been worn so smooth by the pressure of his hand, it fitted so snugly that it looked almost part of him. Hazel eyes peered out of sunken sockets, and his face, what could be seen of it below the hair, was deeply lined. The tide surged unexpectedly, wetting his naked feet and the bottom of his tunic. Looking down, he examined them ruefully.

"Drendas!" Ferdia was running across the sand towards them.

Behind him, a woman watched and waited in front of the roundhouse. Lifting his face from his feet, Drendas took two steps forward, taking himself out of the reach of the water.

"Ferdia," he called.

Ignoring Seamus and Jasmine, he began to pick his way awkwardly up the beach, towards his son-in-law.

"Are you coming, Seamus?" he called over one shoulder.

Seamus grinned. "A bit of a showman, wouldn't you say, Jasmine?"

"As are you, Seamus, as are you," Drendas replied tartly, still not looking round.

Seamus laughed. He looked at Jasmine and his face became serious. "C'mon, we'd better follow him. We can talk later, when it's just you and me."

She nodded and, waiting for him to move first, slipped in behind him so he couldn't see her face.

"Drendas, father," Ferdia said as the two of them embraced.

"You are home," Drendas replied. They let one another go. "And my son, Daire?"

"He waits for the Third."

"He has not come?"

"No."

Drendas touched his arm. "It is as it should be. As was foretold. Come, we have guests, and Emer is waiting."

*

Seamus and Jasmine followed them to the house.

"Emer," Drendas greeted the woman.

"Father," she replied with an elegant dip of her head.

Wearing a long dress tied in the middle with a belt, her dark hair was intricately plaited. A red stone, maybe a ruby, adorned the brooch that fixed a light shawl to her dress. Around her neck she wore a necklace called a torc, the metal flattened and beaten. She was young, although older than Jasmine, and even if she'd hadn't spoken, her heritage was obvious. She shared Drendas' hazel eyes and Daire's hair, his sharp cheekbones and oval face, but whereas Daire had seemed open and friendly, her manner was quieter, more reserved. In comparison, Jasmine felt a mess, like a child of the forest in her rough tunic and trousers and her wild, knotted hair.

Half-turning, Drendas held out his hand. "My daughter, Emer. Emer, our guests, the druids Seamus and Jasmine."

"Seamus." Emer dipped her head again, but her eyes never left Jasmine's face. "Jasmine."

Self-conscious, Jasmine nodded awkwardly.

"Emer." Seamus smiled, bowing.

Hazel eyes examined him seriously, before returning to Jasmine's face. Oblivious, Drendas spread his hands wide and waved them inside, like a farmer herding cattle or a flock of geese. "Welcome; my home is your home. Come, come, sit, rest and eat."

Seamus went first. Dark inside, the house was one circular room with a place for the fire in the centre. Made completely from wood and reed weaved expertly together and with a bare earth floor, it was surprisingly warm. On the other side of the room, willow panels created an enclosed space, like a rough, makeshift box or cupboard, and next to that lay a pile of reed mats. Their beds, Jasmine guessed.

"Sit," Drendas ordered, coming in, indicating a space next to the fire.

They did as he said. Using his stick to lower his body stiffly to the ground, he sat opposite them. Ferdia sat next to him as Emer went over to the willow panels and, pulling one back, knelt down.

"I felt your coming." He glanced at Jasmine then back to Seamus. "I felt too, the dark one, but I could not come quicker."

"Drendas walks beneath the waves," Ferdia explained.

Seamus' eyebrows lifted. "Beneath the waves?! How?"

Drendas smiled. He had only three teeth left, and one of those was brown and decaying. As he talked, it bobbed in and out of sight, and she found herself watching for it with a sick fascination.

"On the cusp of manhood, I fished in my father's currach. There was a storm, of a power rarely seen. My father's boat sank. I could not swim, but like my father and his father before him, I had Iomlan and by, the Goddess' grace, I was saved. She showed me how to protect myself and now, in her honour, I walk." He smiled at Jasmine, his eyes gleaming. "The darkness quietens my thoughts and, as I walk, I feel her breath on my ear and my cheek as she speaks to me."

No one spoke. Jasmine glanced at Ferdia, but his eyes never left Drendas' face. He believed him, she told herself incredulously; he actually believed Drendas' Goddess talked to him while he ambled around the bed of a fjord!

Drendas smoothed down his beard, breaking the spell. "But all druids have their gifts, no?"

"Yes, we all have our own, individual talents," Seamus replied, sharing a look with Jasmine. "But I think there is much that has been forgotten."

There was another pause. Jasmine waited, wondering if Seamus was setting Drendas some sort of test, to find out how much he knew, or thought he knew.

Drendas leant forward. "The Goddess spoke to me of your coming. She told me of the thousands of seasons that would pass before you were born, and I saw such strangeness. People thronging, as the mayfly at dusk throngs the deep, cool pond, stone that was not stone and a land forged in metal." He sat back and regarded Seamus with amusement and something that was almost triumph, as if he'd seen the test and was laughing at its childlike simplicity. "I saw too, as was foretold, the return of the Tuatha de Danann, the Goddess herself brought forth by the child of Erin and Brigantes."

Seamus started. "The what?"

"The Child of Erin and Brigantes."

"Who's the Child—?" Jasmine began, but Drendas cut across her, his eyes fixed on Seamus.

"The child the dark one seeks. Have you not seen the signs? Can you not feel her? She is coming, but only through the child can she return.'

"I don't believe in Gods."

Drendas laughed with his head back, giving Jasmine a full view of the toothless back of his mouth. "Then much wisdom has been lost. Ellyllon did not believe, but you will see, and Ellyllon will see, when she returns."

"Ellyllon?" Seamus' eyes narrowed, "Has he been here?"

"He has. He spoke, and his voice weaved a great magic. Swift, like an arrow shot from the bow, so he finds the treachery in men's hearts."

"And did he? Did he find the treachery in your heart?"

Drendas smiled, but his eyes burned. "What harm would I wish my brethren in Erin, or in Brigantes, or the lands beyond? The Goddess is wise; what has passed has passed and what is to come must also come to pass." His voice hardened. "His heart is dead, poisoned by that he feeds on. What cares he for the peoples of this Isle? As a man, a druid bound to the sacred path, what care did he have for our ways? For his own people? He means to be a God among men, a God that will bring darkness." He glanced at Jasmine. "The Goddess has spoken; the Gods will not allow it."

"So you'll help us?"

"To the east lies a lough of many isles. One, the smallest, near the shore, is sacred. I have sent word to my brothers, calling them to the isle. I await their answer, but I know they will heed me and we will meet on the Sacred Isle and I will speak of the dark one, the hunger in his heart. The Goddess speaks only to me, but they will see her through me and they will know. The signs are there; do we not have the Three?"

"But…" Seamus shook his head. "You don't. It's just the two of us."

"Ah." Drendas waved his hand at him, as if to dismiss him. "But he has come."

"Malachy?!" Seamus leant forward. "Are you sure?"

"He has come. My son brings him, but the way is hard."

"Oh God, is he OK?" Jasmine asked, looking at Seamus and seeing her fear mirrored there.

Drendas nodded. "When he comes, we will go to the isle and together, my brothers and I will destroy the dark one and all those who follow him."

*

Later, leaving Seamus and Drendas to talk, Jasmine left the hut and wandered out, along the beach. It was a beautiful evening, nestled between the mountain slopes; the sun had turned a vivid hue somewhere between pink, red and orange. It streaked the sky around it, threw light and shadow across the stone. Sitting down, Jasmine hugged her knees and watched it set. It was so quiet, the water gently lapping, and with the last heat of the day she could almost convince herself she was somewhere in the Mediterranean, with her mum and John sat behind her, in some beach taverna, chatting and sipping wine. But this wasn't the Mediterranean and it wasn't her mum and John, it was Seamus and Drendas, with Ferdia watching as they talked, and Emer hovering, unnoticed, in the background.

*

They hadn't been here long and already she wished they hadn't come. The way Drendas kept looking at her was unnerving, and more than a bit creepy. His gleaming hazel eyes were similar to Seamus, but with more green flecks than brown, they had none of Seamus' warmth. His was the soft flash of amber, the burn of his inner fire, whereas Drendas' burn was cold, the fixed flame of the zealot, the fervour of the fundamentalist. And he spoke in riddles; it hurt her head just to try and follow his logic and yet he seemed so certain of everything. No wonder Daire believed everything he said. Growing up with a father like that, what choice did he have? Sighing, she placed her chin on her knees. He was so certain about Malachy, but it couldn't be true. Malachy was back with Grainne just as Seamus intended, living with her in her castle, adapting to life in the fifteenth century. She imagined him out riding, speeding along the bay, the wind in his face. When this was all over Seamus would find him and bring him home and he'd go back to school and life would continue. She sighed. It seemed to have come out of nowhere, but she had the strangest feeling she wouldn't be joining them.

"Jasmine?"

It was Ferdia, coming after her for a second time. She didn't look up and after a moment, he sat down beside her. Silence.

"You are thinking of Malachy."

"Before I left, we fought."

"Lovers fight."

"Yeah."

She wished they'd parted better. But at least he wasn't here to see her, to see what she was becoming. The sun had almost set. A breeze ruffled her hair, stroked her arm with a cooling breath and she shivered.

"It was about Iomlan – my power. He doesn't understand. I don't suppose he can." A thought struck her. "How is it, being married to someone with magic?"

She wanted to ask *how do you cope*, but she daren't. What happened with Malachy had been so fast. It seemed she'd been moping after him for ages and when she'd given up, finally, he was there. But looking back, they hadn't had a chance. And yet Daire and Ferdia seemed to manage it.

"We fight."

"And what do you do when you stop fighting?"

"Make love." He grinned. "Sometimes I fear Daire fights just so it will be so."

She laughed at that. Ferdia's arm snaked around her shoulders and he pulled her close. They stayed like that for a few seconds and then, abruptly, he pulled away.

"Ferdia?" She touched his arm, looked into his face.

His eyes were bright with unshed tears. He wiped hastily at them and turned away.

"It's OK, it's not that bad," she joked.

"No," he replied, his voice determined. "We must trust to Drendas, and the words of the Goddess." But still he wouldn't look at her.

Chapter Seven

The river widened, its meandering becoming slower, deeper. Malachy sniffed, catching the first faint scent of the sea. Benbulbin lay to their right, looming over them in the darkness like some huge, high wall. Almost to the mouth, the flow quickened and soon they needed the oars only to steer the boat and stop it floating helplessly into the riverbank. For Malachy, it was a welcome rest. They hadn't travelled that far, but already his arms were beginning to ache, the muscles protesting. He flexed first one arm and then the other, stretching to unlimber them, glancing behind him. He could just make out the torches of the party following them. They bobbed as if those that held them were running, but thankfully, they were still far away. *No, wait.* He stopped, squinted. There were two sets of lights, one slightly ahead.

"Daire, look."

Daire's head swivelled. "Currachs!"

"What do we do?"

"Hide."

Malachy looked around wildly. "But where? We're almost out to sea."

"There are many places to hide where water and land meet. Connemara lies south; we will go north."

"But what then? Have you horses nearby?"

Daire shook his head. "We will travel by water."

"What? In this?!"

Daire grinned. "I am druid; what harm can the waters do you?" He lifted his arm and pointed into the distance. "Look, Malachy, the river's mouth."

At the river mouth, the tide took the boat and began pulling it in a sideways sweep, south and out across the bay. They rowed furiously, going against the tide. The boat rocked, but was surprisingly buoyant, riding the waves as if nothing could sink it. Malachy bit back a groan, the ache in his arms intensifying. He didn't think he could row for much longer.

"There!" Stopping for a moment, Daire pointed to where, just ahead, the land reached out into a thin, rocky promontory. "Behind lies a cove. We will hide there." He glanced back. "Quickly!"

They were coming. Malachy could just make out the torchlight as the currachs approached the mouth of the river. Again they rowed, bending their backs as they drove the oars hard into the water. In, back, out; in, back, out. The boat sped across the surface of the water, tipping up and down with the waves. The promontory moved closer. Malachy gasped for breath, desperate to look back, but he daren't. In, back, out. In, back, out. The words seared through his brain, like the pain that was moving up his arms towards his shoulders. He had to hold on, he couldn't, mustn't stop. They reached the promontory, steered the currach awkwardly around it, fighting the waves that threatened to dash them bodily onto the rocks. Finally they were past it and following Daire's lead; they moved the boat back in towards the land. Malachy risked a last look back. The light of the torches made the water around the boats gleam, but they were still too far away to see them. Another moment and the promontory hid them from view. Slowly, painfully, they rowed their boat inland.

*

They pulled the boat up onto the beach and tucked it in close to the rocks. Exhausted, Malachy fell onto the sand and lay there panting. Daire slipped onto the rocks above him and, keeping his body low, watched the boats out on the bay. Three all together, they spread out. They began to move inland, as if planning to comb the shore.

"Malachy, come." Daire scrambled off the rocks and back onto his feet.

Reluctantly, Malachy joined him and the two moved swiftly up the beach and into the forest.

"What about the boat?" Malachy asked as he and Daire crouched in the undergrowth and looked out.

Daire's eyes never left the water. "My magic hides it. I thank the Goddess Cathbad and Ellyllon are not here."

"Cathbad?"

"Shhh," Daire admonished him as one of the currachs came into view.

Two men swept their torches, illuminating the shoreline as oars dipped and splashed. Malachy started, remembering their footsteps, but when he looked, the sand was empty, undisturbed. Someone shouted, the voice echoing across the water. For a moment, Malachy thought Daire's plan had failed and they'd been spotted, but then the currach turned abruptly and went back the way it came. Daire breathed out.

"What happened?" Malachy whispered.

"I know not." Daire shrugged. "But the Gods smiles down on us. Wait; I will return."

Malachy watched him slip back onto the beach before turning left and disappearing. He sat back, resting his back against a tree, and waited. Minutes passed, and he stifled a yawn. He had to stay awake and alert, but he was so tired. He hadn't slept since last night, and that seemed like a lifetime ago. He shifted, thought about getting up and walking about just to keep himself awake. His eyes closed.

*

"Malachy!"

A hand shook his shoulder. He woke, blinking, against the sunlight. The sun was still low in the sky; dawn had not long passed. Daire was crouched next to him, his face pressed close.

"I'm — awake." Sitting up, he ran his fingers through his hair and looked about him. It was morning. Daire sat back, reaching for a rough cloth bag.

"I have food. Eat."

He passed Malachy what looked like a rough, grey-white bread. Too hungry to look too closely at it, he chewed at one end. Toughened by age, it tasted of oats and water and had the consistency of somewhere between putty and wallpaper paste. His stomach growled and forcing it down, he took another bite.

"Why did you let me sleep?" He asked in between chews.

"Our journey is long." Daire pulled out another bag stained with patches of purple and folded the cloth back revealing a small pile of blackberries. "Eat."

Malachy took a few, popping them one at a time in his mouth.

"More."

"What about you?"

"I have eaten."

He did as he was told, savouring the juices that wetted his mouth before reluctantly returning to the oat bread.

"Garach's warriors move among the inlets, hugging the land. To pass, we must go to deeper water."

"Deeper water." Malachy repeated, imagining rowing out into open sea.

Daire smiled, as if reading his mind. "Eat, and you will see."

*

They set off as soon as Malachy had finished. Climbing to his feet, Malachy's whole body protested. After the rowing, he'd stiffened as he'd slept. He staggered after Daire, marvelling at his fitness. Half-curled, like a leaf, the boat was bigger than he realised, the lattice framework more intricate. The outside was made of skin, stained by a liquid or paste that Malachy presumed kept it waterproof. Without a word, Daire climbed inside and, rummaging in the bottom, pulled out a thick wooden pole. Curled around it was a large, heavy looking piece of cloth. Confused, it took him a moment to think what it could be and then it hit him. It was a sail, attached to a makeshift mast. Marvelling at the ingenuity, Malachy helped Daire place the mast into the groove carved into the bottom of the boat and held it while he tied it securely in place using thin leather straps. And then, slowly, they pushed the boat back to the water. The waves took it and gasping against the cold they followed it to knee height, then climbed inside. Rowing, they went north, hugging the land to stay out of the view of Garach's men. With Sligo Bay far behind and the wind whipping along the coast, Daire told Malachy to stop rowing and unfurled the sail. Using Iomlan, they sped out, at last, towards open water.

The land receded. Confident they could not be seen, Daire turned the sail and steered the boat south.

"Who is Cathbad?" Malachy asked after a while.

Daire pulled his eyes from the sail. "A druid from Ulster. He follows Ellyllon. It is said he descends from the Gods, the Tuatha de Danann, maybe Dagda himself."

"What do you think?"

"His hair is golden and his magic very powerful." Daire shrugged. "Once the Gods laid with people, but the Tuatha de Danann returned to the earth long ago. They see us, but do not walk among us."

Untying the sail, he turned it, keeping the boat on course. "Cathbad is the light to Ellyllon's dark, yet they are the same. Only, Cathbad is the fruit you must taste to know its bitterness."

Yeah, like that juicy blackberry, Malachy thought sourly, *with the maggot inside*.

High in a cloudless sky, the sun was way too hot. Daire had asked him to keep an eye out for Garach's men and he scanned the sea and the land rising up behind it. It was hard to tell, but he thought by the height of the land they were passing the cliffs of North Mayo. Black rock, topped with green, rolled with the movement of the boat. He tried to keep his eyes open, but the waves and the emptiness seemed determined to lull him to sleep. Daire was silent. Malachy's eyes closed. He dozed.

*

"Malachy, wake."

"Yeah?" He sat up, stretching. "Sorry."

There was a pause.

"How long will it take to get to Connemara?" he asked, just for something to say, hoping that talking would keep him awake.

"One, two nights. Beneath Cruachan Aigle lies an isle. It belongs to the druid Cethern. It is said he commands the creatures of the sea. Garach's warriors will not go there. We will sleep there."

"But won't he know we're there?"

Daire nodded. "Long ago, he was a friend to my father. His mind moves as the ocean; restless, with sudden storms, but he will not harm Drendas' son."

The morning wore on. They'd passed the headland as Malachy dozed and were following the low-lying land south. At Daire's insistence they ate again, but sparingly, Daire mindful of the little they had. They drank beer, sipped from a tall earthenware bowl Daire had pulled out of the boat's depths. Watery, Malachy didn't really like it, but almost immediately he felt better as his body responded to its natural sugar. By the afternoon, clouds had moved in, blown by a quickening wind, their thick white puffs edged with a thin trace of silver. Daire studied them dubiously.

"It's going to rain?" Malachy asked, already knowing the answer.

Daire nodded. "With Lir's blessing we will reach the isle." He looked up again. "But I fear his displeasure. We must stay close to the land."

Immediately, Daire began to move inland. Swivelling, Malachy watched the coastline carefully, but there was no sign of Garach's men or their boats. There was no sign of anyone; no fishermen, no settlements, just water, rock and grass.

"If Seamus and Jasmine knew I was coming, why didn't they wait for me?" Malachy asked, gazing at the empty land and finally asking the question that had been bothering him.

Daire gave him a shrewd look that reminded him of Brennan. Was he really so transparent?

"They did not believe you would come and they could not wait. It is not safe."

Malachy sat up. Beneath him, the boat rocked as a large wave caught it, tossing it up and over, the water slapping against the side, but he didn't even notice.

"Ellyllon and Garach's warriors waited for them," Daire continued. "The attack was sudden, ferocious. Many men died. I feared Seamus would fall, and in his death all that was foretold would not come to pass, but in aiding them I showed Ellyllon I stand against him. His power grows. He speaks to chieftains and warriors and no man can resist. He speaks to druids, and many, like Cathbad, fall from the path. And so, his word follows them, like fire."

Malachy frowned, remembering the look on Jasmine's face after she'd destroyed Cormac, and wondered how coming straight from that into such a violent, bloody battle had affected her. He desperately wanted to ask Daire, but daren't. Part of him feared the answer, the rest thought Daire couldn't possibly understand. He was too used to the violence; it was too everyday, too normal. He shivered in the ocean's breeze. And now, running from Ellyllon and Cathbad, anything could be happening to them. Already, without Daire, Ellyllon would probably have killed Seamus, leaving a vulnerable Jasmine all alone. Malachy imagined them desperately trying to stay one step ahead as tribe after tribe swept in on them, harrying them and forcing them on to the one place they had left to go: Drendas and Connemara.

"All will be well." Daire gave him an encouraging smile. "Ellyllon will not attack Drendas for fear of uniting all druid against him."

They just have to get there, Malachy told himself darkly.

In the distance lay the islands off the coast of Clew Bay and to the left, only just visible, was the triangular peak of Croagh Patrick. Overhead, the clouds continued to build.

*

The coastline was becoming increasingly jagged, layers of rock protecting small, narrow inlets. They crossed a second bay, passed a round sandy shore and skirted the high cliffs to the west. If Malachy had his geography right, they were passing Achill Island.

"There – the isle." Daire pointed as it came into view around the edge of the cliffs.

Little more than a large hunk of rock in the ocean, it wasn't far, maybe a few hundred metres away. But if there was anywhere to land, it must be on the other side. The boat lurched, caught by the wind, and the surge of a wave and water sprayed. Away from the shelter of the bay the waves were wild and, drawn on by the wind, becoming worse. The wind whistled across the rock, tugged at the sail, pushing the boat perilously close to the land. Black cliffs loomed, dwarfing them. Feeling the first spot of rain, Malachy looked up and saw how dark the clouds where. Daire cocked his head, and for a moment Malachy thought he was going to say something but, turning back to the sail, his lips remained firmly closed.

Flattened by the wind and buffeted by the waves, they passed the cliffs and an inlet came into view. Black rock, eroded and sharpened into thick, hard shards, surrounded a small cove, ending in a crescent shaped, sandy beach. Behind the beach, huge boulders dotted the grass; to the right a track, worn white by use, stretched up over the cliff and disappeared down the other side. Maybe they should stop there and take shelter. Malachy stared at the boulders, squinting. Something was wrong. They didn't look right, as if the sand and the edge of the boulders didn't quite meet. The boat lurched, caught by a sudden gust of wind. It caught the sail, pulling it taut, and the boat heaved, swinging violently, throwing them back against the side as the prow came around to face the beach.

"Malachy!" Daire shouted. "The sail!" He leapt to his feet, his knife swinging. It sliced the cords holding the sail to the mast, and the sail crumbled. Without thinking, Malachy grabbed at it, stopping it from falling overboard and stuffing it down towards the bottom of the boat. He looked up. Speeding down the inlet, they were being drawn towards the beach.

"Daire, what's happening?"

Daire waved his hand, as if flicking a fly away. A man appeared, stood on top of a flat boulder and dressed in a long grey cloak. Tall and thin, with a large, hooked nose, his hands were raised, like a priest lifting up towards heaven. Behind him, a handful of men crept slowly forward, their weapons raised.

"Rochtad!" Daire exclaimed.

Beneath them, the sea was churning, the waves increasing to an impossible size as they rolled towards the beach, carrying the boat with them.

"Daire, what about the oars?" Malachy shouted, looking around desperately.

"We cannot row against him!" Daire threw out his hand, "Hold on!"

Malachy grabbed the side and almost immediately the boat leapt backwards, the stern lifting as if to cut through the waves, like a speedboat. But Rochtad was too strong. Curling his hands into a fist, slowly, inexorably, he began to pull them back. Daire's face twisted and the boat stopped, trapped between two forces. Rocking wildly, the sea rolled in over the sides, splashing into their faces, making their eyes sting. Salt water caught the back of Malachy's throat, making him cough.

"I cannot free us," Daire groaned. "His magic equals mine."

Something hit the side of the boat with a loud whack before falling back into the water. There, at the water's edge, was a warrior, his arm working furiously as the string on his sling whirled. Beside him, another warrior held a spear. Slowly, deliberately, he pulled his arm back, almost to the ground, then threw it forward in a powerful, wide arc. Released, the spear hurtled towards them, heading straight for Malachy.

Chapter Eight

Lifting the bottom of her dress, Jasmine paddled restlessly through the water. Deliciously cold against the heat of the day, it tickled her toes and lapped gently against her shins. At Drendas' command Ferdia had taken a small, rough looking boat out onto the fjord. To her surprise, Seamus had gone with him. They'd disappeared some time ago, leaving her alone with Drendas. She didn't blame Seamus for going; there was a sense that today was an all too brief lull, a chance to at least try to relax and refresh themselves. Seamus had slept until late, but she'd been up early, her head filled with half-remembered dreams and wanderings that flitted like shadows through the corners of her mind and drove her out into the sunshine. She'd bathed in the fjord, luxuriating in the sensation of being properly clean for the first time in days.

Off to the left was the huge wooden pyre they'd built that morning. It was a beacon for Malachy and Daire, a light in the darkness to bring them home, for Drendas was certain they'd arrive tonight. Behind it, in the willow enclosure next to the house, Emer tended their horses. In her own quiet way, she seemed to do everything – cook, cleaner, farmer, gardener, nursemaid – while her father communed with his precious Goddess. Emer had given her this dress; she'd made it herself on a rough woollen loom and the belt to tie it with. Purplish blue, it was so typical a Jasmine colour it was as if Emer knew her. Not that she wasn't grateful; it felt good to be out of her tunic and leggings and into something clean. She'd washed them in the fjord, and they were now hung on the string Emer used. After she'd thanked her, Jasmine had tried to strike up a conversation with her, but with a faint smile Emer had shook her head and moved away, as if she were too busy to chat. But Jasmine couldn't shake the feeling she was avoiding her. If only Drendas would do the same.

She glanced out across the fjord, but there was still no sign of Seamus and Ferdia. By late afternoon it was hotter than it had been at midday, as if by lowering the sun wasn't losing strength but gaining it. She stifled a yawn. It was so quiet here, so peaceful, she longed to lie down in the soft, warm sand and let herself drift away.

"Jasmine."

She stiffened. It was Drendas, not for the first time, creeping up behind her. Even last night, tossing and turning in the dark, she'd felt his eyes on her.

Reluctantly, she turned. "Yes?"

He was stood a few feet away from her, his eyes, squinting against the sun, locked onto hers.

"You must rest."

She resisted the urge to sigh. "I'm waiting for Seamus."

"He fishes."

I know that. She thought irritably. *How did he manage to make it seem as if he saw everything, even when he couldn't possibly?*

"It is the Goddess that sees, not I. Come." He gestured with one hand. "Sit with me."

Chastened, she did as he said and leaving the water, came over to him. Immediately, he grabbed her arm and sitting down, pulled her with him. Sat by side, with only a breath between them, her stomach twisted. It was all she could do not to move away.

"Jasmine, you are young, but you must prepare."

"Prepare?" She looked at him.

His face was pressed so close she could see the errant hairs in his moustache, the ones that curled up or out instead of down.

"For the coming." His brown tooth flashed at her. She could smell his breath.

"For Malachy?" Surreptitiously, she leant back, trying not to make it obvious.

"For the Goddess." He looked at her with such affection, that for a moment, she felt bad.

He was helping them with Ellyllon, after all. And without him, who knew what could've happened to her and Seamus?

"I'm sorry, I don't understand."

He smiled. "She comes through the Child of Erin and Brigantes."

"Oh, I see," she said, even though she didn't really. It was so vague it could mean anything. "Where is the child?"

Drendas grinned, "The child is here."

"What? Where?" She looked around. There was no one there, apart from Emer. "Emer?"

He giggled, his bright eyes boring into hers, as if he were trying to see past the outer shell and into the centre of her. Suddenly, she didn't want to know. She looked away. In the silence, she dipped her hand into the sand, then slowly brought it out again, watching as the grains trickled off her fingers. She could feel his eyes on her. He was waiting for her to ask, knowing that she'd have to know, but she was determined not to give him the satisfaction.

*

"OK, where is Erin?" she asked finally, not looking at him.

He shrugged. "Erin is here."

Of, course. She knew it. *Erin, Eire, Ireland*.

"And Brigantes?"

"The land that spawned Ellyllon."

Her heart sank.

Brigantes, Britannia, Britain.

It was obvious; now the way he kept looking at her made sense. But he'd made a mistake; it wasn't her, it couldn't be, both her parents were English. Unless… She remembered Ellyllon's taunts on the sand dunes outside the church, the last remnant of the village of Killaspugbrone. At the time she'd thought he was full of spite, then afterwards that he'd been deliberately trying to rile her so that she'd attack him and help him open the rift, but now?

Drendas put his hand on her head and pressed once, very, very gently. "Do not fear, Child of Erin and Brigantes, for those that welcome the Goddess will be honoured above all others for their sacrifice."

It was too much. Pulling her head away, she scrambled to her feet.

"Jasmine, Jasmine!" Drendas called after her.

She sped up until she was no longer walking but running, as fast as she could, away from Drendas, the beach and everything he was saying.

*

Almost to the slope that would take her out of the valley, she realised what she was doing and slid to a halt, her feet skidding on stone. Whether she liked it or not she couldn't leave the valley alone; she needed Drendas' protection. Breathing heavily, she turned back. Drendas had returned to the house and was stood talking to Emer. She watched them talk, or rather Drendas talk as Emer listened, her head bent. Then, when he'd finished, they turned and entered the house together. Determined not to go back, she moved over to a large cluster of stones and, sitting down on the biggest one, tried to ignore the tremble in her hands. She wished Seamus was back. She still couldn't see their boat, even from up here; they must've gone almost to the sea. *Why isn't he here? He should be here, should've stayed with me and not left me alone with Drendas.* She pushed the thought away. Panicking didn't help anyone. Putting her head in her hands, she closed her eyes and tried to calm herself.

The strangest thing was that part of her wasn't really that surprised at Drendas' revelation, as if she already knew that John was her dad. It made perfect sense. There had always been a connection between them, a shared... something. And while it had been the unrequited love for his best friend's wife that had driven John away, maybe it was the possibility that the child could be his that had brought him back again. But John had promised her an end to the lies. Why hadn't he told her? She lifted her head. Seamus knew! The way he'd reacted when Drendas mentioned the child; it was obvious. But then, if John knew then of course, Seamus did too. But what about her mum? Did she know? She'd slept with John; she must've known there was a chance she was his, or had she just buried her head in the sand, telling herself Jasmine could only be Justin's? But how could she? How could any of them? For a second time, she'd had to learn for herself who she was. Didn't she have enough to deal with?

*

The shadows lengthened. Unnoticed, the hillside behind her darkened. Raindrops, cold on the top of her head, roused her from her thoughts. Evening was drawing in, bringing a cooling night rain with it. She looked out across the fjord. She had no idea how long she'd sat there, but there was still no sign of Seamus or Ferdia. The rain was getting stronger and she wasn't wearing her cloak. There was no shelter up here either. She didn't want to go back and face Drendas alone, but she didn't want to get soaked either. There was nothing else to do. Getting to her feet, she scrambled down the hillside.

Skirting the beach, she half-ran towards Drendas' house. All was quiet, the only sound the soft patter of rain. Drendas and Emer must be inside. She stepped under the low hanging thatch and out of the rain. Still no sound. No sound of activity or even the low murmur of conversation coming from inside the house. Overshadowed, the doorway was dark, the inside darker. Reaching the doorway, she hesitated, listening. Nothing.

"Hello?"

She caught a scent, musky with a touch of spice. There was a rustle, the sound of movement. Footsteps.

"Hello?" She stepped into the doorway.

A body bundled into her, knocking her sideways as it shot past.

She glimpsed Emer's black hair, a flash of her pale, set face and her long, lightly woven dress and then she was gone in the direction of the outhouse. For a moment, she was tempted to follow, but then Drendas was there. "Come, Jasmine." He beamed at her, beckoning.

Inside, at his insistence, she sat down. He joined her, his movements surprisingly spry as he sat cross-legged opposite her. The scent was coming from a small clay bowl next to the fire. Inside it, small pieces of roughly chopped wood smouldered, giving off thin trails of smoke. Stood beside it, a wooden cup was filled almost to the brim with water.

"Emer—?" she began.

"She is well." He dismissed her with a wave. "I gave you pain, forgive me."

She looked away. "It's OK." She lied.

Picking up the cup, he held it out to her. "You thirst, Jasmine. Drink."

Something told her not to drink, but she was so thirsty. "Thank you," she said, accepting the cup.

She took a sip. The water tasted strange, like the scent that was filling room, but it wasn't unpleasant.

Drink, a voice inside her urged. *And you will feel better, stronger.*

Obeying, she drank it straight down.

"You are prepared," Drendas intoned, taking the cup from her.

Purified, agreed the voice.

A roar came from outside, followed by a loud whoosh.

"The pyre is lit."

Jasmine blinked. "Isn't it a bit early?"

Drendas shook his head. "It is time. Come, Jasmine."

"But – Seamus?"

"He comes."

Getting to his feet, he held out his hand.

It's time. The voice in her head buzzed with excitement. In a daze, she took his hand, heaving herself up.

"Come, Jasmine," Drendas repeated, his eyes gleaming. "Can you not feel her? She waits."

*

Stood next to the pyre, Emer watched them come. Reaching high above her head, the flames roared. Drendas had hold of Jasmine's hand. Her head floated; she looked down at her feet, watched them step, one foot in front of the other, but they didn't seem to belong to her. It had stopped raining, she noticed vaguely; behind her, if she'd turned to look, was the ghost of the moon. They reached Emer and without a word, Drendas let her go. Moving behind them, he turned to face them. Raising his arms, he began to chant and Jasmine felt the surge of his Iomlan. Slipping out of him, it slowly encircled him. Turning, it gathered speed.

Emer's hands slipped around her and positioned her in front of the fire. "Jasmine, look."

She stared in the fire. The heat was immense; she could feel the force of its burning on her face and hands. Laughter bubbled up inside her, thrilling her body with an anticipation that made her want to throw back her head and shout.

I am ready.

"Come, Brid!" Drendas screamed behind her, thrusting his hands forward.

Emer let go as his Iomlan hit her full in the back. She pitched forward, helpless against the force of it. Flames flared, she heard herself give one loud, thin scream of terror and then she was falling, into the fire…

There was no crash, no jar as her body hit wood and branches. There was only unbearable pain as her hair caught fire and her skin began to burn, and then, suddenly, it was gone, and she felt nothing but warm, like a baby wrapped in a soft, fluffy blanket. She opened her eyes. She was in a huge cavern, the stone cut and chiselled into the shape of a long hall. Water dripped; she could smell the damp, the scent of stone and earth hidden below ground, but it was warm and bright. Above her, strata of rose quartz twinkled like stars and to her left, in the centre of the room, lay a stone table. Made of granite, etched into the top of its smooth, sculptured surface, were three interlocking spirals, a wooden bowl in the centre of each swirl. Behind the table, a woman stood looking at her. Completely naked, her once athletic body had curved with age, her arms, legs and waist thickening even as her round stomach drooped, its skin lined and stretched with children. Grey flecked her dark hair, around the crown, forehead and ears. In one quick movement, she darted around the table and, grabbing Jasmine by the back of the neck, pulled her towards her. Their lips touched. Fire danced across her lips and into her mouth, its blistering heat searing her tongue, her gums and the roof of her mouth. She tried to scream and to pull back, away from the pain, but the hand holding her was too strong.

"Rogha." She heard the word in her head as flames licked the back of throat and tumbled downwards, burning and burning. They hit her stomach and the heat engulfed her.

The hand released her and groaning, she slipped to the floor, her stomach

"Drendas, what happened?!"

The voice was Seamus'. He was close by, talking softly. Jasmine opened her eyes. She was in Drendas' hut, a reed mat beneath her. Emer knelt beside her, her face a picture of concentration as she looked down at something in her hands. Behind her, Seamus was stood facing Drendas, the light from the fire illuminating one side of his face.

"Jasmine feared for you. We looked for you, by the water."

"And?" Seamus' voice sharpened.

"She fell, as the tree without roots falls, swift."

"And she hasn't woken up?"

"No."

Emer looked up and, seeing Jasmine's eyes open, raised a finger to her lips. Shhh. They stared at one another.

"Could it have been Ellyllon?" Seamus wondered out loud. "Did he do something to her?"

"No." Drendas sounded definite. "He was not there."

"Then what?! Something happened to her!"

Something had happened to her. She felt terrible, her body sore and her stomach raw, but for the life of her she couldn't remember what.

"Seamus," she tried to say, but it came out as a dry whisper.

Emer got to her feet. "Father."

With a loud exclamation, Seamus dashed over to her and careless of his knee, threw himself down next to her. "Jasmine, Jasmine. Are you alright?"

"I—"

"What happened?"

"I – can't remember."

"What? Nothing at all?" Seamus persisted.

There was something, an image of flames reaching up into the sky and a brief sensation of pain, but it was as gone as quickly as it came. She looked down. The skin of her arms was smooth and unblemished. It made no sense, but she was too tired to care.

"Maybe I can help." He lifted up his hand, as if to touch her forehead.

"Don't!" she heard herself cry, pulling away.

Inside her head, a fire roared, the pain of it making her flinch.

"Seamus," Drendas interjected quickly. "She must rest. Come, eat, Emer will tend to her."

Frowning, Seamus lowered his hand. Leaning in, he began to speak to her, his face urgent. She saw his lips move, but the roar was getting louder, drowning him out. She closed her eyes.

*

"Jasmine?"

She woke for a second time. Drendas was sat beside her, a bowl and spoon in his hand. Apart from him, the roundhouse was empty. Swallowing, she licked her lips, moistening them.

"Where's Seamus?" she croaked.

"Eating with Ferdia and Emer. As must you."

"I'm not hungry."

"You must eat," he said softly, lifting the spoon.

"But I don't want it."

His lips tightened. "Your body must be strong. Eat."

He thrust the spoon towards her. Grey-white lumps sat in a thin, watery sauce. Reluctantly, she lifted her head and took it. Her stomach churned. She swallowed, fighting the urge to gag. Sauce ran down the corners of her mouth and onto her chin, before dripping on to her neck.

Drendas' eyes flashed. "More."

Keeping her eyes on him, she forced another four spoonfuls down.

"Seamus must be calmed. When you are well, you will talk to him." Putting the bowl down, he lifted his hand to her forehead and this time she didn't pull away.

Cold, damp fingers caressed her skin. She felt his power and a sharp stab of pain shot across her forehead.

"Aahh." He closed his eyes and let his hand drop.

"Drendas!"

He opened his eyes and looked her. And then, with a cry, threw himself down beside her. Lowering his face, he lifted her hand to his lips and gave it a lingering kiss. Dry, old lips wet her skin with spittle. The sensation was unpleasant, but the gesture not unwelcome.

Turning her head, she smiled tightly, conscious of the need to be gracious. "Thank you."

"My honour." His hazel eyes shone, and bending his head again to her hand, he slobbered some more.

Chapter Nine

Frozen, Malachy watched the spear come towards him. Daire lifted his hand, as if to knock it away, but at that moment, Rochtad leapt forward, one arm swinging, and the spear veered sideways, hitting the water with a loud splash. Free from his grip, the boat lurched backwards, towards the open water. More stones landed just behind them, missing the boat by inches.

"Malachy, down!" Daire shouted.

The boat sped up, and Malachy, crouched at the bottom, watched the end of the inlet approach. *We've done it*, he thought, glancing back, just as Rochtad raised his arms again.

Malachy flinched, waiting for the pull that would drag them back, but it didn't come. Rochtad's arms were still lifting, his chest flung outwards. He fell forward, onto his knees.

"Malachy, look!" Daire shouted, pointing to the top of the cliff face.

Framed against the black clouds, his back to the Atlantic, was a figure. Dressed in a long blue cloak, in his left hand, he held a staff high into the air. The right hand pointed, as if to tell them to go further around the coast. Showing no desire to rush, Rochtad clambered to his feet and slowly, deliberately, turned to face his attacker. Almost immediately, the boat stopped. Still pointing, the figure jabbed its finger furiously.

"No," Daire muttered, almost to himself. "I will not leave you to fight him alone."

Sending out a pulse, it caught Rochtad from behind, knocking him sideways. The warriors whirled, lifted their weapons, but there was nothing they could do; the boat was too far away. They watched as, regaining his feet, Rochtad looked from one to the other of them, and then, with a loud curse, he faced the boat.

"Rochtad, no, I beg of you!" the druid on the cliff shouted, but he ignored him.

He lifted his hands, swung them back then forward, just as the druid on the cliff swung his staff and Daire, in the boat, let fly. Managing to deflect one, Rochtad was lifted high into the air by the other. He struggled against it, Iomlan spilling out of him like sparks from a fire, but the druid was swinging again. He threw his staff forward, sending Rochtad hurtling, limbs flaying, towards the rocks. With a sickening crack, he hit them headfirst, the sharp stone shattering his skull and driving splinters into his brain. He crumbled. Shocked, the others watched as the druid straightened and then slowly brought his staff around to point at the warriors.

"Drop your weapons, go!"

The threat was clear. For a moment, they looked at one another and then one by one they dropped their weapons and began shuffling towards the path. With the druid's staff still trained on them, they followed the path up the far cliff wall and disappeared over the top.

"Wait!" the druid called to Daire and Malachy.

Lowering his staff, he ran along the cliff, skirting the cove and, like the warriors, disappeared down the other side. Their faces pale, Malachy and Daire looked at one another.

"We must thank him for our lives," Daire said grimly, although he looked as if that were the last thing he wanted to do.

Using his Iomlan, he steered the boat in towards the beach. It began to rain, soft at first but getting harder. Malachy kept a close on eye on the path, but there was no sign of the druid or the warrior. He half-hoped the druid wouldn't reappear. He knew he should feel grateful, but the way he'd killed their attacker had been so brutal. The bottom of the boat hit sand. Clambering out, they slipped up to their knees into surprisingly warm water and began pulling the boat out of the current. A few inches and they finished. Malachy looked up.

"Daire!" He pointed.

The druid was back. Holding his staff in one hand, he ran swiftly down the path towards them, his movement light, effortless. Without a word, they left the boat and walked up the beach to meet him. Malachy averted his face, trying not to look at the body on the rocks or the red that was staining the sand.

They reached the grass. Joining them, the druid slowed and stopped. One hand held the edge of his hood, holding it forward, as if the druid was unwilling to let them see his face.

"They will not return," he said, his voice low.

Beneath his cloak, he wore nothing but a tunic the colour of rust. Long, much longer than Daire's, it reached down to his calves. Malachy stared at the bottom of his legs. Hairy, there was something about them.

"I, Daire, son of Drendas, thank you," Daire said with a bob of his head.

"Son of Drendas?!" The druid took a step back.

"Yes. We seek shelter and the protection from the druid known as Cethern."

There was a pause. The hand flexed and slowly the druid pulled back his hood, releasing grey-blond hair hanging loose to mid-thigh. The face was narrow, with wide, full lips and freckled skin browned and lined by the elements. Grey eyes moved slowly from one to the other of them, as if determine their reaction. The druid was a woman.

"I am Cethern."

Daire started. "My father spoke often of Cethern. You cannot be he."

"Your father," she repeated, her voice dripping with sarcasm. She took a deep breath, calming herself. She had no love for Drendas, Malachy thought, watching her. It took a moment, and then she continued. "I am Cethern, daughter of Cethern."

"But you are a woman."

"My father wished for a son." She straightened. "Are you, the son of Drendas, as the acorn to the oak, or will you accept the protection of a woman?"

"It would be my honour."

Her eyes softened, the light inside them giving the grey an almost violet hue. "Then come, brother. I will guide you to my home."

*

Walking behind, Malachy followed them back to the boat. If Cethern noticed him, she showed no sign until they were back aboard and he and Daire had retrieved the oars from the bottom of the boat. Turning to look at him, she watched as he settled the oars with a faint smile on her face. Malachy's lips tightened. Her staring wasn't exactly helping. Trying to synchronise with Daire, he pulled at the oar, but it slipped in the wet. Swearing under his breath, he tried again.

"And from which tree did this poor fledgling fall?" she asked Daire as they began to row.

Daire laughed. "Malachy is one of the Three."

"The Three?" Her smile faded. "The Three is a legend."

"The Three was foretold."

"By Drendas." She shook her head. "The voice of his Goddess has driven him from his wits."

Her voice was sharp with bitterness.

"You know my father?"

She looked away. "No. My father spoke of him. How he turned druids against women. '*A woman cannot be druid*'. I am a woman and I am druid."

"My father is wise, but no man can be wise in all things."

She looked back at him. "No, he cannot."

"But you have heard the coming of Ellyllon, the dark one?"

"I have heard, and I have seen. He believes in the prophecy?" Daire nodded. "Then that is why he hunts you." She stared into the water. "Rochtad, son of Maine, was a friend, his gentle heart strong with kindness. His was the gift of healing."

"And yet his heart was turned."

"Yes, but I thought only to wound him." She glanced at Malachy. "He is but one. What of the other?"

"They are with my father. When the Three are reunited, we will travel to Lough Orbsen, to the Sacred Isle."

"Drendas asks a hearing?"

Daire nodded, grunting with the effort of rowing. Almost to open water and away from the shelter of the cove, the waves were getting stronger. They buffeted the boat, driven on by the wind.

"It is a waste of strength to row in restless water," Cethern said bluntly. "The dark one cannot follow us here. Come, use your magic."

Doing as she said, Daire steered them towards her island. Sitting low in the sea, it was very bare. Grass was dotted with granite and the occasional scrawny bush or windblown patch of gorse. Hunched inside his cloak, as far as Malachy could see, there was no real shelter, no place to escape the rain that was beginning to pour. Cethern guided them around to the south shore of the island and into a small, narrow inlet. The water was deep, but jagged rock waited just below the surface, ready to rip and tear through the waterproof skin. Malachy peered over the side and watched as they floated inches over the top of it. Without Cethern, her perfect knowledge, he doubted they'd have made it through in one piece. The bottom of the boat bumped the beach and once again, they clambered out, this time pulling the boat fully out of the water and up to the farthest end of the narrow beach.

Following Cethern, they climbed the grassy slope, heads bent against the wind and the rain. Malachy shivered, chilled by the rain that was already seeping through his thick woollen cloak. Across the ocean came a clap and a rumble of thunder. Malachy counted; one, two, three. On ten, lightning flashed. Cethern sped up, striding across grass that must surely just lead off the other side of the island and back into the sea. She passed a cluster of bushes and for a second disappeared. They reached the bushes and she reappeared again. Walking down a slope towards a hollow, built into an almost perfect circle, was a thick, crumbling stone wall. Straight ahead, lay a gap just wide enough for a horse to ride through. It looked like the ruins of an ancient settlement or some kind of fort. Confident that they would follow, Cethern slipped through the gap and disappeared inside.

Speeding up, they followed her into the stone circle and stopped. There was no sign of her. The only place she could've gone was a huge pile of stones built tight into the wall.

"Maybe she's in there?" Malachy offered.

"The resting place of the ancestors?" Daire shook his head, his face ominous.

At that moment, as if to contradict him, Cethern's head reappeared around the side of the stones but almost as quickly disappeared again.

"Come on," Malachy said, eager to be out of the rain.

Still reluctant, Daire followed more slowly.

Seen from the front, there was a low, narrow doorway. Built off-centre, it seemed deliberately placed to utilise the shelter of the wall. Ducking down, his feet scraping across loose stone, Malachy inched awkwardly inside. Sitting cross-legged a few feet away, Cethern watched him come. He straightened, moving forward to allow Daire to come in behind him. His eyes already adjusting, he realised it was bigger than it looked from the outside. Along one wall were rough, woven baskets. Behind Cethern, a long piece of cloth hung, half-obscuring, over the entrance to another, deeper, darker chamber.

Cethern waved one hand. "Come, sit with me."

Malachy did as she said, Daire joining him. Sat on the same level as the doorway, it was surprisingly bright and warm. He sneaked a look at Cethern. She in her turn was watching him with the same, barely disguised amusement.

"You are welcome, Daire, Malachy," she said, inclining her head. "My home is your home."

"It is my honour," Daire responded, with an answering bob.

Realising that this was some kind of formality, Malachy did the same. "And mine."

Cethern's lips twitched. Getting to her feet, she moved into the corner and, one by one, brought out two small baskets, two rough, wooden plates, a clay jar and a chipped cup, and laid them in front of them.

"Your journey is long. You must eat, rest."

*

They ate bread with some kind of salted fish and wild leaves Malachy didn't know the name of, but tasted mainly of green, and drank beer from the shared clay cup, passed quickly from one to the other of them. The speed of the drinking went to Malachy's head, giving him a warm, cosy glow and a sudden blast of affection for the people sat either side of him.

"The ancestors left this isle long ago," Cethern was telling Daire. "and none else would live here."

Daire glanced up at the roof. "For fear of disturbing their resting place?"

Cethern shook her head. "There is an isle to the south. Once sacred, now I swim to it. Their resting place lies there. This—" She paused to take another drink then passed the cup to Malachy. "—was their place of hiding. Beneath us, lie passages and a way outside, to a cave, near the shore."

The cup was almost empty. Malachy knocked back his head to finish it and immediately Cethern refilled it. His head swam as he passed it on to Daire and he closed his eyes against the feeling.

"Cethern, how come you live here alone?" Daire asked suddenly, "Do you not wish for friends? A clan?"

There was a silence and, for a moment, Malachy thought Daire had offended her, but then she started to speak.

"My father lies with the ancestors in their resting place. I speak of Cethern as my father, and he was in all but blood. A woman born druid, I was cast out from my family, my clan, for I would not obey the lore. I have magic; why should I not use it?" She paused again, and taking the cup from Daire, took a heavy swig. "The punishment is death. I fled and sick, hungry, Cethern found me and gave me his hand, for his heart was greater than all the waters of Lir. Friend of the tribe of Laeg, it was he who made Laeg vow to trade with me. Laeg is a man of honour, and so Rochtad would come and we would speak." Her voice broke; for a moment she didn't say anything and then Malachy heard her sniff. "Aahh, I would I were the son my father wished for."

"Do men not weep?" Daire replied softly, his voice sad. "To stand against your enemy takes courage, but to stand against a friend? No man could be stronger of heart. Dheirfiur Bheag, Little Sister, is the same."

"Little Sister?"

"My sister, Emer. My mother died birthing her."

"My sorrow." Cethern inclined her head and her hair fell forward, hiding her face. "I knew your mother."

Daire smiled. "Emer is like her."

"E-mer." She said the name like she was trying it on, for size. "And Emer, with no mother to tend her; she is of age? Wedded?"

"Not wedded, although she is of age. But she is well, for my father and I love and tend her enough for twenty mothers."

Cethern stared at the ground, deep in thought. No one spoke. In the silence, Malachy found himself lying on the ground, his cheek against the soft, powdery earth.

"Daughter and sister of such powerful druid, has she no magic of her own?"

If Daire replied, Malachy didn't hear it. He drifted away.

*

It was morning when he woke, the cairn empty. Head thumping, he dragged himself outside. The storm had passed, leaving a bright, sunny, fresh day, with a light breeze coming in from the west. There was no sign of Daire and Cethern, but there, in the distance, he thought he heard a shout. Staggering towards it, he followed it out of the stone fort and down a rough, path. He passed a patch of yellow, blooming gorse and the bay opened out in front of him. Grass sloped away to a small headland, green on top of black, stratified rock stark against the pale blue ocean behind it. Islands dotted the bay, framed by the mainland turned hazy in the sunshine and there, to the south, was Croagh Patrick, the top of its peak disappearing into white, cumulus clouds. Malachy heard another shout and Daire appeared, running towards the end of the headland. Naked, his bottom flashed and then, with a wild shout, he jumped, his arms and legs wide, like a starfish. Cethern's voice laughed and, turning towards it, Malachy saw her head. She was walking up the slope, coming, Malachy guessed, from her own jump in the water. The full length of her neck appeared, the top of her shoulders.

"Jesus!" He turned away, but not before he saw her lean, naked body, the tight folds in the skin around her stomach and her small breasts hanging.

"Malachy?"

"I've got to go!" Keeping his face carefully averted, he fled.

*

"Malachy? Malachy?"

Sat on a low, crumbled part of the fort, Malachy was tempted to pretend he hadn't heard, but he knew that would just look silly, childish. He sighed. "Cethern?"

She came into view, and thankfully had put her tunic back on. She'd pulled her wet hair back and tied it into a rough knot that reminded him of the women in his own time. With the tunic, it gave her a hippy look, an ageing Sixties Earth Mother. She sat beside him.

"Have I given offence?"

"No." He shook his head, but his face burned. "I'm just not used to—"

He stopped. He was going to say old women running around naked, but he doubted she'd like being called old. Not that he was used to young women running around naked, either.

"You speak strangely, with no meaning." She flapped one hand irritably at him.

"Oh, everyone tells me that."

She laughed and he guessed enough of the meaning had got through.

"Why does Drendas speak against women?"

She frowned at that. "Ask Daire."

There was a pause as she pulled a stray hair off her forehead. Beginning to dry, the hair around her crown had grown fuzzy and she smelt fresh, of sea and salt and summer days. And her skin, despite its age, glowed a deep, freckled brown.

"Drendas serves the Goddess, Brid," she said eventually, giving him a look as if that explained it. It didn't.

She sighed, sensing his confusion. "I fear his heart is angry."

"But, why? That's stupid. And why does anyone listen to him?"

She laughed at that. "Drendas is a powerful druid. His word is strong, for he has grown old and his power has not faded. The elder druids listen to him and the younger follow the elder. Until the dark one came."

Malachy thought of Cormac, of what Jasmine had said when she'd aged him. "As the body ages, so does Iomlan. As the body weakens, so too does Iomlan."

"Yes." She looked at him in surprise. "You *are* one of the Three."

"Not in the way—" He stopped. Of course, she knew he didn't have Iomlan. She'd've sensed it. He thought of Jasmine. She'd be with Drendas right now, a powerful druid who didn't believe that women should have any such power.

He faced Cethern. "Jasmine's one of the Three, but she's a girl, a woman. She has Iomlan, so you'd call her druid, and she's with Drendas."

Her eyes widened and she grabbed his arm. "A woman druid?

Malachy, hear my words. Watch her. Do not trust Drendas. He cannot, he will not, accept a woman druid. He pledges his help to rid you of the dark one, but know this; he serves only the Goddess, and what are you or I to the Gods unless they will it?"

"I should tell Daire, maybe—?"

"No!" Her fingers tightened. "A son must honour his father; he will not listen. I thank the Gods that his sister, Emer, knows nothing of our power, for I would fear for her too."

They stared at one another. In the silence, they heard a voice whistling. It was Daire returning.

"Do not speak of this," Cethern said, letting him go. "Do not trust Drendas. When the dark one is defeated, only then will you know his true heart."

Daire appeared, coming through the gap in the stone wall. Oblivious to their conversation, he looked happy, his face glowing from the sting of the cold water. Without another word, Cethern jumped off the wall and went to meet him.

Chapter Ten

Cethern didn't mention Drendas again. After insisting they breakfast with her, she walked with them across her small island to the boat and helped them reset the sail. Hugging them both, she lingered a little longer with Daire. Even when she let him go, she watched his face, as if to try and fix it her memory. She waved as they left her and stayed waving until they were out of sight. Bolstered by the breeze, the boat skipped across the bay and, very quickly, the island disappeared from sight. Neither of them spoke. Malachy gazed at Croagh Patrick, watching the colours change as it moved closer. Cethern had looked so forlorn standing there. Exiled to a small island just because she had Iomlan, something she couldn't help any more than Daire could, or his father, the old bigot. He sighed. She was being true to herself, but at what cost? A life of loneliness made worse by the fact that to save them from Ellyllon, she'd killed one of her only friends. Croagh Patrick drew close, loomed overhead, then, as they turned around the headland, slowly turned its back on them. He lifted his chin. Drendas and his cronies might've turned their backs on Cethern and women like her, but he would never, ever turn his back on Jasmine. No matter what.

*

The day wore on and they continued south. There was no sign of Ellyllon's followers. Maybe they'd sailed beyond his influence, or maybe they were too busy. Maybe.

"Cethern's beer was good," Daire said abruptly, rubbing his stomach.

"Yes."

Malachy's head had stopped thumping, but the movement of the water was making him nauseous. He wished he could get off the boat and go find a dark corner somewhere and sleep.

"To live without family or clan is to the heart as the stab of the blade."

"Does she have a choice?"

Daire gave him an even look. "She broke lore."

"I know, I heard." Malachy took a deep breath. It wasn't Daire's fault.

"My father spoke his heart. I fear it was not right, but his heart is pure. He would cut it out rather than give pain to the innocent, for his is the courage of the warrior. He spoke this because he believes it is so. I know, for he blessed my union with Ferdia when others would not."

"Ferdia?"

"My husband."

Malachy looked down, not knowing what to say. Maybe she had made a mistake. Daire's version of Drendas didn't sound like the man Cethern had described, and surely Daire should know; he was his father.

Daire smiled. "By my oath, when you know my father, you will love him as all love him."

"Yeah." Nodding, Malachy returned his smile. "I'm sure you're right."

They sailed past an outcrop of rock and the land disappeared, opening up in a wide, vast estuary, with mountains straddling both sides. Malachy gasped in surprise. He'd seen Killary Fjord many times, but never from this angle.

"We must row," Daire said, reaching for the sail. "For the tide and the wind follow the sun."

He gestured with his hand, showing the wind sweeping down the fjord towards the sea mouth. Again, they reached for the oars.

Hugging the sides of the fjord, they skirted the land, careful to stay out of the middle, where the pull of the tide was the strongest. At first they'd rowed, but it was too hard and it wasn't long before Daire reverted to Iomlan. Almost a third of the way down, they reached Mweelrea. Black against a darkening sky, it towered over the mountains around it. Night was drawing in and, with thick cloud obscuring the moon and stars, there would be little light.

Suddenly the boat lurched, the water around them lifting into a large swell. Catching the boat, it propelled it round into a sharp spin that had Malachy and Daire grabbing hold of the sides. And then, incredibly, the water began to flow back the way it came, inland not out, taking the boat with it.

"What?!" Malachy exclaimed, looking all around.

Behind them, the water continued to flow towards the sea.

Daire clambered to his feet, making the boat rock even more. "It is my father!"

"What?! How?"

"He sensed my coming and is bringing us to him."

The boat sped inland and Malachy, staring down at the churning waves, wondered exactly how much power Drendas had.

*

The last of the light disappeared from the sky. Shivering, Malachy pulled his cloak tight to him. Beneath them, the water looked almost black, the land a shade lighter.

"Malachy, there!" Daire pointed.

A fire burned brightly in the distance. Still too far to see clearly, it felt like a beacon in the darkness, bringing them home. They were almost there. Craning his neck, Malachy watched as they approached the end of the fjord. The fire was huge, its flames reaching high into the air and casting its light far across the water. Three figures stood next to it, their forms silhouetted against the brightness. Three; Seamus, Jasmine and Drendas; the right amount. Malachy's stomach fluttered, relief mingling with excitement and a small stab of dread. *What if they didn't want him?*

A hundred metres away and finally Malachy could see them: Seamus stood next to a tall thickset man with black hair and an old wizened man with long flowing white hair. Jasmine wasn't there. Malachy searched the darkness, eager for his first sight of her, but there was no sign of her. His heart sank. She must still be angry with him. The boat bumped to a stop; Drendas spread his hands wide and the sea literally parted for them. Laughing, Daire jumped nimbly out and, landing lightly on the sand, ran towards his father.

"My son!" Drendas cried and the two embraced.

Malachy clambered out, his feet sinking as he drudged towards Seamus.

"Seamus, I'm sorry, but I had to–"

He didn't get any further. Seamus threw his arms around him and held him tight. "Malachy, it's good to see yer."

"Where's Jasmine?"

"It's alright. She's asleep." He let him go.

"Did something happen? Is she OK?"

"No, no," he said smoothly, his voice soft and reassuring. "She's fine. Just tired."

"Yes," Drendas agreed, nodding furiously. "She is well."

Malachy stiffened. Something was wrong. They were trying too hard. He looked at Seamus, but his face gave nothing away. Behind them, Daire and Ferdia broke apart.

"Father, where is Emer? I would see her."

"And she you. Come, she watches Jasmine, come."

Leaving the fire, they walked towards the house. Sandwiched between Daire and Ferdia, Drendas chattered and beamed, looking every inch the kindly old man doting on his family. Seamus and Malachy walked a few paces behind.

"Daire found you," Seamus said. "He said he would."

"Yeah. Without him, I'd've gone to the village."

"And straight to Ellyllon." Seamus nodded. "We've a lot to thank him and Ferdia for. We'd never have made it without them."

"How long have you been here?"

"Just over a day."

"Seamus, is Jasmine angry with me?"

"No, no. It's just the journey was very difficult. Ellyllon's influence is growing faster than I could've imagined. But it's late; you look tired. We can talk tomorrow."

"But, there's something I must tell you—"

Suddenly, Daire laughed. Malachy looked across and saw Drendas' head cocked, as if he were trying to listen to their conversation.

"Malachy, I said wait until the morning," Seamus snapped.

Hurt, Malachy didn't know what to say, but then Seamus touched him lightly on the arm. *Be patient*, his touch said, *you don't know how things are*.

*

They were at Drendas' house. Visible through the wattle and daub walls, light from the fire gently illuminated the inside, like a lamp through its shade. Somewhere in there was Jasmine. They reached the doorway.

"Can I see her?" Malachy asked Seamus.

Drendas turned. "She sleeps."

"Yeah, I won't wake her. I only want to see her."

Behind him, Daire thrust his head through the doorway. "Emer?" He called gently, "Emer?"

"I won't be long," Malachy insisted.

Drendas shook his head. "I will not allow it."

Seamus stepped forward. "Allow it?!"

Drendas' eyes flashed, one hand clenched the top of this staff. "You do not know our ways. She lies in *my* house."

"Father." Daire's head reappeared. "Come, where is the harm?" He smiled at Malachy, "Would you refuse Ferdia if it were me?"

Drendas' hand relaxed. Without a word, he dipped his head and, moving aside, allowed Malachy access.

"Daire!" Coming through the doorway, Emer threw herself into his arms.

"Little Sister." He grinned, lifting her off her feet and spinning her around.

With Seamus following, Malachy slipped past them and through the doorway. The fire was very low, the embers glowing a fierce red as it slowly faded. There was just enough light to see.

"There," Seamus whispered, pointing to a wooden screen positioned in the far side of the house.

His heart in his mouth, Malachy went towards it, sensing Seamus hang back. Daire and his sister were talking outside, their voices murmuring excitedly. Shimmying around the screen, Malachy peered inside.

Covered by a blanket, she was laid on her back, asleep. Her face was turned away, in towards the wall, and he could hear her breathing. He couldn't resist. As quietly as he could, he knelt down in front of her and reaching out, gently stroked her hair. She stirred.

"Mal." Her eyes opened, and she gazed at him.

"Jas."

Crouching forward, he bent until his lips touched hers. They tasted faintly of spice and something that made him think of Christmas.

"You came. Drendas said you would." Already her eyes were closing, as if the effort to keep them open was too much.

He kissed her again. "Go back to sleep, I'll see you tomorrow."

He straightened. She was already asleep. He watched her for a moment. Shadowed by the half-light, she looked young and impossibly vulnerable.

"Mal." Seamus' hand touched his shoulder. "We should go."

"Yeah." Getting up, he followed Seamus back around the screen, pausing for one last look.

"Our thanks," Seamus said to Drendas as they joined the others outside.

Drendas smiled, his lips tight across what was left of his teeth. One, Malachy noticed, stained brown and sat all on its own, was particularly prominent.

"Seamus, does he wish to eat?" asked Daire's sister, looking at Malachy.

"No, thank you." He stifled a yawn. "I'm too tired."

"We should sleep," Seamus said quickly. "We might not get the chance later."

*

"Malachy, Malachy," a voice whispered, its owner's lips close to his ear.

Woken suddenly, Malachy turned his head away irritably, but the lips followed him. "Malachy, we need to talk."

It was Seamus. He opened his eyes. It was still dark outside, although dawn couldn't be far away. Around them the others still slept.

"Shhh, don't speak." Seamus breathed, "Come on."

Climbing carefully to his feet, Malachy tiptoed past the sleeping bodies. Curled into one another, Daire's head was nestled under Ferdia's chin.

*

Even this early it was still warm, for the cloudy night had kept in the heat. A thin patch of light illuminated the sky above the hill, heralding the sun. Without speaking, Seamus led Malachy away from the fjord and up the hill. Wet with a light morning dew, the grass tickled their ankles. Water from a spring babbled brightly, trickling over stone and gravel. They reached the rocky outcrop next to the spring and Seamus indicated they should sit. Finding a flat spot on the rock, side by side, they stared out across the valley and the fjord. Below and to their right, Malachy could just make out Drendas' house, another patch of darkness in the shadow of the hill. It wouldn't be long before they'd be able to see it, and anyone who came out.

"We need to talk, before the others wake."

"Seamus, what's going on? What happened to Jasmine and why bring me up here to talk?"

"I'll explain later, but let's just say the walls have ears. For now, I want to hear about your journey."

As briefly as he could, Malachy told Seamus what happened.

"Do you trust Cethern?" he asked after he'd finished. "What she said about Drendas?"

Malachy frowned. "I thought I did. She killed her friend to save us, but I like Daire and he trusts his father."

Seamus nodded. "So does Ferdia." He paused. "You know why Rochtad knocked the spear away, don't you?"

"To stop it killing us."

"To stop it killing you. Ellyllon doesn't want you dead; he wants to use you like he did in the abbey, to get to Jasmine. That's why I didn't want you to come."

"I know. I'm sorry, but I had to. I had to help."

Seamus smiled faintly. "I know yer did. Ah, Mal, I was angry with you for coming into the abbey when I told you not to, and worried if you came with us it would happen again. When we left, I thought Ellyllon had got all he wanted from Jasmine, I'd never have brought her with me if I'd realised. Looking back, I shouldn't've, but I needed her help."

Malachy shifted. "Why's he so obsessed with her?"

"Because he believes she's special. He told her Iomlan's still growing inside her."

"But it can't; you said it's fixed."

"And I thought it was, or at least, I've never heard of it before. And you'd think, surely, I'd feel it if it were happening and I've felt nothing. No, Mal, I think either Ellyllon's mistaken, or he's lying."

"So, what *is* happening to her?"

"I don't know. But I think we first saw its effect in the abbey. Jasmine believes Ellyllon. She thinks it's growing inside her, changing her. She was going to tell me more, but Drendas arrived and I've not had chance to speak to her since. But I've seen it myself, although I haven't wanted to believe it."

"Seen what?"

Seamus sighed and straightened the leg with the bad knee. "We were attacked as soon as we came through the portal. It was so quick, the fight vicious, bloody, but as the warriors retreated Jasmine continued to attack them. It was far worse than anything we experienced with Grainne, I thought it was just a reaction to the shock and panic, but later–" He stopped.

"Oh, Jesus, Seamus, what?!"

"On our way here, we were ambushed in a forest. I lit a fire, tried to use it to shield us so we could escape, but Cathbad intervened and it got out of control. It was chaos; Jasmine was protecting our backs, the warriors were fleeing, desperate to escape the fire. I shouldn't've let her do it, but I thought she'd be OK. But she didn't just protect us, she attacked the warriors as they were fleeing. It's like shooting someone in the back. They were no threat to her or us, but she deliberately sent the fire towards them. Mal, I heard their screams as they burned. I doubt one of them survived. What she did to Cormac I can understand, even if I don't agree with it. And again, when we came through the portal, the shock and the fear, especially for someone so young, but this? This was cold-blooded murder."

"But, she wouldn't, she wouldn't *do* that. Look at the way she was over Killaspugbrone."

"Yes, I know; she blamed herself. But maybe that wasn't a good thing. Maybe that guilt's got all twisted." He sighed again. "I don't know, Mal. She's got so quiet, so withdrawn. When I asked, she always had an excuse, a something and nothing. And now I realise I was struggling meself after what Cormac did to me. I'm getting old; the body doesn't recover the way it used to. Daire was certain Ellyllon wouldn't risk an open attack on Drendas and I thought, if we could just get here, we'd have time to think, to breathe. Looking back, she was obviously worried and trying to hide it from me, probably worried about me too. But we have to find out what's causing it."

"Maybe it's using Iomlan. You said it's like any power; if you use it badly–"

"You'll corrupt yerself," Seamus finished for him. "Possibly. Iomlan doesn't need to be growing for her to become corrupted. Maybe Killaspugbrone was the catalyst, or when she was with Ellyllon. I don't know exactly what happened, what he did. Do you? If it was, it was all my fault. I expected too much from someone so young."

Malachy rested his head on his chin. There were so many questions. He couldn't imagine her doing the things Seamus said; it just wasn't her. She'd taken his warning about the power of Iomlan to heart, and as for Killaspugbrone, she blamed herself when it wasn't even her fault, for Christ's sake. But still there was this image in his head of Jasmine looking down at Cormac's agonised face, her own completely devoid of pity. A thought occurred to him.

"But this doesn't explain why we had to come up here to talk. Or why she was asleep."

"No. Yesterday, Drendas arranged with Ferdia to take me fishing. I thought there was no harm in going; Jasmine was still sleeping (she'd barely slept the whole journey and she needed her rest) and Drendas promised to take care of her. But as the day passed, and we stayed longer than I was expecting, I got the feeling that Ferdia was finding things to keep me there. First he wanted to check Drendas' nets, then there was something else and, in the end, we only left because I said I'd go without him. When we got back, we found Jasmine unconscious in the house. Drendas said she'd just collapsed, but I don't believe him. He was up to something, something he didn't want me to see, and Ferdia knew it. Anyway, when she woke, she couldn't remember a thing. She seemed alright, although a little tired. I left her sleeping and you've seen her, she's been sleeping ever since."

Malachy took that in. "What do you think he did?"

"I don't know, but the more I think about it, the more I think he's deliberately keeping us apart. He seemed fascinated by her from the word go. The way he reacted when you wanted to see Jasmine... if it hadn't been for Daire, he'd never had let you see her."

"But I thought he wanted the three of us?"

"He does. It's something to do with his prophecy and his Goddess." Seamus' eyes slid away and, for a moment, Malachy was convinced he was hiding something from him, and then he continued and the moment was past. "We can't trust him, Mal. And yet we need him. Without him, his influence with the other druids, we don't stand a chance of stopping Ellyllon." He gave Malachy a grim look. "If we don't end this, Ellyllon will. He wants Jasmine and he wants me dead. I'm in the way of his revenge and him getting her. She told me he groomed Cormac for months just so he would kill me."

Malachy looked away. He wanted to say, then let's go, get out of here and go back to our time, where it's safe, but he knew that it couldn't be. What Ellyllon did now affected the future.

"Mal, why did you follow us?"

"I told yer, to help. It was Grainne. She made me see I was turning my back on Jasmine when she needed me the most."

Seamus placed his hand on his shoulder. "And so she does. We both do. I'm asking you, Malachy; we need your help to finish this."

Malachy sighed. "What do you want me to do?"

"The same as me. Watch her. Anything you notice, no matter how small, tell me. She might tell you things she won't tell me. Together, we might start to get the real picture. Oh, and keep as close to her as yer can. I don't want anything else to happen that we don't know about."

"Alright. And what will you do?"

"I'm going to talk to Daire. He may love his father, but he's not completely blind; you saw how he interceded for you last night. I doubt anyone else could have made Drendas do that. And Daire likes you, Mal; your journey together has brought you close together. I'm sorry to say it, but I think we can use that."

Malachy nodded; he knew Seamus was right and there was nothing else they could do, but he couldn't stop thinking of Cethern's warning.

When the dark one is defeated, only then will you know Drendas' heart.

Chapter Eleven

The sun was just climbing over the top of the mountains when Seamus led Malachy back down the hillside. The house was still quiet. No one was up. Without warning, a figure stepped out of the shadow of the roof and walked slowly towards the beach. She was wearing a dress very like Emer's and it took him a moment to realise it was Jasmine.

"Seamus!"

"I see."

There was a pause.

"Why don't you go and see her?" Seamus suggested.

"What, on my own? Don't you want to talk to her?"

Seamus smiled. "You go first. I'll follow."

"Oh, OK, thanks." Flashing him a wide, grateful grin, Malachy shot off, running across the grass and onto the sand.

*

He caught her just before she reached the water. Hearing him coming, she stopped and turned.

"Jas." He slowed to a stop.

She didn't answer. She looked different in the dress, as if she were born here and was part of this time and not thousands of years later. Her face drawn and pale, she looked exhausted, and she'd lost weight. Malachy frowned. In just a few days she was too thin, the skin stretched over her bones, giving her a gaunt, brittle look that made her seem much older than her years.

"How are you feeling?" As soon as he said it, he could've kicked himself; it seemed such a stupid thing to say.

"I'm OK."

"I'm sorry for what I said."

She passed a hand over her eyes. "It doesn't matter."

"Yeah, it does."

He took a step towards her and she lifted her hand, as if to hold him at bay.

"You shouldn't've come."

"I had to. I had to help."

"But how can you? You make us vulnerable and we don't have time to protect you. You should go."

Malachy flinched, taken aback by her bluntness. He'd expected anger, shouting and yelling, but not this cold matter-of-factness. He tried again. "Maybe it's not me that needs protecting. Seamus told me – I can help you, I know I can."

"No, you can't. No one can, I mean, no one *else*."

She looked so deflated, listless, as if even holding herself upright was too difficult.

"You don't know that."

She smiled at that. Weak, faint, it was still a smile. Grainne was right; she did need him. Putting his arms around her, he pulled her to him.

They ended up together on the sand, Jasmine tucked under his chin with his arm around her shoulders. Pressed into him, her body felt light, insubstantial, almost as if something was eating away at her, consuming her from the inside out.

"Jas, what's happening to you?"

She sighed. "I don't know. I'm so tired, I can't think straight."

"But, you've been sleeping for hours."

"I know, but Mal, my head's so muddled. I have such thoughts, and such dreams."

Her body shuddered.

"What kind of dreams?"

"I don't know." She pulled away so she could look at him, and the eyes that stared into his were haunted. "It's like I'm someone else, doing things I've never imagined, but I can see them so clearly. It sounds stupid, but it feels like this is the dream and what I see in my head is real."

"Seamus said that you told him that Iomlan's taking you over. Could it be that?"

"Did I?" She looked down at the ground. "I don't remember."

He tried another way. "So what happens in these dreams?"

"I don't know; I can't remember. But they're so close I can almost see them. If I could just reach out–" She stopped, and her eyes widened slightly. "I remember fire."

"Fire?"

"Fire. I'm inside it; I can feel it burning me, and it hurts so much I can barely breathe. And then it's gone, and I feel wonderful. Everything's soft and warm and I'm so happy." She smiled vaguely. "It's like being in the womb. Like I'm new, back to being a baby, waiting to be born all over again."

A swirl of green flashed through her eyes. Malachy started, but it was gone as soon as it had come.

"Jasmine! Jasmine!"

It was Drendas. He scampered towards them, using his staff to give him impetus.

"Don't let go." Twisting upwards, she pressed her lips to his.

They kissed, a serious kiss, her lips working furiously against his. She clutched him to her as if she'd drown without him and for a few seconds Malachy forgot everything, but the feel and taste of her.

"Jasmine!" Drendas had reached them.

She pulled away and without a word clambered to her feet. Confused, Malachy followed more slowly.

"Jasmine, I woke, and you were not there," Drendas complained, panting. "You are weak and Emer has prepared food."

"I'm not hungry." She rubbed at her forehead.

"You must eat if you are to grow strong." Taking her by the arm, he pulled her close. Stiffening, she moved her head away, but she didn't protest. "Come, we will return."

"Wait," Malachy interjected, looking around for Seamus.

He spotted him, near the house, talking to Daire, the two of them looking across at them. *What was he doing? Why didn't he come to help?*

Raising his staff, Drendas waggled it at him, looking like nothing more than a cross old man chiding cheeky schoolchildren.

"Look to the deer. If the newborn does not stand, he will die; so must Jasmine be strong for her journey. Do not weaken her."

"What are you talking about? I'm not weakening her. We were just talking. Jas?"

She wouldn't look at him. "Drendas knows best."

"Come, Jasmine." Lowering his staff, he turned towards the house, pulling her with him.

"But–!"

Too late. His mouth pressed close to her ear, Drendas led her back to the house.

*

Leaving Daire, Seamus quickly joined him.

"Seamus, why didn't you help me?"

"Shhh!" He looked back, checking, but Drendas and Jasmine had gone inside. "I was helping; I was talking to Daire."

"But did you see what he did? And Jasmine just let him. She didn't want to go with him, I know she didn't, but I couldn't do anything without her saying, I dunno, *something*."

"Mal, calm down, it's alright. I know I said stay close, but you can't force it."

"But you didn't see!" Malachy flapped both arms in frustration. "She couldn't refuse him even if she wanted to, and she did want to. She didn't want to go. It's as if he owns her!"

"Alright, alright." Seamus placed one hand on his shoulder. "Mal, you have to calm down. This isn't helping Jasmine. If you're right, then getting into a fight with Drendas will only drive a wedge between you and her. We have to be cleverer than that. Do you not see that?"

Malachy swallowed. "Yeah, of course I do."

"I know it's difficult, but I've spoken to Daire and I'm hoping that will help. He tells me that the druids are meeting early tomorrow, so we're leaving today. I don't know what lies ahead, but we have to be strong. Emer's made breakfast, we should eat. We can talk later. Alright?"

Malachy nodded. "Alright," he agreed reluctantly.

Side by side, they walked back towards the house.

"Did Jasmine tell you anything?"

"Only that she's so tired that she can't think straight. And she keeps having these dreams."

Seamus cocked his head. "What dreams?"

"She couldn't remember, but she said they felt real. No, there was one, or part of one. She said she fell into a fire."

"A fire?"

"Yeah. She said it felt like being reborn."

"That's an odd dream. Powerful."

Malachy looked sideways at him. "You think it means something?"

"Hmm. I don't know, but fire and rebirth are an age-old belief. Think of the phoenix, rising from the ashes." He stopped suddenly and lifting his hand, pointed. "Malachy, look."

Pulling two horses behind him, a rider skirted the far edge of the fjord.

"Who is it?" Malachy asked.

"I don't know, but hopefully Drendas will. C'mon, we'd better tell him."

*

Back inside the house, Emer had built a low fire and was just serving breakfast. Daire and Ferdia sat on one side with Jasmine and Drendas on the other. Jasmine sipped milk from an earthen cup, but her bowl of food was untouched.

"There's a rider coming." Seamus told the group. "With horses."

"Badb." Drendas said, looking at Ferdia.

Immediately Ferdia lowered his plate and, scrambling to his feet, disappeared outside.

"The tribe of Noisiu lies through the mountains to the south," Drendas explained. "Their ancestors, blessed by the Goddess Epona, tamed the wild horses of Connemara, and Noisiu and his warriors tame them still. I was promised horses, and so they have come." He nodded, indicating the empty spot Ferdia left. "Come, Seamus, eat."

"Thank you." Ignoring the offer, Seamus moved past Daire and sat the other side of Jasmine.

Behind him, Malachy took the gap.

Drendas looked, but he didn't say anything. Immediately Emer passed them each food in a rough wooden bowl.

"Thank you, Emer." Seamus smiled then turned to Jasmine. "And how are you feeling this morning?"

"Much better."

"We worried about you."

"I'm fine." She glanced at Drendas. "I think the sleep helped."

Seamus took a bite from his bread. "Can you remember what happened?" He asked casually.

"No, not really." Another glance at Drendas. "Maybe I was just exhausted from the journey."

Reaching for his cup, Drendas nodded approvingly. Like a teacher, Malachy thought darkly, pleased with the performance of their favourite pupil.

"Drendas, when do we leave for the Sacred Isle?" Seamus asked.

"Now Badb has come, we can prepare. As was foretold, we will meet my brother druids on the Sacred Isle on the birth of the new moon." He looked at Jasmine and smiled. "The Goddess sees all, and her wisdom guides us."

That, thought Malachy ironically, was as clear as mud.

*

Ferdia returned before they finished, bringing Badb with him. He was young, maybe a couple of years older than Malachy, with dark hair tied by a cord into a high ponytail so tight that it pulled the skin on his face.

A single glass bead, tied to the end of the cord, rested on the left side of his chest.

"Badb, you are welcome." Drendas said, getting to his feet. "How is Noisiu?"

"The honour is mine," Badb replied, bowing low, the bead swinging with the movement. "Noisiu is well, but he is fearful for the herd."

"Be easy; Emer has the potion. But first, come, sit and eat with us. Emer, tend to our guest."

She stepped forward and Badb bowed again, going so low that Malachy thought he was going to fall flat on his face.

"Badb."

"Emer." He straightened, his cheeks flushed. The bead bounced once more then settled.

"Come, Badb, sit," Daire interjected, laughing.

Badb's eyes darkened, but twisting his mouth into a smile, he did as Daire said. Emer passed him a bowl of food and he took it from her eagerly.

"I would speak with you, Drendas," He said in between bites, his eyes following her as she moved to the fire. "I have spoken with Noisiu."

Daire snorted, and again, Badb's face flushed.

"And how did he answer?" Drendas asked.

Taking another bite, Badb swallowed hastily. "As I wished."

"Then we must speak." He waved one hand. "But we cannot speak in front of our guests. Eat and then we will walk."

There was a pause.

"Badb, druid to Noisiu, you know of my prophecy."

Badb lowered his bread, looked from Seamus to Malachy to Jasmine, and his eyes widened, "The Three."

Drendas smiled. "And you know of the dark one?"

Badb shrugged, returning to his bread. "I have heard speak of him, but few enter the mountains."

"And Noisiu is loyal," Drendas agreed. He glanced at Jasmine. "You must eat, or you will not become strong."

Reluctantly, she lifted up a piece of bread and took a bite.

"Good." He watched her for a moment. "Come, Badb, we will walk." He got to his feet, Badb following. "Emer, the potion."

He led Badb outside. Emer got to her feet, preparing to leave, but Daire was there, stopping her.

"Little Sister, what answer would you give?"

She scowled. "I will not tell you."

Daire laughed and, throwing his arms around her, thrust his face into hers. "What a face to give your brother, or your husband to be. The face of a pig, a big fat hog." He screwed up his face and snorted loudly.

Emer laughed. "Better the face than the wits."

Daire opened his mouth, pretended to look shocked, then pressed his face close again. "Do you wish it, Little Sister?" he asked softly.

Looking away, she quickly shook her head.

"Then father will not grant it and I will not allow it." He touched her cheek. "It is Badb that has the face of a pig, and the wits too."

"Daire!" she admonished, shaking her head again.

He laughed again and, releasing her, stepped back. Immediately, she darted away, through the doorway and out into the sunshine.

"Daire, come, we must prepare for the journey," Ferdia said, his voice thick with disapproval.

"Malachy, why don't you help as well?" Seamus suggested quickly.

Staring at Malachy, he gave one, almost imperceptible nod in Jasmine's direction. Now she'd started to eat, it looked like she couldn't stop. Her mouth was stuffed with food; even as Malachy looked, she managed to cram the last piece of bread inside. Her face flushed with contentment, she chewed with her mouth open, sucking in air between the gaps. Even before she'd finished, she was reaching for more. "Oh, yeah, OK," Malachy answered, staring at her. He'd never seen her eat like that, but then he'd never seen anyone eat like that, as if she were literally starving. "I mean, I'd like to help."

"Very well." Daire smiled.

Malachy followed Daire and Ferdia out, and with a last look at Jasmine, still chewing obliviously, left Seamus and her alone together.

*

Outside, they went over to the wooden lattice pen that housed the animals. Emer was there, tending to the pigs, her head bobbing as she gave them their feed. Stood next to the water, Drendas and Badb were talking and as Malachy looked, Drendas placed a hand on Badb's shoulder and patted it sympathetically. Obviously, Daire was right, and there was no way Drendas was going to let him marry his daughter. Head bowed, Badb turned away.

"I would speak to my father," Daire said quickly, darting away.

"Daire, Daire!" Ferdia called after him, but it was too late. He gave Malachy an ominous look, "Watch; he will speak to Badb when it is wisest to stay silent."

"But why?"

Daire and Badb moved towards each other. It was like watching two cars collide in slow motion.

"Because Badb has dared to lift his eyes to the daughter of the most powerful druid in the whole of Connacht, and the sister Daire has been both brother and mother to."

The two met. Daire spoke first, his hands gesturing. Badb responded, his voice, loud, angry, carrying across the valley to where Malachy and Ferdia watched. He raised his hand, but Daire was already shifting, preparing his own attack. "Stop!" Drendas' voice rang out.

He held his staff high above his head, the warning clear.

Ferdia shook his head in disgust. "Come, Malachy, it is finished."

Malachy followed him inside the pen. Seeing them coming, Emer turned back towards the pigs, as if she too had been watching but didn't want them to know. Ferdia went over to the four horses and, taking three of them, began to lead them out.

"Bring the dillats," he ordered, nodding towards a pile of rough thick cloths approximately one metre long.

They were in the far corner. Stooping, one by one, Malachy began to pick them up and throw them over his shoulder. They were surprisingly heavy.

"Emer?"

Malachy whirled. Slipping in between the latticed walls was Badb. Not noticing Malachy, he darted over to Emer and tried to take her hand, but she snatched it swiftly away.

"Your father has refused permission, but Noisiu has given it," he said, his face red with excitement. "Come with me and Noisiu and I will protect you."

"No." She drew herself up. "I will not. Go, before my brother and father hear you."

He grabbed her arms. "But Emer, I know—"

"What do you know?!" she snapped, trying to wiggle free. "Your tongue runs loose, as a dog's eager for water. My father will hear it."

"Then I will wait, and when they are gone, I will come back for you and we will flee together," he purred, not listening. "I am no child. Do I have not eyes to see?"

"Not if you defy my father, for he will burn them from your head. Go, before he and Daire come."

Malachy stepped out of the shadows. "I think you should do as she says," he said quietly.

With a low cry, Badb let go of her and threw out a hand. His Iomlan caught Malachy full-on, sending him and the dillats flying. He hit a section of lattice and it collapsed under him. He rolled, feeling the sticks rough beneath his back. Across the room someone shouted; he heard a loud thud and looked up.

Breathing heavily, Emer was stood over Badb. Led across another collapsed section of lattice, he stared up at her in disbelief as she slowly lowered her left hand. Outside, people were shouting. Quick as cat, she ran across the pen and, grabbing Malachy's hand, pulled him to his feet just as Ferdia appeared.

"Go!" Ferdia told Badb, taking it all in with one look.

Without a word, he scrambled to his feet and, staggering over the fallen lattice, disappeared.

"My thanks, Malachy," Emer said loudly.

"But I didn't do anything."

She looked into his eyes, her gaze intent.

"I mean, I guess so," he said stupidly, finally catching on. "Yer welcome."

"Emer!" Daire joined them.

"She's well," Ferdia interjected quickly. "Badb is gone, driven from her by Malachy."

"Did he hurt you?" Daire demanded. "If he has, by Dagda, I will gut him like a fish and leave his entrails on the sand for the gulls to pick at."

"No, he sought only to persuade me."

"Against father's word?" Daire shook his head. "Then I beg the forgiveness of our pigs, for he has not even their wit." Spinning, he grabbed Malachy and gave him a quick hug. "My thanks."

"Daire, Emer?" Drendas' head poked around the entrance, his eyebrows lifted in a silent question.

Emer and Daire looked at one another.

"Father, Badb is gone; he will not return," Daire said quickly, his voice firm, like a parent determined to stop something before it starts.

Drendas' eyes narrowed. He opened his mouth to speak, then closed it again. Watching, Malachy realised that Seamus was right. If anyone had any influence over Drendas, it was his beloved son.

"Emer, have you the food for our journey?" he growled, turning to Emer instead.

"Yes, father."

He studied her bowed head, as if wanting to say something more and suddenly, it hit Malachy. He didn't know! How could he not know she had Iomlan?

"Bring it to me."

As she dashed past, he looked at Malachy. "Where's Seamus?" He asked suspiciously.

"He waits inside, with Jasmine." It was Ferdia who answered.

Muttering a curse, Drendas span and scuttled away.

Ferdia and Daire helped Malachy pick up the dillats and take them to the horses. Once they were on, they showed him how to fit the single bridle. There were no stirrups, he noted, to help you get on. They weren't big horses, more ponies than anything, but still, it wouldn't be easy. He'd have to stand on a rock and look a complete and utter idiot. Still, better than trying and getting stuck on his stomach, floundering and flapping helplessly like a fish. He glanced back towards the roundhouse. Jasmine would laugh if she saw it. He sighed. It seemed ages since he'd heard her laugh.

"Malachy."

It was Emer. Stood in the shadows of the back of the roundhouse, she beckoned. Daire had sent him back to get the food. A quick look around, and he joined her. Somehow it seemed to sum her up, a life spent in the shadows, her true gifts and talents unmarked and unnoticed.

"Yes?"

"My thanks for not speaking of–" she made a vague gesture, "to Ferdia or Daire."

"But why don't you tell them?" he asked, but what he really wanted to ask was how come they didn't know, what with Iomlan sending out signals to the other druids like some giant bloody beacon.

Her dark eyes held his with a strange glow, like the deep, even throb of a heart. "It is not permitted."

"But your father knows?"

She looked away and he knew he was right. It was just as Cethern said. Only this was Drendas' child, his daughter.

"But what about Jasmine? And there's another druid, a woman called Cethern. How can they be–?"

"Shhh!" Lightly touching his shoulder, she looked behind him.

In his anger, he'd spoken too loudly.

"I'm sorry," he whispered. "But your father is wrong. Why shouldn't women be druid?"

She shook her head. "My father is as wise as I am wilful."

"But what about Daire, or Ferdia? Would they agree?"

She sighed. The light in her eyes died, but she didn't answer.

"What about Badb, do you love him?" Malachy insisted.

"I do not. But sometimes I wish–" She left it hanging.

"You could get away? But you can. You don't need Badb for that. With Iomlan you could go anywhere. The druid, Cethern, you could go to her, live with her on her island, you'd be safe there and she'd have com–" He stopped, a thought occurring to him. "Why is it OK for Jasmine? Is it because she's one of the Three?"

Again, no answer. Malachy shifted. She knew something, he could feel it.

"Emer, why's it OK for Jasmine to be druid? She's a woman, and yet your father seems to hang off her. Surely he'd want nothing to do with her?"

"I must go, my father calls me."

"I don't hear him." He grabbed her arm. "Tell me, why's it OK for Jasmine?!"

"My father calls me," she repeated. "I must go to him."

There was something in the way she stood there, not fighting or pulling away while he held her that turned his disgust in on himself. He let her go.

"I'm sorry, Emer, I'm just afraid for Jasmine. Can you understand?"

Her eyes softened. "My father wishes her no harm, but only through the Child of Erin and Brigantes can the Goddess come."

"What does that mean?" Malachy frowned, "What Child?"

"Emer! Emer!"

"If I do not go to him, he will come."

Sidestepping, he let her go and she moved swiftly away. It was only after she'd gone that he realised she'd known Drendas wanted her long before he'd called.

*

Seamus was stood next to the horses with Daire and Ferdia, but as soon as he saw Malachy, he came over. "We'll be leaving soon. Daire told me what happened."

"Where's Jasmine?"

"With Drendas." Seamus frowned. "He wasn't best pleased to see me alone with her, but he tried to hide it. Made some excuse to get rid of me."

"How is she?"

"Not good," Seamus said in a low voice. "Drendas told her that her Iomlan is still growing inside her."

"So Ellyllon was right?"

Seamus glanced at Daire and Ferdia. "It seems so. Drendas told her that he can help her learn control, but it will take time."

"What do we do?"

"Go to the Sacred Isle, meet with the druids. If Drendas is right, then maybe he can help her."

"And if he isn't, or he's lying?"

"We're—"

"Father." Daire called, looking past them.

Drendas and Jasmine appeared in the doorway of the house, the latter blinking in the sunlight. Emer followed, carrying two cloth sacks.

"Seamus, there's something I need to tell you," Malachy said urgently.

"Not now, tell me later," Seamus muttered as Drendas and Jasmine came towards them.

*

Midmorning and, leaving Emer behind, the five of them travelled east along the river valley that ran all the way to Lough Orbsen. Out of Drendas' valley, the mountains quickly gave way to round, gentle hills and then to forest. Mimicking the curve of the river, the path meandered across the wide valley floor and through the trees. Clouds had rolled in off the Atlantic and, filling the sky, had blotted out the sun, although the day was still very warm. Even under the trees it was too warm. Malachy rolled back his sleeves. Humid, it felt hotter than it actually was, the air close, oppressive, as if the weather had caught their mood. Daire might be using his Iomlan to hide them, but Malachy knew from experience that they couldn't be too careful. And as Seamus said, while Ellyllon might not risk an open attack on Drendas, it didn't mean he hadn't got other tricks up his sleeve. Ultimately, who knew what eyes had watched and waited for them to leave the safety of Drendas' valley?

Once again, the landscape began to change. Tall, sweeping, grass slopes heralded the start of a new mountain range. Streams trickled downwards, cutting deep into grass and rock, their trails punctuating the mountainside like rivulets on a rain drenched window. Alongside Drendas, Jasmine rode with her head bowed, lost in thought. Back in her tunic and leggings, Malachy tried not to watch her, but he couldn't help it. She hadn't spoken to him since they'd kissed and the way she kept just the other side of Drendas made it pretty obvious she was trying to avoid him. Part of him wanted to ride over to her and demand she talk to him, but with Drendas next to her that would probably only lead to another confrontation. If he wanted her to face him, he was going to have to be a lot cleverer than that.

Chapter Twelve

Ferdia led them across the river at a low point, and moving sharply upwards, they began to climb. The horses slowed, the nod of their heads lengthening. Below them, the river widened, its path moving from the fast, quick step of the young towards the ponderous tread of the old. Half an hour later they left the trees, and skirting the line of the forest, rode slowly across the slopes. Undulating, the low mountains rose up above them, the jagged peaks of the spectacular Twelve Pins just visible through the V-shaped valleys. For a moment the sun appeared, sending a shadow across the slopes and turning the dark green to light then back to dark, then the clouds closed in again.

When Jasmine had first woken, she'd been so confused, but Drendas had explained everything to her. And then, waking up this morning, she'd been confused all over again what with the muddle in her head and the dreams. Seeing Malachy hadn't helped. He had this way of getting under her defences. Drendas had warned her to stay away from him, but she hadn't listened. She sighed. Everything should be so much clearer now. The muddle in her head had receded and the voices fallen silent, and she knew exactly what she had to do, yet it still didn't feel right. Everything felt surreal, overbright, and she could sense the voices hovering on the edges of her consciousness, like actors waiting in the wings, watching eagerly for the moment they would step out into the light and address the world. It was a disturbing thought; she should be disturbed by it, but somehow she couldn't find the energy. She hadn't told Drendas about the voices. There'd seemed no point; she knew he'd tell her not to worry, that it was just part of the process, the different parts of herself coming to terms with becoming who she truly was. If only she could do that with Seamus and Malachy instead of him.

Unlike her, Seamus was disturbed. She could see it in his eyes, hear it in his voice as he'd talked to her that morning, but she'd had no answers for him. Or at least no answers he would've liked.

Waiting for the others to leave, he'd bent his head towards hers.

"Jasmine, can you tell me what happened," he'd said softly, keeping his voice low.

She'd shaken her head. "I don't remember."

"I'm worried about you. You were going to tell me something, before we met Drendas, do you remember? You thought Iomlan was still growing inside you."

"Oh, yes, I remember now. Drendas explained it to me."

Seamus stiffened. "When?"

"While you were gone." She stopped, as if confused, then with a small shake of her head continued. "I *think* that's when he told me. It's not very clear. I can't seem to get my head straight. It feels like someone picked it up and jiggled it, messing it all up."

Reaching out, Seamus gently pulled her hair off her forehead. "You didn't hit it, did you? When yer fell?"

"No, I don't think so." Her voice lifted. "I don't know! I can't remember. Drendas said it was exhaustion – from the journey."

"I can't see anything, so maybe he's right." Seamus let his hand drop. "You said Drendas explained it to you. What did he explain to you?"

"About Iomlan. Sometimes it continues to grow. It's rare, it doesn't happen often, but it does happen. It happened to him, that's why he's so powerful."

"So you'll become as powerful as him?"

"I don't know. I don't think it's – set. But Drendas said that as it grows it becomes harder to control. He said the danger is that Iomlan begins to follow not just our will or our emotions, but our innermost urges, especially the dark ones, the ones we never let out."

"Because our darkest, most primitive urges are often the stronger," Seamus agreed, nodding. "I can't fault his logic. The greater the power of Iomlan, the greater the chance of corruption. It answers everything perfectly."

Almost too perfectly. He didn't say it, but she knew he was thinking it. Drendas had warned her of this. Seamus didn't mean it, but he was prejudiced. If something didn't fit into what he believed, he rejected it. *Hadn't he done it to her before, with Ellyllon?* Drendas was right. Although she'd be the first to admit that she owed Seamus more than she could ever repay, he just wasn't able to take her safely onto the next level. How could he, when he hadn't got there himself? Only Drendas could do that. Her stomach fluttered with a small thrill of excitement. Soon, her power would surpass Seamus', and who knew, in time, it may even come to surpass Drendas'. She could become one of the most powerful druids ever.

Or more powerful than any druid, a voice crowed inside her. She had to do as Drendas said, no matter how difficult. It was her duty, her responsibility, she told herself, her heart glowing with pride, she had no choice.

"So Ellyllon was right after all," Seamus was saying, oblivious.

"That's why I have to be so careful. Why I have to listen to Drendas and learn how to control it." Her voice broke. "I can't let Ellyllon use me again, not with Iomlan like this. I could do anything."

"It's alright." He gave her a brief hug. "We won't let that happen."

No, the voice inside her agreed, *we won't*.

*

Jasmine's stomach growled, the sound ending in a pathetic gurgle. Midday; it was time for lunch. At first she'd found it hard to eat, but now she couldn't seem to stop. She longed for the food from home with all its exotic flavours, not to fill her stomach but to taste and savour.

In fact, there was so many things from home she wished she'd tried. So many things to tempt the senses, to slip, slide and luxuriate in. She glanced back at Malachy. His body was young and firm, and inexperienced; he would be eager to please.

"The horses need rest and to drink, as do we," Ferdia said, lifting his arm and pointing ahead, where water flowed between two ridges. Spilling out from two slabs of rock, it was like a waterfall, only in miniature.

Jasmine stared at it. Her head throbbed and she felt strangely disconnected, like a person watching the world from the inside out.

"Jasmine, come." Drendas beckoned.

He, like the others, had dismounted. They all looked at her, expectant. *Why are they staring at me?* she wondered irritably.

"Are you alright?" Seamus asked, stepping forward.

"Yeah, of course." She shrugged, quickly dismounting.

They moved towards the waterfall, pulling the horses after them. Crouching around the water, they drank from cupped hands. The taste of the crystal-clear water was unbelievably good and Jasmine drank, slurping greedily. Afterwards, leaving the horses to have their drink, the group sat down in a circle of pairs to rest and to chew on pieces of Emer's salted pig.

Malachy was watching her again, small surreptitious little glances from the other side of Seamus. He looked worried, but she was sure that Seamus would tell him of their conversation and hoped that would reassure him. Although, probably not. Infected by Seamus' obvious dislike for Drendas, and already repulsed by what she'd done to Cormac, how much more repulsed would he be if he knew the other things she'd done? Abruptly she was back in Sligo Abbey, seeing the look on Malachy's face as he told her she was being corrupted, as if she were some kind of monster. If only she could make him understand, and Seamus too, that without his help, she probably would become that monster. She looked upwards, to the top of the hill, the mountains behind it. How would he react when she finally reached her full power? What future could she and Malachy have together? It would be like a time traveller from the future hooking up with a caveman. Once again, Drendas was right, his logic and his wisdom irrefutable. He might not mean it, but Malachy, just like Seamus, would only stand in her way. She had to be strong. Ferdia said something she didn't catch and the others laughed. Leaning forward, Malachy's eyes sparkled and she looked away. Stronger than she'd ever been, in her whole life.

*

They finished eating and, restless with her thoughts and an itch in her stomach, Jasmine clambered to her feet and wandered aimlessly away. Only Daire and Ferdia showed no interest; the others, she knew, watched her go. Annoyed at Daire and Ferdia's indifference, paradoxically, she found the others' gazes stifling, knowing that each one thought they had more right to her than the other. The sky was darkening, despite the heat, rain not far away. A storm was coming. Suddenly she longed to escape, to wander free, away from these men and the close heat and feel the fresh mountain air on her face, the wind in her hair and the grass, earth and rock beneath her feet. She moved out of their sight and without thinking, began to climb, following the urge to go higher and higher and further and further away from them.

At the top of the ridge, she stopped, breathing heavily. A hundred yards above them, she'd gone much further than she'd meant to. Drendas and the others were on their feet; she knew they were looking for her, but not one of them thought of glancing up, the luthramons. She giggled. They thought they were protecting her! Spinning slowly, she lifted up her arms, saluting the land, as a traveller would his long-left relatives; the Twelve Pins to the southwest, the mountains to the west, north and east, and there beyond them all, the outline of Lough Orbsen, the home of the Sacred Isle. Iomlan rose up inside her, the strength of it taking her breath away. Below her, someone shouted; she glimpsed figures moving but ignored them. In the distance, thunder rumbled, coming closer. Glowing with the power coursing through her, it was as if her body were a beacon, drawing everything on this spinning planet to her. It would draw Ellyllon to her, but she didn't care. Let him come, she crowed, triumphant, or better still, she would go to him.

Jasmine blinked. Gone was the mountainside, Malachy and the others, the wilds of Connemara. Instead, she was on the side of a small, round hill, her back to a high log fence looking into the centre, towards a huge, round house. Metres wide, with its roof reaching high into a grey, cloudy sky, around it had gathered warriors from almost every tribe. Druids in black and brown cloaks dotted their ranks. Stood in front, facing them, was Ellyllon. A druid with long blonde hair was stood next to him. Cathbad: it had to be. He saw her and his black eyes widened. Slowly, a silence descended on the gathering, as one by one, they all turned to look at her.

"Jasmine." Ellyllon mouthed her name.

Oh, my God, what have I done? Her stomach dropped. She reached down for Iomlan, but nothing happened. Cathbad nodded; she felt the druids focus. Panicking, she tried again, scrambling desperately for Iomlan as the warriors closest to her drew their weapons and began creeping cautiously towards her.

Iomlan exploded through her and Ellyllon and his followers disappeared. She was back on the mountain, her head reeling. Rain poured from the thick, black clouds above her, wetting her instantly. Ferdia was there, his hand outstretched back towards Daire, who was still clambering upwards. And then, in a blink of an eye, as though the ground had simply opened up and spewed them out, the warriors appeared, standing between them.

More appeared below. Behind Seamus and Drendas, Malachy stood all on his own. Jasmine opened her mouth to shout, but was overtaken by the warning sound of Ferdia's horn. She watched, transfixed, as those below her whirled. Drawing his sword, Malachy began to move away from them. Behind him, Drendas lifted his staff. Jasmine's mind whirled. She'd brought them with her! The warriors parted and she saw two druids among them. Crouching low, one sent a pulse towards Ferdia and Daire, the other towards her. She tried to parry, but she was seconds too late. His Iomlan caught her hard across the legs, sending her tumbling towards the edge. Her body bounced and rolled across grass, landing with a crunch against hard stone. Pain shot through one side. People were shouting; she heard a cry, the clash of metal and someone groaning. Placing her hands on the stone, she pulled herself painfully upright.

Holding her side, she stood on the edge of the mountain, feeling her heart pound, her head floating with the height of it. For a moment she thought the world was going to tip and her body slide inexorably down and over, into space. Behind her the shouts were coming closer, the sounds reverberating in the hot air and the stone around and beneath her. She turned and running towards her, with their legs stretching over thick clumps of grass, taking them with ease, were the men dressed in cloth and leather, their long hair flying in the wind. They were shouting her name, not calling for her, but coming for her, their voices rhythmic, chanting. She looked wildly about her, glimpsing Malachy with his sword, Seamus charging towards him, throwing bodies away from him, and Daire fighting, with Ferdia on the ground behind him. There was nowhere left to go. The men were much closer now, the first of them only a few paces away, his knife raised high above his shoulder. Behind her, both druids were back on their feet; she felt them focus and she did the only thing she could think of, the last thing they'd expect. She jumped.

She fell, the wind pummelling the breath from her body, the speed of her descent knocking all but one thought from her head, that she could hear her own voice screaming. A second passed and the ground was already coming closer, and incredibly, impossibly, as if he were only a few feet away, she saw Malachy watching from far below. Heard him shouting her name. He calmed her, and quickly she focussed, trying to stop her descent. Her body began to slow, but still the ground was coming and with a sickening lurch of her stomach, she realised that she'd left it too late. She pushed harder, feeling the pressure squeeze her body, her limbs as she continued to slow, but it wasn't enough. The ground was a heartbeat away and she shut her eyes, anticipating the crunch her body would make as it hit the earth.

Chapter Thirteen

Iomlan flared. Flashing through her, it burned with an intensity that was almost pain, and then it was gone, out, away, in all directions. Her body jerked to a stop. She cried out in terror and pain, but there was no thud, no broken and mangled bones of her body hitting solid earth.

Cautiously, she opened her eyes. Lying sideways, her body was suspended inches from the ground, floating as if lying on an invisible sea. If she reached out her hand, she'd be able to touch it. She shuddered, realising how close she'd come. Someone was screaming her name. Forcing herself to stay calm, she focussed. Lifting her body, Iomlan turned it over, before gently lowering it to the ground, feet first.

Followed by a slower Seamus, Malachy was racing towards her. Behind them, bodies littered the ground. She saw Daire cradling Ferdia, but of Drendas there was no sign.

"Jas, Jas, are yer OK?" Malachy cried, throwing his arms around her.

He pulled her to him, the violence of it catching her side and she bit her lip against the pain.

"Mal." She twisted, trying gently to slip out of his grasp, but it was too tight.

"I saw you fall. I thought you were dead. Are yer sure yer alright?"

"I'm OK. Where's Drendas?"

"Are yer sure?" Ignoring her question, he let her go and began feeling and pressing her arms, as if looking for damage.

"Mal, I'm OK – really. Where's Drendas?"

"I think he went to help Daire," he answered, hearing finally.

Again, he pulled her to him, holding her as if he'd never let her go and this time, she let him.

"I thought I'd lost you." Stroking her hair, he pressed his face to hers. "I love you."

Her heart swelled. *I love you too.* Then they were kissing and all she could think that finally, incredibly they felt the same.

Do not toy with him, the voice inside her head snapped.

Or else, sate your hunger. Lie with him and have done with it. A second, harsher voice rejoined.

Shocked, repulsed, she pulled away.

"Jas?"

"No, Mal. I can't, I mustn't!" Turning her back on him, she breathed deeply, forcing the feelings down.

"Jasmine, are you alright?" Seamus demanded.

"I'm fine." She turned back, in control once more.

"What happened? Where did those men come from?"

"I don't know." The lie slipped from her. Even now, after what had just happened, it was surprisingly easy. "But a druid attacked me, and I fell."

"You looked like you jumped." Malachy was staring at her, the hurt and confusion in his face changing to suspicion.

"Jump? Maybe." She shrugged, deliberately casual. "I think I panicked."

Seamus and Malachy looked at one another.

"I felt your Iomlan," Seamus said slowly. "To stop so quickly – you must've defied gravity."

"Seamus!" They turned to see Drendas bounding towards them, his staff swinging. "We are found. We must leave."

"Where's Daire and Ferdia?"

"They wait with the horses. Ferdia was wounded, but it was easily healed. Ellyllon's forces will be gathering, drawn to our use of Iomlan."

"I thought they wouldn't attack you directly."

Drendas scowled. "His influence spreads as fire on the wind. As the wolf in a pack, so he loses his fear and grows bolder and bolder. But, by the Goddess, his boldness, his arrogance is his undoing, for I will speak to my brothers of this attack, and even those that would argue for peace, for reason, will be silenced." He waggled his staff impatiently. "But come, we must leave."

Already mounted, Daire and Ferdia were waiting for them with the horses. Jasmine looked at Ferdia, searching for some sign of a wound, but there wasn't one.

"Be swift." Daire ordered, looking and checking for more warriors.

They mounted.

"On the mountain to the west of Lough Orbsen, lies a cave, the Cave of Morrigan. No one will enter it, for it is said that the Morrigan herself may lie within it," Daire explained. "We will rest tonight and tomorrow we will ride to the meeting place, on the northern shore."

Kicking his heels against the flank of his horse, he moved off, the rest following.

*

Back in the forest, they skirted the hills. Below them, the river widened, its shores littered with stones, bleached white by the sun. Jasmine rode ahead of Drendas, careful to keep him between her and Malachy. It had been all her fault. What if one of them had been seriously injured or killed? She had to learn to control herself better. It was exactly as Drendas had warned. Iomlan was becoming more erratic, more unstable the stronger it got. And as it did, what of her and her emotions? She hadn't thought of it before, but they were irrevocably linked, and if Iomlan followed her emotions, then why not vice versa? It all made sense. The feeling of elation, of invincibility that had sent her to Ellyllon's camp. The fear and triumph that had responded to Malachy's declaration and confused things all over again. Drendas was right; she had to quash her feelings for him, stamp them down and force them out, for him as well as her. Her emotions would be erratic enough with Iomlan; she couldn't afford to be in love as well. Malachy would be angry, but he'd thank her when he realised what she'd done. Drendas and Malachy had finished talking, but she noticed Malachy didn't try again. That's all she had to do; keep her distance and eventually he'd get the message.

*

Late afternoon, and passing the end of the hills, they returned to ground level. Ahead, peeking over the tops of the trees, lay another mountain range, this one running from north to south. And behind that lay Lough Orbsen and the Sacred Isle. They crossed a path heading south, through the mountains, and Malachy nudged his horse forward. For a moment, Jasmine thought he was going to try and ride alongside her, but Seamus said something and he dropped back to answer him. And then it was too late; they were back in amongst the trees, riding again in single file.

Hurt, going over and over it, Malachy silently seethed. He'd opened his heart to her and she'd pushed him away. And now she couldn't even look at him. This morning, he'd been so determined to find a way to get through to her, but now he wondered if it were even worth bothering. He should've stayed with Grainne and waited for their return. He could be riding Eoin along Clew Bay, without a care in the world. Reaching the second hill range, Ferdia led them upwards, back above the trees, and Lough Orbsen came into view. Deep, dark blue water glistened. He'd forgotten how big it was and how wide. Tiny islands dotted the blue, filled so tightly with trees they reached almost to the water's edge, as if they'd piled on, like drowning sailors, and had to huddle together to make room. Crannogs; one of which must be the Sacred Isle. Picking their way through thick purple and brown scrub, they moved around to the east slope. Below them, the forest reached almost to the lakeshore and above, a rocky outcrop jutted outwards. Just below it was a narrow patch of black; the Cave of Morrigan.

*

By the time they reached the cave, there wasn't much daylight left and, unable to use Iomlan, they had to work quickly. Making a rough torch out of a long stick and strands of dry grass, Ferdia lit it with the small flint he carried while everyone but Drendas gathered wood and bits of dry grass. The others waited while he and Daire went inside the cave to light a fire. With a loud caw, a crow landed on a branch near Malachy and fixed him with his beady eye. For a moment they stared at one another. According to legend, one of the Morrigan's favourite forms was a crow. Malachy swallowed. The crow dipped, and then, with another even louder caw and a quick, powerful push of his wings, he took off. Flying upwards, he disappeared over the top of the outcrop.

Reappearing, Daire beckoned them to the entrance. Just wide enough to lead a horse through, Daire went first, the others following. Malachy came last. Layers of rock, the strata vivid hues of reds and purples, reached high above his head. A few steps inside and already he was sweating. He hated small spaces, hated the feeling that the walls were closing in on him, shrinking to fit his body, leaving just enough oxygen for a slow, terrifying death. His horse neighed nervously, as if his fear was catching, and he stopped to reassure it. Strangely, it seemed to help.

The cave widened and to Malachy's relief, Ferdia's fire revealed a huge cavernous space. A loose, grey soil covered the floor, a mixture of fine dust and earth. The back of the cave lay in darkness; it was impossible to know how far back it went without checking and there was no way Malachy was going to do that. Instead, he led his horse into the space to the right with the others then moved hastily back to the fire. Next to its light, he could almost pretend he was outside, and the darkness beyond was the black of the night's sky.

Later, while the others rested, Malachy left the cave and went out into the fresh night air. Glad to be out, he breathed deeply. The cloud had finally lifted, leaving the sky full of stars. Malachy gazed up at them. There were so many. He thought he saw the plough, but couldn't be sure. The plough. His dad often came home from the fields this late.

He imagined him now, turning off the tractor and plunged into sudden darkness, looking up at the stars. Maybe he was doing it now, gazing up the selfsame constellations as his son. The same stars twinkling down on them both two millennia apart. He suppressed a sigh. He wasn't sure he liked the idea. You'd think it would be comforting, but it just felt sad.

A silhouette appeared, a figure emerging from the cave. It moved around a boulder and into the starlight.

"Malachy?" Seamus whispered softly.

"I'm here."

"Come on, we need to talk."

Leading the way, Seamus passed by the trees, their branches and leaves whispering in the night air, over to where a large boulder sat illuminated by moonlight. Sitting down, he perched on one side, leaving just enough room for Malachy.

"The stars are amazing," Malachy said as he joined him.

"Beautiful," he agreed.

Gazing into the sky, they sat in silence for a moment.

"Seamus, what's happening to her?!"

"I told you, Drendas thinks it's Iomlan."

"I know. I don't mean that." Malachy threw up his hands in frustration. "She's different. Not just the power, but inside. Can Iomlan change who she is, her actual personality?"

"I don't know. I didn't think so before, but now I'm not so sure. Of course, if you become corrupted by power, then yer personality will change. Jasmine certainly believes Iomlan is changing her. But is changing the same as corrupting? I mean, Drendas might be able to stop it corrupting her, but can he stop it changing her?"

"Can't you help her?"

"I've never experienced this. I didn't even know it was possible for Iomlan to grow until she told me. I have no idea of that kind of power, or how to stop its corruption. But Drendas does. Or at least, he says he does." Seamus smiled grimly. "Looking at him, the way he behaves, you might wonder if he's managed that himself."

"But if he can't, does that mean there's nothing we can do? That Jasmine will become what – evil?"

"No, I don't believe that. I don't believe in evil, I don't believe in destiny or prophecy. But if Drendas is right, and I'm starting to think he must be, then the corruption doesn't need to happen. It can be stopped." He sighed. "I don't like it, but we have to trust him. Look at what she did today. She jumped off a mountain and at the very last minute stopped her fall. Think of gravity. How much force it would take to stop falling at that speed? Not to mention what it'd likely do to the human body to stop so abruptly?!" He paused and, after a moment, looked down at his stomach. "Did she tell you what she had to do heal the wound?"

Malachy shook his head. "No, there wasn't really time."

"She had to heal it from the inside out, healing each layer of tissue, one at a time. It's grim work, especially if the wound is deep. The first time I did it I almost threw up. And it's not something that comes easy, natural; someone has to show you what to do. The first instinct is to try and stitch the wound, like a doctor would."

Malachy nodded. "I remember it took her a few goes. She was desperate. She thought, we both thought, we'd lost you."

"Yer almost did!" Seamus smiled faintly. "But the point is, there's no way Jasmine should have been able to do it. Not on her own. She wouldn't have the knowledge."

Malachy thought about it. "But if her power is getting so strong, maybe the knowledge comes with it? Maybe it's part of the change?"

"Maybe, although I find it hard to see how more power automatically brings more knowledge. Iomlan has never been like that, I've always had to learn. Sometimes through others, sometimes trial and error, but it's always taken time. You remember the lessons? How Jasmine almost dropped you on yer arse? She had to learn how to use Iomlan. Why now, all of a sudden, do things just come to her?"

There was a pause.

"So if it's not the power giving her the knowledge, what is it?" Malachy asked.

"I don't know, Mal, I really don't. It has to be Iomlan changing her. What else could it be?" He stared moodily into the trees.

Malachy studied the side of his face. This had to be why Jasmine was giving him mixed messages. She was trying to hide the changes from him, or trying to protect him. A thought occurred to him. "Seamus, who's the child of Erin and Brigantes?"

Seamus stiffened. "Who told you about that?"

"Emer."

"It's part of Drendas' precious prophecy."

"I've been thinking about it and I know what Erin is."

"Yes?"

"I think it's an old name for Ireland."

"It is."

"So, where's Brigantes?"

Seamus rubbed his face. "Can't you guess?"

"Brigantes, Brigantes," Malachy repeated, listening to the sound. "Brigantes. It's Britain, isn't it?"

Seamus nodded.

"A child of Ireland and Britain. Irish and British." He looked at Seamus, his eyes widening and Seamus sighed, like a man bowing to the inevitable.

"The child Drendas is talking about is Jasmine."

"But it can't be. She's English; her parents are English." Malachy cocked his head. "Aren't they?"

"Her mother's English."

"Then who's her father?" Malachy stopped, his eyes widening even further. "It's John, isn't it? He's her father."

Seamus nodded.

"Why didn't you tell me?"

"Because it wasn't for me to. I don't know if Jasmine knows or if she's guessed and it's not my place to ask. If she wanted me to know, she'd tell me. But if she doesn't, how could I tell you when she doesn't know herself?"

"How long have you known?"

"From the beginning. To each person, Iomlan is as different and unique as they are themselves. But when it follows families (and it doesn't quite a lot of the time) there's a certain similarity. It's like facial features, I suppose, or family traits. Jasmine's Iomlan is very like John's was."

"Does he know?"

"He's never told me if he does. Sometimes I think he suspects. It would explain why he's so difficult when it came to Jasmine, so stubborn." He smiled. "That's why they fought so much. They're too alike."

"So, John and Jas's mum," Malachy mused. "Jas told me about her father, all the women, but her mum?"

"With the two of them marrying after, yer could say it was the other fellow, Justin, that was the mistake."

"And Jas was angry because she thought John was trying replace her father and all the time, he was her real father."

It was so ironic.

"You mustn't say anything to her, not now. There's too much

happening. Who knows how she'll react? It could push her even further towards Drendas, especially if she feels I've been keeping it from her. Promise me."

That was a sobering thought.

"I promise." It was Malachy's turn to survey the line of trees. "Emer said something about a Goddess."

"Emer's been telling you a lot lately," Seamus said wryly. "Drendas believes that his Goddess will return through the child of Erin and Brigantes."

"But that explains why Drendas is so interested in her!"

"If you remember, I did say it was about the prophecy," Seamus reminded him gently.

"But what does that mean?"

"I don't know. Maybe he believes that by helping Jasmine gain her full power, she will help him recover his Goddess. But don't worry, it's not real. A prophecy is just a prediction, like a horoscope. It can't actually do anything to ya."

Malachy rubbed at his eyes and yawned. "A strange horoscope."

Seamus smiled. "Come on; you're tired and we'd better get back before anyone notices how long it's been."

"Wait, there's something else. It's Emer. She has Iomlan."

"Emer? Are you sure?"

Malachy nodded. "I saw her. When I tried to top Badb, he attacked me and she stopped him."

"Then why don't I feel it? Does anyone else know?"

"I don't know. I don't think so. Apart from Drendas."

"Then don't tell anyone. I have to think about this." He stood up. "We'd better get back."

When they returned the rest were fast asleep. Sleeping either of side of Daire and Ferdia, like bookends, Drendas and Jasmine had turned away and buried their noses inside their cloaks. Anything Malachy wanted to say to her would have to wait until morning. Tiptoeing past her, he couldn't resist a look, but she didn't stir.

*

Malachy woke, sweating. The cave was dark, the only light coming from the dying embers of the fire. There were no rumbles, no shaking or falling, suffocating rock; all was quiet. Pulling his cloak off him, he sat up. Someone had let the fire die, but even in the dim light he could see that Jasmine wasn't there. It must've been her turn to watch, but there was no sign of her. A streak of daylight illuminated the wall near the entrance. It called to him, enticing him away from the heavy, pressing rock and out into the sunshine.

Outside, he blinked in the bright sunlight. Early morning scents filled the air, accompanied by the soft, warming coo of a wood pigeon. She wasn't here either. Turning right, he moved past the line of the trees and looked out across Lough Corrib to the Sacred Isle. Was it his imagination, or were the druids already starting to gather? He squinted. There, he saw a figure leave the trees and walk across a grassy bank towards the edge. And there, off to the left, halfway between the north shore and the island, a small boat moved towards him. According to Daire, they would be arriving throughout the morning, preparing for midday and the start of the meeting. Although, also according to Daire, it was more of a gathering than a meeting. There were certain rituals and formalities that had to be undertaken, even with the urgency of Ellyllon, it was doubtful the meeting would be completed before dawn the next day. Inwardly, Malachy shook his head. Red tape, it seemed, went surprisingly far back.

He picked his way down the slope, following a sneaking suspicion that Jasmine had gone down to the lake to wash. He'd thought about it during the night. He had to talk to her, to tell her he knew what she was doing, while he had the chance. Once they met with the druids, who knew what would happen? He could understand her desire to spare him, but he could've told her it was too late for that. Any doubts he'd had, any chance of escape had disappeared the moment he'd stepped through the portal. Probably even before that; from when he'd first laid eyes on her. He ducked under a branch. Or maybe it was Drendas' idea, using her fear to keep them apart. Either way, he had to find her and make her see sense. His bladder stirred with the first urge of the day, but he ignored it.

A third of the way down and Malachy's bladder was fit to burst. He couldn't wait. Thick clumps of stinging nettles lay all around him, grown tall in the fertile land, so he went sideways, inching pass them along the slope to the right, in search of a better spot. Not long and he found it, completely nettle free, ferns almost to his shoulders. Lifting up his tunic, he undid the flap in his leggings.

Finishing, Malachy closed the flap. Something cracked, off to his right, sounding like a stick snapping. He looked up, over the top of the sea of ferns. There was nothing there. Even so… he let his tunic fall and turning, began slowly to climb. Above him, something moved. Stopping, he froze, listening intently. Trees disappeared upwards, tall and silent. Not a rustle, not a sound. Nothing but the thud of his own heart. He swallowed noisily and going left and upwards, horizontally, continued to climb.

Voices came from above and off to the left, talking softly, and through the trees Ferdia and Daire appeared. Malachy stepped out between two trees and lifted his hand in greeting. Simultaneously, they glanced right.

"Malachy!" Daire bellowed, pointing.

Beginning to turn, Malachy heard the body just before it hit him. It knocked him off his feet and sent the two of them crashing and tumbling through the undergrowth. Stings caught across his face, his right arm, and then the world stopped spinning and he was flat on his back, a man on top of him. Dark eyes glared, the whites stark against the brown of the face. Baring long wolfish teeth, hands flew to his throat and squeezed. Choking, his chest heaving as his lungs fought desperately for air, Malachy's ears rang. And then suddenly, the hands were gone. Coughing, gasping, Malachy rolled over and watched as Ferdia took the man by the throat and lifted him off his feet. Ignoring his struggles, his wildly kicking feet, it was Ferdia's turn to squeeze, the muscles in his arm straining. There was another shout, off to Malachy's right, as Daire sent a second man crashing into a tree, his head hitting bark with an audible crack. Three more men appeared, flowing through the trees. Whirling, Daire turned to meet them. Still suspended, Malachy's attacker's eyes were closed, his kicking feet lying limp. Ferdia's opened his hand and the body dropped.

"Malachy?" Coming over to him, Ferdia held out the same hand.

Hesitating, Malachy looked from the hand to the body lying crumpled amongst the ferns. If it hadn't been for Ferdia, that would have been him lying there. Reaching up, he took Ferdia's hand.

"Thank you."

Ferdia grinned, pulled him to his feet as another man slipped out from behind a tree. It was Badb.

"What–?" Ferdia began, stepping forward.

Raising his hand, Badb thrust it towards him then jerked it away violently. With a cry, Ferdia went with it, plunging headlong into the undergrowth.

"You," Badb said quietly, pointing at Malachy. "I will be the one to give him you. Only you won't be alive to see it."

He took a step closer and Malachy, his heart pounding, drew his sword.

Chapter Fourteen

"Liar! Traitor!" a voice cracked.

It was Jasmine, walking calmly up the slope towards them. "Cowering, whimpering dog!"

Badb whirled, his eyes widening. Moving sideways, away from Malachy, he thrust again, this time towards her. Nothing happened. Another thrust, this one deeper, harder, with both hands. Jasmine's body rocked slightly.

"You think I cannot protect myself from the likes of you?" she purred. "Your heart is weak, your power nothing. Run, while you have the legs to carry you, and never speak of this."

"Weak? I have no fear of you," Badb sneered, although Malachy could see the thin sheen of sweat across his face. "A girl!"

"A girl?" She stepped past Malachy. "No, Badb, look closer, if you have the eyes and the wit to see."

His eyes narrowed, as if he were concentrating. Jasmine said something in a language Malachy didn't recognise and the colour drained from his face.

"Forgive–" He stopped and looked down.

His right hand was trembling. Even as he looked, the trembling changed to a shake that reverberated into his wrist and up his lower arm. With a sudden jerk, his hand moved down, towards his belt and the dagger he kept there, but he grabbed it and forced it upwards.

"Release me!" he cried, looking from his hand to Jasmine and then back again.

She didn't answer. His whole body jerked with the effort of keeping his hand up. Gasping, his eyes continued to roll between his hand and her.

"Jas, what are you doing?" Malachy asked, shifting uncertainly.

He didn't like it; this wasn't her. It was as if she were deliberately toying with Badb, savouring her power over him.

Badb's breath came out in one long gasp. His legs collapsed under him and he fell to his knees. Free, his hand lowered. His fingers grazed the handle of the knife and slowly tightened.

"I beg you," Badb pleaded, his eyes fixed on Jasmine. "I will go and not speak of this."

She dipped her head. Badb's wrist flexed, and slowly, his hand drew out the dagger.

"Jas, stop it!" Suddenly, Malachy wished Seamus was here. He'd know what to do, what to say to stop her.

Ferdia's head appeared above the ferns. Jasmine glanced towards him, her focus slipping, and Badb was on his feet in a heartbeat, his hand twisting the knife as if to throw it. Without thinking, Malachy leapt forward, his sword raised and using the hilt, hit him hard across the side of the head. He fell like a stone.

"Why did you do that?" Jasmine cried angrily, looking down at Badb's inert form. "I had it under control."

"He was going to throw it at you!"

"He wouldn't have got that far. I wouldn't've let him."

She sounded so sure, so confident. Arrogant, almost, like Ellyllon.

"Why didn't you run him through?" Bending, she picked up Badb's knife and hefted it.

"Jas, what are you doing?!" Malachy cried, his eyes wide with horror. "He's unconscious, you don't need to kill him!"

"He betrayed us, and given the chance will do so again." She lifted her arm. "Spite makes even a coward strong."

"I don't care. I know you. You can't just kill him!"

That stopped her. For a moment, the knife hovered and then, refusing to look at him, she let it drop. Thudding softly, it embedded itself deep into the soil. Kneeling down, she placed one hand on Badb's forehead.

"Malachy, are you hurt?" Ferdia asked, joining him.

"No, but he was going to kill me and give my body to Ellyllon."

"His vengeance on you, for Emer."

"Amadan! Ellyllon would've disembowelled him," Jasmine sneered, without turning. "What use is your body to him?"

Removing her hand, she sat back onto her haunches.

Does she have to talk about my body like that? Malachy thought plaintively. *When I'm not even dead?*

"What did you do?" he asked, deliberately changing the subject.

"I made him forget."

"What?"

"Everything. Emer has nothing to fear from him; his mind is empty. Not that it took much, it was halfway there already. Ferdia, help me up," she ordered, holding out her hand to him, looking for all the world like a queen.

He darted forward and pulled her gently to her feet.

"Ah, that's better."

They stared at one another, and then Ferdia lowered his eyes, and for one mad jealous moment Malachy thought he was going to lift up her hand and kiss it.

"Thank you, Ferdia." Smiling graciously, she took it away.

The look she gave Malachy was impish, a flash of her old self that made his heart leap. For a moment he thought he saw the green of the forest reflected in her eyes, and then she was gone. Moving past him, she slipped lightly through the ferns, towards the lake.

"Jas, where are you going?" He couldn't let her out of his sight. The way she was behaving, who knew what she'd do? And besides, he needed to talk to her. "Wait!"

She moved so fast he couldn't keep up with her. The steepness of the slope and the undergrowth that caught at his feet and ankles didn't seem to bother her. He stumbled, almost fell headlong, but at the last minute caught the branch of a tree. At the bottom of the slope, she paused and looked back, as if sensing his near miss.

"Jas, c'mon, I need to talk to you!"

She turned away; he thought he heard her laugh, the sound low, earthy, coming from somewhere deep in her throat, and then she was dipping under a huge, low branch and away.

Annoyed and worried for her in equal measures, Malachy threw himself downwards, his feet slipping and sliding. He crashed through the undergrowth, grabbing at overhanging branches and stems of ferns to keep his body upright. At the bottom, he dipped under the same branch, and ignoring the breath whistling through his chest, followed her.

He reached the edge of the trees. Bathed in sunlight, the surface of the lake shimmered a dark midnight blue, the closest cold water could come to mirroring the sky's brighter, paler cousin. And there, beyond the grass, was Jas. Running hard across sand, she was almost at the water.

"Jas, stop! Wait!"

A single, fleeting look back and she hit the lake, her quick, eager strides sending the water splashing. Jackknifing in one fluid motion, she dived smoothly into the waves. Her feet and ankles flashed and then she was gone, into the dark, murky water of the lake.

What was she doing? Bending over, Malachy placed his hands on his thighs and waited for his breath to come back. And what a time to decide to go for a swim. The water was smooth, its surface unbroken. His breath easing, Malachy straightened. There was no sign of her. He began walking towards the shore, scanning the waves. She'd been down there a long time.

He reached the water's edge. "Jas, c'mon, you're scaring me! Jas!"

No answer. Where was she? He peered into the water. She'd been down too long. No one could hold their breath that long.

"Jas!" He shouted again.

Something moved through the water to his right, darting like quicksilver. He glimpsed a tail, a streak of grey-silver, the curve of a scaly back and then it was gone, down into the depths. Two heartbeats and then Jasmine broke the surface a few metres in front of him, gasping, her body lifted as if propelled by an invisible force. Letting it fall, she spread her arms wide and lay backwards.

"Come in, Malachy, it's lovely," she called, examining the toes that peeked at her over the top of the water as if she didn't have a care in the world.

She'd lost it. The power of Iomlan hadn't corrupted her, it had sent her spinning over the edge.

"Bloody hell, Jas, you scared me. I thought you'd drowned!"

She laughed, but whether it was at the idea that she could drown, or that he'd thought it, he couldn't be sure. He tried again. "C'mon, I want to talk to you."

"If you want to talk you have to come in here, to me."

"But the water's freezing. Why don't you come out and we can sit on the nice warm sand?"

"Just sit?" she retorted, with another laugh.

Lowering her legs, she pushed downwards and sank slowly into the depths.

"Oh for feck's sake!" Malachy muttered, throwing up his hands and turning away. "Now she thinks she's a fish."

Hearing splashing, he turned back just in time to see her crawling out of the water on all fours. Wet and dripping, her hair covered her face.

"Malachy, help me up," she demanded, stopping and lifting up one hand.

Wincing at the cold, he stepped into the water, feeling it mill around his ankles. He reached down and their hands met. Her fingers tightened, and with a wild yell, she pulled him over and down, into the water.

"Shit!" He sat up, gasping in shock.

Laughing, she pounced on him. Pressed her mouth to his and began kissing him. It took him a moment, and then, eyes closed, he was kissing her back, their mouths working furiously. Her tongue in his mouth, she pressed closer, her wet body slipping over his as she tried to force him back. Water splashed upwards, wetting his neck and the back of his head.

"I've waited so long," she murmured, her hands moving to the edge of his tunic.

"Me too, but here?"

She nipped at his neck. "Why not?" she asked archly, for the first time looking straight at him.

Green swirled across her eyes, gleaming like the light from the portal. With a shout, he dropped her, his feet and legs scrambling as he tried to get away. Water splashed; cold raining down on them.

"Mal?" The green was gone, her eyes returning to their usual brown.

He stopped. "Jas?"

Pressing one hand to her temple, she screwed up her face. "Ow."

He peered at her, "What's the matter?"

"My head, it really hurts."

He looked back towards the hill. "Maybe we should get Seamus–"

She dropped her hand. "It's OK, it's stopped."

"Just like th–?"

"Mal, I'm cold," she interrupted him, shivering. "I'm getting out."

"You're getting out?! You're the one that pulled me in and jumped on me!"

"But I'm cold."

Helping each other up, they moved up the beach to the edge of the sand.

"I'm freezing," Jasmine complained again.

She looked it. Sitting down, her teeth chattering, she began rubbing her arms.

"I wonder why!" He joined her on the grass. "Here, let me." Knocking her hands away, he began rubbing furiously. "Yer an idiot, going swimming in that."

It wasn't what he wanted to say, but how could he say it? *I don't like* this, you're getting worse, behaving really weird and oh, by the way, does that headache have anything to do with your eyes turning green?

The offending eyes slid away. "I suppose."

"Why did you do it? Anyone could be here. Ellyllon? Or his followers?"

"Mal, that's too hard. Stop, it hurts."

He stopped rubbing. "I don't like this; you should tell Seamus."

"Tell him what?"

"What you did."

She frowned. "What did I do?"

"Very funny!" he snapped. "I'm serious. Jas, you're not yourself. You have to talk to Seamus."

"About what?"

He took a deep breath. "He told me what Iomlan's doing to you. He can help, I know he can."

"He told you?!" Her face cold, she quickly extricated herself. "Seamus can't help me. No one can, apart from Drendas, and he only understands because he's been through it himself."

"But you don't even like him. I see your face when he touches you or gets too close. He repulses you!"

"Don't be stupid; you don't have to like someone to know what they're saying is true!" she snapped, her eyes bright with sudden fury. "He has more power than Seamus could ever dream of."

"So, that's it, is it? Seamus doesn't have enough power? He can't take you to next level? Cop on to yerself!"

"Cop on to myself?! You think I should apologise for the power I have? Pretend it's not there because Seamus doesn't have it? It's not my fault I've outgrown him!"

"You? Outgrow him?! He's forgotten more than you'll ever know, you and your precious Drendas!" he roared, leaping to his feet. He'd never been so angry. "If Drendas is so perfect, why doesn't he think women should be druid? Is that why his daughter hides her power, because he wouldn't approve? Or maybe it's because he'd try and stop her, or try to force it out of her?"

Getting up, she thrust her face at him, her anger easily matching his. "Don't be stupid, he'd hardly force it out of her. That would kill his own daughter!"

"That's twice you called me stupid! If you're so clever, tell me why that misogynistic old bastard, who doesn't believe women can be druid, would want to help you?!"

Her face fell and she took a step back. "I don't know."

Quickly, he pressed his advantage, "And Seamus loves you. Worries over you like you're his own."

"I know he does. I love him too, but he can't help me. Don't you see, without Drendas, there's nothing?"

"But why should I be surprised?" he continued, ignoring her. "I tell you I love you and I get nothing. So, tell me, right here, right now, do you love me?"

"That's not fair. With everything that's happening, you can't ask me that."

"Too late; I already have. Do you love me?"

"I – I don't know how I feel. I'm so confused."

"What's there to be confused about? Either you love me or you don't."

"Mal, you know it's not that simple. We have to stop Ellyllon, but there's all these things happening, happening to me, I can't just–"

"Oh, Jas, just tell me!" He clenched his fists; he wanted to scream. "Yes or no."

She hung her head. "Yes," she whispered.

"Because if not, then–" He blinked. "Yes?"

"Yes, I love you." She turned away. "Happy now?! You've only gone and made things a hundred times worse."

Grabbing her shoulders, he turned her back.

"No, I haven't," he said with a grin, pulling her to him. "Actually, I've made things a hundred times better. You're not alone. We're in this together."

Sinking to the ground, they held each other.

"Seriously, Jas, why didn't you tell me?" Malachy asked finally.

"Drendas told me what will happen if I don't learn to control Iomlan, what I could do. It's so hard, Mal. I need all my energy, my focus–" Her voice broke. She swallowed, but with an effort continued. "It's happening already. It's corrupting me. I've done things – you don't know about."

He hesitated. "Jas, I'm sorry, but I think I do. Seamus told me."

She pulled away. "What happened at the portal?"

"Yeah, and the forest."

Her face twisted with pain.

"But listen, it's not you, you're not a killer. It's Iomlan. All that power inside you – how could anyone control it?"

"But it's changing me, inside, can't you see that?"

"Yeah, of course it's affecting you, but you're still you. It can't change that."

She shook her head. "But it is, I can feel it. Sometimes it feels like it's not Iomlan inside me, but me outside Iomlan, as if it's the important, the real thing, and I'm nothing more than a host. Sometimes, in my head, I hear–" She stopped as if she'd wanted to say something more, but thought better of it. "I'm losing myself, Mal, I'm slipping away and I don't know how to stop it."

"No, you're not." He pressed his forehead to hers, as if by doing so he'd be able to force this idea, this dangerous fancy, out of her. "I won't let you."

"But Drendas says–"

"Fuck Drendas! Look, I know you need him to help you control Iomlan, just don't believe *everything* he tells you, and don't trust him, OK? His daughter has to hide her power, Drendas made sure women can't be druid and is obsessed with a prophecy that he thinks is about you. Does he sound like someone you should trust?"

"I suppose not."

It was an admission of sorts, but it wasn't enough.

"Then trust me, trust Seamus. Talk to us."

He heard voices. He turned just as the others appeared, coming out of the forest, pulling the horses behind them. Seamus had Malachy's horse as well as his own, while Ferdia had Jasmine's. His arm lifted, Daire pointed right, out across the lake. Malachy followed his finger and saw a boat coming across the water towards them, rowed by two men. Jasmine was on her feet next to him. It was too late. He'd left it too late.

Chapter Fifteen

Getting to his feet, Malachy waited while Jasmine went to meet them. Out on the lake, the boat moved closer. Leaving the horses near the edge of the beach, the others joined him.

"Is everything alright?" Seamus asked quickly.

Malachy shook his head. *No*, he tried to tell him with his eyes, *we need to talk*. Amazingly, Seamus caught it.

"You left your cloak in the cave. Here, I left it on your horse." Cocking his head, indicating Malachy should follow him, he went back to the horses.

"What happened?" he hissed as their heads met over the horse's back. "Ferdia told us about Badb."

"But did he tell you she was going to kill him? Stab him with a knife!" He lowered his voice. "Seamus, she's getting worse. Doing things that make no sense."

He glanced at the boat. Only a few hundred yards offshore, it was speeding inland. There wasn't much time.

"She went swimming and she tried to–" He stopped, flushing.

"What? She tried to do what?"

Malachy squirmed. "She tried to seduce me."

"Seduce you?!" Seamus spluttered, biting back a laugh. "Jasmine?!"

"That's exactly what I'm saying. But there's something else."

"Go on."

"Her eyes went green."

"Green?" Seamus' eyebrows disappeared into his hairline.

"The same green as the light in the portal."

The boat had reached the shore. As the rowers raised their oars, Daire and Ferdia leapt forward to hold the boat.

"Seamus, Seamus!" Drendas called urgently. "We must leave."

Seamus looked as if the horse had kicked him. "We'd better go; we don't want to be left behind. But this isn't finished," he said darkly. "We'll talk later."

The boat headed out across the water. Shoulders bent, the rowers rowed in silence, keeping time to their own internal beat. Sat next to Drendas, Jasmine glanced at Malachy, who'd raised his hand and was squinting against the low, early morning sun. She wished they'd had more time together. Everything was moving so quickly, it was hard to make sense of it all.

The oars swung upwards in a wide arc and then lowered again, entering the water with the smallest of splashes. The surface of the lake rippled with small, sharp waves. Midnight blue had changed to platinum. She gazed into the depths.

She hadn't meant to admit how she felt, but now she was glad she had. There was a completion to it, a sense of closure that she suspected she might need in the coming days. It scared her to admit them, even if she'd been able to find the words, but the symptoms were getting worse. Growing quickly, they clouded her mind like a fog. She'd tried to tell Malachy, to explain something of what was happening to her, but he hadn't understood. How could he, when she didn't really understand it herself? But the worst of it wasn't what she did or the gaps in her memory, whole pieces of time she couldn't remember, or could only remember dimly, like a half-forgotten dream. It was the voices. They'd become so strong, so clear and distinct, she could almost name them. There was the first voice, the one she thought of as the main one, the one that held the other two in check. The second one sounded old in her head and the third seemed younger, more like herself, only softer and more musical. She shivered. Drendas had warned her Iomlan could corrupt her soul, but he hadn't warned her it could corrupt her mind.

"I will speak to those gathered," Drendas was telling Seamus, who'd twisted backwards to look at him. "I would ask you speak only when I ask it, for our ways are not your ways."

"Agreed." Seamus' face was calm, his voice neutral, but even now, Jasmine noticed, he couldn't quite manage to disguise his dislike.

She turned back to the water.

Malachy won't be our first loss, the first voice said, *we've had many. Handsome, brave men, willing to die for us, their bodies taut and muscular.*

Although, the second voice said wistfully, *there was always one that was special; Diarmuid.*

Ah, yes, Diarmuid, I'd almost forgotten.

Malachy said something to Seamus in a voice too low to hear. Seamus answered and the two of them smiled, sharing a comment that no one else could hear. It made her wish it was how it was before, just the three of them, but the lake was still calling to her, the voices showing her their memories. Diarmuid sliding from the water, his hair and body dripping. His eyes glowing as he reached for her. Something moved. Indistinct at first, it slowly took shape. A face came towards her, floating up through the water, its long blond hair drifting outwards, like a fan. It was him. But it couldn't be; Diarmuid died centuries ago. She'd seen his death, seen the blood running from the wounds in his chest and side, dying as he'd lived, her own fierce, brave warrior.

"Jasmine!" Drendas muttered, leaning in towards her.

The others were staring at her. Seamus was frowning, and she knew he'd sensed something. *This wasn't the first time; she must learn to control herself better. The urges of her sisters were dangerous, unpredictable.*

She glanced again at the water, but this time the waves were empty.

*

They were almost there. The island was bigger than it looked from the shore. Green, bushy trees sat in a cluster in the centre of the island, its grassy banks sloping down to the water so that it could be reached from all sides. The other druids were gone, melted away into the trees, apart from one man who stood waiting. Dressed in a russet red tunic and leggings, topped with a yellow cloak, his light brown hair was pulled into a high knot, then bunched in three places.

Maine.

Inwardly, Jasmine lifted her head. How did the voice know that?

Shhh!

Abruptly, the voices fell silent.

The shore was metres away. Still the man didn't move, didn't lift up his hand or raise his voice in greeting. The boat hit the lake bottom and Daire helped his father out. One by one the others followed.

"Maine," Drendas greeted him.

"Drendas."

They embraced.

"Maine, my son, Daire."

Maine grinned. "Thank the Gods he has only his father's eyes."

"My daughter, Emer, stays at home."

"Little Emer?" He and Daire clasped hands.

"Grown a woman."

Reaching out, Seamus took Malachy's arm. She watched him gently lead him away. Heads bent, they talked in low, urgent voices. Daire had introduced Ferdia.

"He is not druid," Maine said, his face darkening. "Drendas, you know the lore."

"No, he is not, but would you have him wait on the shore with only his strength, his guile, for protection, for I sense the dark wolves gathering."

"Then he must wait at the water's edge."

"Agreed." Drendas nodded.

Maine looked at Jasmine and then Seamus and Malachy still talking.

"Maine." Drendas paused and with a proud tilt of his head, he slowly, deliberately lifted a hand towards them. "As the Goddess foretold, the Three."

Maine's mouth dropped. "The Chosen?"

"Yes. The Goddess sees all."

"Then the Goddess forgive me." Maine thumped his breast dramatically. "For I doubted her word. I doubted you, even when I heard the call."

Drendas smiled, looking for all the world like the proverbial cat. *He's loving this*, thought Jasmine, half-disapproving, half-admiring. But then again, who could blame him? He was proving all his many doubters wrong.

"And the Goddess?"

Drendas smile faded. "Ah, Maine, I have much to tell, but it must wait until all are gathered."

Maine nodded. "It is the lore." He looked at Malachy and frowned. "How can a chosen not be druid?"

"The Goddess willed it. Would you question her wisdom?"

Maine shifted, awkwardly. "Then he too must wait at the water's edge."

Daire and Ferdia were gazing at each another.

"All will be well," the latter said, his hand going to the horn in his belt. "I will call if we have need for you."

"The dark one's power grows," Maine was telling Drendas. "Cat brought word that he sits now at Cruachan, the ancient seat of Queen Medb, calling her spirit, and the spirits of all the ancient kings to his cause, and our young brothers flock eagerly to him, feed on his words as the crow feeds on carrion."

Deep and low, a horn sounded. Malachy and Seamus separated.

"It is time," Maine intoned. "Come."

Impulsively, Jasmine threw her arms around Malachy.

"You won't be that long!" he joked, kissing her.

But still she held him, pressing her body tight to his.

"Come, Jasmine." Drendas waved his staff impatiently.

A final kiss and, reluctantly, she let Malachy go. The horn sounded again, and this time, obedient to its call, they left Malachy and Ferdia on the grassy bank and stepped into the trees. Jasmine took one, brief last look at them sat together in the sunshine and then, with Maine leading, she followed the others as they fanned out behind him and walked peekaboo through hazel, willow and oak. The horn sounded for a third time, echoing eerily through the trees, then fell silent. No one spoke. Jasmine glanced over at Seamus, but he didn't notice. Now this moment had arrived, she felt unaccountably nervous, as if it were her, not Drendas, who would have to convince the other druids to stand against Ellyllon.

*

Figures appeared through the trees, their faces turned towards them in anticipation. Some, Jasmine knew, were believers, but most had at best dismissed Drendas' prophecy as the ramblings of an increasingly deluded druid, and at worst mocked and denigrated him for it. And yet his power had been such that no one would dare challenge his authority, his right to have his voice heard above everyone else's. Slightly ahead, Drendas entered the meeting place and the other druids fell silent. She couldn't say how she knew all this; it was just there, as if she'd always known. As for Drendas, he knew well what some of the druids thought about him, but after today no one would doubt his authority, not even to themselves. Ducking under a low branch, she joined him inside the meeting place. Inside, the voices were still silent, but she knew they weren't far away. No one spoke as all eyes turned to look at her.

*

Huddled together in small groups, the druids were stood around an oblong, man-made clearing. Older; their hair, beards and moustaches moved from brown flecked with grey to grey, silver and white. Jasmine counted nineteen, maybe twenty; a fraction of their total number. In the centre of the clearing was a fairy fort, a circle of stones sat perfectly equidistant from one another. Varying in size and shape, they were almost exactly the same height, that of a small child's chair. At the north end lay an altar stone. Thick, rectangular, it reminded Jasmine of the huge Blue Saracen stones found at Stonehenge. Drendas and Maine were stood next to it, and beside them a man with thick black hair tied into three elaborate plaits, wearing a green tunic and leggings. A torc, the metal twisted into a tight curl, adorned his neck, showing him to be a man of some distinction. In his hand was the horn that had called them there. Thin, almost completely circular, with a strange bulge midway, one end widened into the small head of a trumpet. A lip surrounded the head, etched with delicate swirls and shapes that to Jasmine looked vaguely Celtic. With a glance at Maine, the man placed one hand on each side of the bulge, and to Jasmine's amazement, the horn turned, the two ends pulling away from each other into a loose 'S'. Stepping forward, he lifted it high into the air and then pressing the mouthpiece to his lips, threw back his head and blew. The sound came again, low, deep and plaintive. Two more blows, the last one lingering, and as the man lowered his horn, the druids slipped through the gaps in the stones and took their rightful places inside the circle.

Drendas beckoned and, as Daire followed the druids, Jasmine and Seamus joined him and Maine at the altar. They all looked at one another, waiting, as Maine stepped forward and raised his arms.

"Brother Druids, you have crossed the waters to the Sacred Isle, answering the call of Drendas, son of Aurith. The dark one's power rises, even as our brother foretold. It is the kings' right to rule and their right alone. But it is our right to guide them, to uphold the teachings and law made by our gods. If our young brothers have lost their way, then we must guide them back. We must look to the prophecy, heed the wisdom of Brid." Lowering his arms, he turned to Drendas. "Drendas, son of Aurith, will speak."

Drendas stepped forward. "Brother Druids, you know the prophecy, for have I not spoken of it many times? What was foretold has come to pass. The dark one, Ellyllon, seeks to destroy our ways and those of our brethren in the land of Brigantes."

A white-haired druid, dressed in a brown tunic and leggings covered with a yellow cloak, took one step forward. "The dark one's power has spread throughout our lands; our brothers, our kings, our people follow him. Drendas, what would you have us do? Speak with them?!"

"Scibar, the dark one's power is too strong. Lies spill from his tongue as rain from the sky. There is but one way; to fight."

Another stepped forward. "You would fight our brothers, our kin, for what?" He jerked his head eastward. "Those of another land?"

Drendas raised his staff. "No, for our ways. Are not our ways the ways of our brethren in Brigantes? Do we not follow the same oath? To your king, your clan, your brothers?"

A murmur rippled through the group.

Scibar nodded. "We must honour our oath."

Drendas' voice lifted as he warmed to his subject. "The one known as Ellyllon was once one of us, but he turned from our path, from our ways. He has no honour. He will not stand with you when you are fallen, he will not tend the lambs that sicken or teach the children of our lore, the oneness of things. He will not guide our kings, or seek to temper the flame of justice with the wisdom of humility. He will set king against king, brother against brother. See, has he not already done so? The prophecy–"

"The prophecy?!" A druid with brown hair flecked with grey scoffed. "The ravings of an old man. You speak of kings, of clans and children, of guiding and teaching, yet you will not guide, or teach or live among us. I hear you, Drendas; I hear your talk of signs, but I see none."

"Ronan, what of the dark one? Is he not a sign?" He waved his staff at Seamus and Jasmine. "And see, I have brought the Three."

"Three?" Ronan sneered. "I see only two."

Some of the druids tittered, but stopped when Maine glared at them.

"The third waits at the shore," he explained coldly.

Someone shouted from the other side of the circle. "Why is he not here? Bring him to us."

"He cannot. Only druid may enter the meeting place."

Suddenly, everyone was talking or shouting at once.

"He is not druid?"

"How can that be?"

"The Gods would not allow it."

"Wait, brothers, wait." Ronan's voice cut through them. Moving into the centre of the stone circle, he pointed at Jasmine. "Drendas, friend and brother, by your word, your *oath*, women cannot be druid, and yet you bring *her* to our meeting place?!"

"Yes, but–"

"I ask you, my brothers," Ronan continued, turning to his peers. "Drendas speaks of tongues and of lies, but by his own words do we hear the lies his tongue speaks. What proof Ellyllon is the dark one? What proof his lack of honour?"

Daire leapt forward. "My word, for I have seen how he twists men's hearts. I have heard his lies. And I have seen one, the best of us, the most gentle and the most pure of heart, turn on his brother druid."

"Daire, son of Drendas, and what proof your heart, your word?"

Ronan flapped one hand, as if dismissing him. "Run to your father's side, for I do not wish to hear you whine and lick, like a dog suckling at the teat of its mother."

"Daire, no!" Drendas shouted as Daire's hand moved to his sword. Darting sideways, he grabbed Jasmine's arm and pushed her forward. "These are not my words, but the words of the Goddess. If you will not hear me speak them, hear–"

"Me," a voice shouted, echoing across the glade.

Everyone turned. Stood, leaning against the trunk of a tree on the edge of the glade, was Cathbad.

Straightening, he moved to the edge of the circle.

"I bring word from Ellyllon," he called, his voice loud and ringing. "Do not listen to these lies. He wishes you no harm and offers his hand in friendship to all the people of Erin. Take it and all you desire will be yours."

Ronan's eyes narrowed. "And if we do not?"

Cathbad shrugged. "Speak to your kings, hear their answer."

"And our brothers across the water?"

"Why do you ask? What care you for the bastards of Brigantes?"

"Nothing, but our lore." It was Ronan's turn to shrug.

But there was something in the way he stood, Jasmine thought, watching him.

"The lore of my ancestors is for the old and the weak." Cathbad held out his hand. "By my birthright, I, at Ellyllon's side, will make new lore. Come, join us."

Ronan stared at his hand, and then, turning to Drendas, bowed slightly. "Forgive me, brother." Turning back, noisily and with great venom he spat onto the ground in front of Cathbad's feet. "That to your birthright! Return to Cruachan, grovel at the foot of your master."

Cathbad's face darkened, but he held his temper. "And what of you?" he asked the other druids.

For a moment, no one answered. They were torn, caught between Ronan's support of Drendas and their unwillingness to do, to say anything that could lead to war. And then, to Jasmine's surprise, Seamus began to speak.

"Listen to me. I know Ellyllon. I have fought him many times. Born druid, he cares nothing for our lore, our ways, or the peoples of Erin. He cares only for power and vengeance on those that took it from him, for he has none of his own, save Tionchar, the power to lie and deceive." He lifted his chin, and his hazel eyes glowed. "Ellyllon is a vampire; he feeds on druid when we are young, gorging on our power like the tick, the horsefly."

Scibar screwed up his eyes. "Feeds?"

Seamus nodded grimly. "Feeds. In the time just before the joining, when Iomlan is ripe for the plucking." A murmur broke out; shocked, the druids looked at one another as Seamus pressed home his advantage. "He cannot survive without it and it has been a long time since his last feed." He cocked his head, as if considering something for the first time. "Or perhaps not. Cathbad?"

"Do not listen to his lies," Cathbad responded angrily, as all eyes turned again towards him. "Look at him. See by his face; he seeks to divide us, even as Ellyllon seeks to unite us. Feeds! What man or beast could feed on druid?! None, I say, but a demon, and I serve no demon!"

"But a man can become a demon," Scibar countered. "Just as a man may turn his head from the dark deeds of his king and so give them strength."

"Tell us, *brother* Cathbad," Ronan sneered. "Do you help your demon to feed?"

"Your words are an insult! They need no answer."

"Ah." Scibar slowly shook his head. "And yet, by your face, you have answered them. Now, hear our answer." He glanced at the other druids; one or two nodded although most stayed silent, the answer clear in the cast of their faces. "Go, return to Cruachan. Tell Ellyllon to await us."

"Ellyllon await you?! You are to him as fleas on the back of cattle. See how with one turn of his tail, he crushes you."

Slowly, he lifted his right hand and four druids appeared in the trees behind him. More came to the left and the right. The meeting place was surrounded. Then suddenly, carrying through the trees, came the sound of Ferdia's horn.

Chapter Sixteen

In the distance, Maine's horn sounded for a fourth time.

"The meeting has begun," Ferdia explained as Malachy turned to look.

He turned back. Clouds were coming across the mountains, rolling inland, but above the lake the sky was still blue.

"How long will it be?" Malachy asked, almost for something to say. He already knew the answer.

Ferdia shrugged. "Today. Not long, I think."

"They'll listen to Drendas?"

"They will listen to the Goddess."

They lapsed into silence. Ferdia seemed even more distracted than he was. Maybe he was thinking of Jasmine. He hadn't forgotten the way Ferdia had kissed Jasmine's hand or the look of total adoration he'd given her. An insect landed on his arm and he flicked it away. Of course, that didn't make sense, Ferdia was married to Daire and you could see their devotion to one another. And Jasmine had told him she loved him, so what was the problem? *That look*, he answered himself immediately, *that look was the problem*.

"Your journey to Drendas was very difficult," he offered, trying to sound casual.

"As was yours. Daire spoke of it."

"Yeah, it makes you close. Like family."

"Yes."

Malachy shifted, bending his legs then unbending them again. "Seamus told me Jasmine didn't sleep much."

"Seamus slept. Her magic was needed to protect us."

This wasn't getting him anywhere. He tried another tack. "It must've been hard for her with Seamus sick. Being so alone."

"She was not alone, for I was with her."

There was a pause. Staring at Malachy, Ferdia's face was a picture of confusion and then his face cleared and he leant forward. "Malachy,

Daire is my husband.”

Malachy flushed and looked away. “I know.”

“Even if he were not, I would not lie with a woman.”

Malachy held up his hand against such unexpected directness. Jasmine and Ferdia sleeping together?! He hadn’t actually got that far. “Yeah, I know. I’m sorry.”

To his surprise, Ferdia smiled for the first time. “Ah, Malachy, the heart runs fast, like an eager dog, and we can but follow. I fear–” He stopped. Then cocking his head, he lifted his hand. “Listen.”

Malachy waited, his ears straining. He couldn’t hear anything. Then water splashed and in a flurry of wings, a heron appeared from around the side of the island, a fish dangling from his claws. Rising quickly, his long, powerful wings took him northwards. Malachy watched him go, a tiny silhouette against the low mountains. Green slopes were dotted with little pieces of white that looked like sheep, but Malachy knew were stones, boulders. At the very top was a figure. Blackened by distance, it was impossible to make out.

“Ferdia, look!” Even as he pointed, his instinct told him who it was: Ellyllon.

Ferdia was on his feet in an instant. “The dark one! Malachy, get up. We must join the others.”

Keeping his eyes on Ellyllon, Malachy did as he said. “But I thought it was forbidden?”

“It is, but still, we must go.”

Already Ferdia was moving off, towards the trees.

“Malachy, come!” He called, looking back.

Malachy dragged his eyes away. Behind Ferdia, men appeared, crouching low as they crept around the side of the island. Seeing Malachy’s face, Ferdia whirled. Three more appeared, stepping out of the trees ahead of them. Grabbing the horn from his belt, Ferdia raised it to his lips and blew once, long and hard.

The note faded. Stuffing the horn back inside his belt, Ferdia drew his sword, Malachy following. Spreading out so as to stop them slipping past, the men raised their swords and moved slowly towards them.

“Go, Malachy,” Ferdia shouted, backing up. “I will hold them.”

“No, you can’t, there’s too many!”

“It is you they seek. You must go.”

He was right. There was no time for anything, no thanks or deep words. Hating himself for it, Malachy hefted his sword and ran.

Racing away from Ferdia and Ellyllon’s men, his feet scrambled across the uneven ground as he followed the shoreline around to the right, aiming for the gap between the line of trees and the water's edge. Two of the men from the forest veered left, tracking across the island to cut off his escape. He sped up, jumping and leaping over the holes in the ground. He heard shouting behind him, the first clash of metal, but daren't look back. Ahead, the men from the forest were almost to the gap. They were too fast, he thought desperately; he'd never make it. Suddenly, the back one fell, his body tumbling helplessly forward as if someone had driven into him. He caught the man in front, knocking him sprawling, and together they hit the ground, one landing on top of the other. Any second and they would be up and his escape blocked. Changing direction, Malachy lifted his sword and charged as Daire ran out of the forest. They shared one brief look, then reaching the men, Malachy raised his sword up over his head and thrust it down into the first man's back. Slicing effortlessly through flesh, the blade caught, shattering bone as it forced its way out the other side. Dead instantly, the man's body collapsed, wrenching the sword from Malachy's hand. Heart pounding, he looked around for another weapon, expecting to see the second man rising, but with a deep cut to his left temple, he remained still. Shouts were coming from the forest, the sound of more people fighting. Confused, Malachy span. Facing four men, with another three dead on the ground, Ferdia was fighting, cutting and thrusting, like a man possessed. Halfway to him, Daire had pressed a druid to the ground and was using his Iomlan to squeeze the life out of him. Another shout and the sound of oars came from behind him. Malachy turned in time to see a man standing in the middle of a boat, a sling in one hand, and then something caught him on the side of the head and he slipped to his knees.

Malachy breathed, the sound loud in his ears. Pain throbbed down one side of his head; he tried to lift one hand to it, but it didn't seem to want to move. Muted, the world passed with dizzying speed. The boat reached the shore and two men jumped out. They ran towards him and knowing he should do something but unable to figure out what, he watched them come.

"Malachy!" Faint, a voice cut through the fog in his head.

Too late, the men had reached him. Grabbing his arms, they dragged him to his feet and began pulling him towards the boat. The world span, it was all he could do to keep upright. His feet and shins hit water, the coldness making him gasp, and then hands pushed him roughly in over the side of the boat. His face hit the bottom, more hands grabbed his legs, pressing and folding them after. And then a body landed on top of him and he lost consciousness.

*

As the last of Ferdia's horn faded nobody moved, and then everything happened at once. Drendas raised his staff and sent a pulse streaking towards Cathbad, who parried it easily. With a cry, Daire leapt forward, Iomlan bursting from him. It caught the druid to Cathbad's left and threw him violently against a tree, his body crumpling. Suddenly the air was full of Iomlan. Druids thrust and parried, fighting with an invisible force that made their movements grotesque, like dancing, jerking marionettes. Daire ran for the gap, and ducking to avoid a blast, disappeared into the trees.

Malachy!

Jasmine willed herself to him. Nothing happened. She tried again, drawing herself up and focussing. Still nothing. It was as if something was blocking her, standing in her way. *But I've done it before*, she thought desperately.

Out of nowhere, a blast of Iomlan hit her side, sending her spinning. She landed, sprawling, across the altar stone. Another blast caught her across the back and she gasped, her body arching in pain. A second pulse joined the first, the two of them forcing and pressing her down and squeezing the breath from her lungs. Her face squashed against the hard stone; she heard Cathbad's voice rise above the noise of the battle and, in a flash, she knew what they were doing. They were holding her there, pinning her to the stone so he could collect her like some helpless butterfly. Anger burned through her, making her head throb. She clenched her fists. *How dare they?* Resisting the impulse to attack, she gathered Iomlan to her and using it like a ram, began slowly to push them back. They redoubled their efforts, but she felt the air around her shimmer and pushed harder. One of them swore, his control weakening. One last push and, abruptly, their power shattered. The pain in her head cleared. In control once more, she clambered to her feet and slowly turned to face them.

Seeing her eyes, they took a step back, but lacked the sense to flee. *Amadan.*

Iomlan flew from her, cracking like a whip, sending them tumbling. Immediately they were back on their feet, but too late. Leaping forward, she knocked one savagely away and grabbed the other one's shoulder.

"My turn," she hissed.

Iomlan, hot and glutinous, like molten lava, slid down her arm and onto his shoulder. He tried to fight back, but she was too strong. It poured over him; sliding eagerly into every line, every crevice, engulfing him. Gasping in pain, he fell to his knees, his body jerking with the power running into him. A stray pulse of Iomlan hit a tree behind her, showering her with leaves and splinters of wood, but she barely noticed. The druid moaned. Beads of sweat dripped from his forehead onto his face. The jerks were becoming stronger, his body thrashing as it fought against her and the pain from the heat inside him. The moans changed to cries, then shrieks. She was burning him from the inside out. Appalled, a tiny part of her wanted to stop and pull away, but the rest of her was singing. The druid's eyes rolled and his head drooped. The heat beneath her hand was terrible, burning her skin; she could feel pain beginning across the pads of her fingers and then incredibly, sickeningly, his skin caught fire. She let him go; falling away, he hit the ground, the flames darting across his body, curling and licking.

The other druid was staring at her, his eyes wide with terror.

He's very young, her younger sister said quietly.

She paused, for a moment torn.

It doesn't matter; the oldest countered, her voice sharp, *he was old enough to choose*.

Across the glade, Cathbad turned away from the battle and looked at her. Their eyes met, and even from this distance he saw her and he knew. She felt the young druid's Iomlan and ignoring Cathbad, she lifted her hand.

The young druid was burning, his screams piercing the air. Across the glade, Cathbad whirled and, with a wide swing of his cloak, leapt into the trees. Abruptly, with a loud choke, the screams stopped.

"Jasmine!"

Seamus strode towards her. Motionless, the body continued to burn.

"Stop it, stop it now!" Seamus' face was white with fury, his eyes glaring at her with something approaching hatred. She let her hand fall.

Around the glade, the other druids watched her in silence. Cathbad had gone, leaving the druids that had followed him to their fate; their bodies littered the ground. Scibar too was dead, his body curled in on itself. She looked at it sadly. Born of an earlier time, he was one of the most loyal.

Seamus reached her.

"How could you?!" he raged, grabbing her hand and holding it, palm upwards, towards her face. "Look at it! Look what you've done to yerself, let alone them!"

He was shaking. Her hand was beginning to swell, the skin tightening into blisters. She focussed.

"What are you doing?" His mouth fell open; he dropped her hand and fell back. "What–?!" His jaw didn't seem to want to work, it just hung there in a way that was almost comical.

Calmly, she showed him her hand, the skin clear and unblemished.

"See," Drendas shouted, his voice ringing. He lifted both hands, like a priest, calling people to him. "As was foretold, she has come."

Stepping past Seamus, she lifted her head and faced the druids. One by one, they sank to their knees and bowed their heads. Lowering his arms, Drendas joined them.

Chapter Seventeen

Malachy woke to the sharp scent of treated animal skin and the sound of men rowing. His stomach lurched with the movement of the water below him. Fighting back the urge to vomit, he opened his eyes. His cheek pressed against a piece of wooden lattice, all he could see was the bottom of the boat and two pairs of feet. He tried to move, but immediately a foot came down heavily on the centre of his back.

"Lie still," a deep voice growled.

He froze.

"He killed my brother," the voice continued angrily. "Ellyllon only said alive."

Someone laughed, the sound unpleasant. Malachy swallowed.

"And you know his meaning?" another voice interjected, sarcastically. "What do you think he would do to you if you are mistaken?"

"I do not fear him."

The second voice laughed. "Then you are a fool. Have you looked into those eyes? A wolf has softer eyes when it rips out your throat." A hand patted Malachy's hip. "I would care for him as I would a precious, young bride, more even. Perhaps, when Ellyllon is finished, he will give him to you?"

"Enough!" a third voice snapped. "I say the dark one is more demon than druid. Rinnach, would you have him hear you? Or see your foot on his back?"

Immediately, the foot was withdrawn, but not before its owner gave him a small but meaningful kick in the side.

*

Malachy drifted. He thought of Jasmine and wondered vaguely what was happening to her and Seamus. Or if they knew where he was. One side of his head was sticky with blood. He could feel it in his hair, matting the strands together. Someone was talking, but he wasn't really listening, and then the oars stopped and the boat slowed. It hit the bottom of the lake with a thud and he heard the splash as the men got out. Opening his eyes, he lifted his head. Trees overhung the lake on three sides. A wide inlet disappeared off to the right. Ahead lay a narrow beach of fine, white sand. Figures moved in and out of the trees; he saw a horse pulling some sort of cart and then the boat lurched as the men began to heave it up onto the beach and the pain in his head intensified. He closed his eyes, and his head dropped.

*

"Malachy, Malachy."

Summoned, he opened his eyes only reluctantly. Ellyllon's face was pressed close, his black eyes huge as they stared into his. Malachy jumped, tried to move back, but with his body sat up against a tree there was nowhere to go. Ellyllon smiled. "Welcome," he whispered softly and the light in his eyes gleamed.

Up this close, Malachy could see the age in his face, despite the smooth, white skin. The centuries old lines and creases had gone underground, but could still be seen just below the surface, mottling and rippling, like opposing sea currents meeting. It was unnerving, as if the surface of his face wasn't quite his own. Ellyllon's black eyes watched him look and if he saw his revulsion, he didn't say anything. Then, abruptly, he straightened. Behind him was a small patch of lake. They seemed to be in a far corner of the lake, but at this angle it was impossible to know for sure. Malachy's heart sank. Lough Corrib, or Lough Orbsen as they called it, was a big lake; he had no way of knowing where he was, or how far from the Sacred Isle.

"Where is Cathbad?" Ellyllon asked the warrior nearest him.

The warrior started, his green eyes rolling sideways, towards the lake. "He brings the other."

Instantly, Malachy recognised the third voice, the voice that had told Rinnach to stop. He was obviously the group's leader.

"The other?"

"The druid."

Ellyllon's eyes narrowed. "The druid? What druid?"

Looking like he wanted to be somewhere, anywhere, else, the warrior shook his head.

"Very well. Tell Cathbad to bring Malachy, and this druid, to Cruachan. Ride fast; do not spare the horses, for I would see you on the full moon." He looked at the warriors stood watching and slowly, deliberately let his gaze pass from one face to the other. "Do not harm them. Not one cut, scratch or bruise." He paused at a man with thick black hair and a deeply scarred face. "Or kick."

Silence. The man's eyes slid to the ground as the other warriors held their breath and waited.

Ellyllon smiled. "One touch and I will lift up my hand," he purred, showing them. "Stretch out my fingers and very, very, slowly reach inside you and pull out your guts." He jerked his wrist and, closing his fingers, let his hand drop. "There will be no honour in your death, no glory. You will not die in battle, or by the blade, but in deep, deep pain. Speak to Malachy; he knows the pain. Afterwards, I will throw your carcass to the dogs and you will have no burial, no place in the afterlife. The Gods will not welcome you and your family, your kin, will wear the stain." His voice softened to a whisper that made the hairs on the back of Malachy's neck lift. "Never, ever disobey me."

No one spoke. Rinnach stared at the ground as if his life depended on it and then finally, the leader cleared his throat. "I, Anle, give my oath they will not be harmed."

"Good." Ellyllon's head swivelled towards him, his black eyes unblinking, and then he was gone.

All the warriors bar Rinnach and Anle relaxed.

"Rinnach!" Anle marched over to him and, grabbing the neck of his tunic, twisted it savagely, "Be at peace, for your brother died a warrior's death and I have given my oath. Now, I swear, harm him." He jerked his head towards Malachy. "And after I watch the demon gut you, I will take my blade to your wife and your children and slit their throats." Letting him go, he glared at the others. "Be ready. Cathbad comes."

Watching the men as they worked swiftly around him, Malachy pulled his knees up. No one seemed to notice him. Cruachan, Anle had said. That had to be Rathcroghan, the royal seat of Queen Medb, near Tulsk. Just down the road from home, Malachy thought bleakly, only two millennia earlier. Stifling a sigh, he glanced all around him. Sat on the edge of the forest, the undergrowth was only footsteps away; if only he could reach it, he might have some chance of escape. But these men were warriors, trackers; to them, crashing through the undergrowth, he'd probably sound like an elephant. And yet he couldn't just sit here; he had to try.

Very slowly, he pressed his hands to the ground, preparing. Another quick glance; no one was looking. The sound of oars came from the lake and, instinctively, everyone turned towards it. A second boat appeared. Stood at the prow, Cathbad's long golden hair was instantly recognisable. This was his chance. Malachy lifted his bottom, preparing to push himself up and away. His eyes fell on the leader, Anle, stood with another warrior. Unlike the others, he'd stayed where he was, facing Malachy. He was watching him, his face impassive as his fingers played almost absentmindedly on the hilt of his sword. Sighing to himself, Malachy sat back.

Cathbad and the boat moved closer. With him, thought Malachy, must be the druid Ellyllon and the warrior talked about. It couldn't be Jasmine or Seamus; there was no way Ellyllon would have left if they'd been the ones caught. But where were they? And why weren't they here, trying to rescue him? His stomach dropped. Unless something had happened to them.

"You."

Anle came towards him. In one quick, fluid movement, he crouched down in front of him and grabbed his hair, pulling his head to one side. Squinting, he examined the wound before touching it lightly with one finger. Malachy's breath hissed.

"It will heal." Anle declared, letting his head go. "Hands, up."

Confused, Malachy stared at him.

"Up, up," he repeated impatiently, grabbing Malachy's wrists and lifting and pulling them together.

Immediately letting them go, he reached into his belt for a long, roughly cut leather cord. Knowing he was helpless but determined not to show it, Malachy deliberately let his hands drop.

"Amadan!" Anle spat, looking as if he'd like to hit him. But he controlled himself with an effort and lifted Malachy's wrists, holding them tightly in one hand while he bound them expertly with the other.

"There will be no honour in Ellyllon's war. All he wants is power and revenge," Malachy said, watching Anle face. "All those deaths for nothing."

Anle tightened the last knot and let his hands drop. "My king wills it, and if the Gods will it, my death will be a warrior's death, by the sword or the spear in the heat of battle."

Cathbad's boat was only metres from the shore. Already he was preparing to jump out onto the sand.

"But don't you want to live, to see your children grow?"

"I will see them again, in the afterlife." He gave him a speculative look. "Will you speak all the way to Cruachan?"

Malachy stared at him. "I might."

"Then I will gag you with a cloth wiped on the loose arse of a pig."

"Maybe not," Malachy countered quickly.

To his surprise, Anle grinned, giving him full view of his chipped and broken teeth. "A wise choice."

The boat hit the beach and Cathbad jumped onto the sand. Using the cord around his wrists, Anle pulled Malachy roughly to his feet.

"Be swift," Cathbad shouted as he strode up the beach, his golden hair swaying. "We leave for Cruachan."

Behind him, two warriors half-carried and half-dragged an unconscious man between them.

"Ellyllon is gone," Anle told Cathbad. "He would have us reach Cruachan by the full moon."

"Yes," Cathbad agreed, examining Malachy curiously. He had the strangest eyes. Mottled like stone, giving them an unfocussed look, as if he wasn't really seeing. "Drendas and his druids will not soon follow."

"What did you do to them?" Malachy demanded.

Cathbad laughed. "By the Gods, the lamb has teeth! Do not fear, she is well. It is as Ellyllon foretold. Greater, even," he finished cryptically, already moving away. "Bring him," he told Anle over one shoulder. "And the other."

Anle tugged at Malachy's wrists. "Be thankful the dark one wishes you unharmed. Another day Cathbad would have cut out your tongue. But speak once more and I will gag you." He tugged again and, getting the message, Malachy nodded.

The warriors carrying the druid reached them. Even before he saw his face, Malachy knew who it was. It was Daire.

"Move," ordered Anle, turning him and pushing him forward.

*

Skirting the edge of the forest, they followed the inlet inland. Narrowing gradually, it took Malachy a few minutes to realise the inlet was actually a river, flowing slowly, lazily down towards the lake. With Anle behind him, pushing him when he slowed, Malachy stumbled along the grassy bank. His head throbbed. Behind them, one of the bigger warriors carried the still unconscious Daire over one shoulder.

The river curled first one way and then the other. Beneath the surface, watergrass glistened, it's long, soft tendrils, like hair, swaying gently with the movement of the water. A dragonfly shot past, its electric blue body bobbing as it soared higher and higher. Following the man in front of him, Malachy ducked under a branch and turned into the forest. Skirting a patch of nettles, they passed a fallen tree.

"Move," Anle ordered, pushing him again.

A horse neighed, the sound coming from somewhere ahead. They scrambled through the undergrowth as, up ahead, men greeted one another. Another push and he staggered through a patch of fern and into a clearing.

Strangely casual, like fans waiting for a match to start, fifteen, maybe twenty warriors were stood chatting. Cathbad was nowhere to be seen. Behind them a chariot, pulled by two horses, stood next to five saddled horses. Made of strong, thick wood, with two high wheels, it was different to the Roman chariots he'd seen in films. Rougher, more basic, there was no front to it, just sides made from two semicircles of woven reed topped by a single semicircular stick.

"Move," Anle growled, jerking his head towards it; then, just in case, he gave Malachy another push.

They moved to the chariot. Sat at the front, with his legs dangling, the driver watched curiously as the warrior carrying Daire placed him in the back. With an effort he pushed his body tight into the right side and tied first his wrists to the semicircular stick, then his ankles. Now it was Malachy's turn. Helping him on, Anle told him to sit, then, using another leather cord, tied his wrists to the stick on the opposite side.

"Anle." Cathbad was back with a second druid in tow. "You will ride with us, and three others." He glanced at the druid. "Ilech, bring my horse and tell Cass and the other to watch and wait."

He waited for Anle and the second druid to go, then, stepping in close, gazed at Malachy with his strange eyes. "Do you know the prophecy Drendas speaks of?"

Malachy nodded.

"The Goddess brought forth by the Child of Erin and Brigantes." He paused dramatically. "I have seen the end."

Good for you, Malachy thought inanely. Tired, hungry, and scared for himself and Daire and what their capture meant for Jasmine, he realised suddenly that he was in danger of losing it. He had to pull himself together.

Cathbad's eyes rolled to the druid bringing the horses and back. "He will not long need you," he whispered. "Once I speak of what I saw. When my ancestors, the Tuatha de Danann left for the Otherworld, they took the ancient knowledge with them. Ellyllon cares nothing for their knowledge; he speaks only of the druid of Brigantes, of what he will do to them and the many moons it will take, but I will have my birthright." He smiled, the mottle in his eyes gleaming like stone. "You have travelled the great and mighty oak, and will do so again, for I will travel with you. And so, as foretold, the time of the Tuatha de Danann will come again and their power will live through me."

"Cathbad." Anle was back, with three warriors. "We are ready."

One, Malachy realised, with a sinking heart, was Rinnach, the brother of the man he'd killed.

Cathbad's stone eyes slid away and he took a step back. "Anle, you ride with us; they will ride behind."

They mounted. Cathbad, Anle and the druid guided their horses to the front of the chariot, while the three warriors went behind. The driver flicked the reins and shouted, and following the riders, the chariot moved off, its wheels bouncing and jerking over the soft forest floor.

*

Stood on the Sacred Isle, gazing at their bowed heads, Jasmine smiled.

Oh, how I have missed this.

"Drendas, her eyes — what have you done to her?" Seamus looked wildly from her to the other druids. "And why are you bowing?"

Seamus, she thought archly, *has finally found his voice.*

As have we, her sister countered. She was right, of course, but then, as the oldest of the three, she always had to be.

Drendas lifted his head. His eyes glowed. "Do you not see?"

"No," Seamus snapped, furious all over again. "I don't. But I know you've been lying to both her and me. This isn't just Iomlan. It's something to do with your prophecy and your precious goddess. I don't know how, but you're trying to use her to bring your Goddess back. And if it hadn't been for Malachy, I'd never–" He stopped, his eyes widening. "Malachy! Ferdia!"

Jasmine's head spun. Everything lurched, as if the world had turned sharply on its axis. A stab of pain shot across her temple. She pressed her hand to it, but the pain increased. Sharp, like a deep slice of a knife, it spread outwards until her whole head throbbed. Her knees buckled and she slipped to the ground. Seamus followed her, dropping to his knees. She could hear him talking and the murmur of the others druids behind, but the pain was too strong; she couldn't seem to focus.

"Drendas, what have you done to her?!"

The voices crowded inside her head. Speaking as one, they called to her, but clinging to the thought of Malachy, she resisted.

"Drendas?!"

Abruptly, the pain stopped. She lowered her hands. "Seamus?"

"Jasmine, what happened, are you alright?"

"I don't know." Confused, she looked around her. "Malachy?"

Together, they clambered to their feet.

"I should've guessed; Cathbad's attack was just a diversion," Seamus said urgently. "He was after Malachy all along."

"We have to go." Already she was moving across the glade.

"Jasmine, wait!" He called after her, but too late; she plunged headlong into the forest.

Her heart pounding, she ran as fast as she could. The island wasn't big; already she could see the blue of the lake through the trees. *Oh God, please be there*. She swerved around a fallen log and then she was out onto the grassy bank and into the sunshine. There was no one there. Slowing, she looked around frantically. He wasn't there. Bodies of warriors — three, no, four — lay close to the beach. Another lay off to her left, near the edge of the forest, but of Malachy, Ferdia and Daire there was no sign. Someone moaned, the sound coming from the beach. Seamus burst out of the trees as she moved towards it.

"Jasmine, we're too late."

From the beach came a second moan. She saw a hand, an outstretched arm and recognised the tunic.

"Ferdia." She was at his side in an instant.

His eyes fluttered. There was no blood on his clothes, no sign of injury.

"Ferdia." She touched his head gently and focussed.

He opened his eyes. "Daire?"

He struggled upwards as Seamus joined them.

"Ferdia, what happened?" Seamus demanded.

"Warriors. We fought, I told Malachy to run, but more came. They took him in a boat." He glanced at Jasmine. "I could not stop them. Daire aided me, but Cathbad attacked us."

He looked around. "Where is he? Where is Daire?"

"He's not here."

Ferdia scrambled to his feet. "Daire, Daire!"

"I think Cathbad took him."

Ferdia rounded on her. "Why?"

Drendas appeared, followed by the rest of the druids.

"Father," Ferdia called. In his agitation he pushed past Jasmine, knocking her sideways, and dashed over to him. "Father."

Jasmine straightened. They didn't have time for this. Already Malachy could be miles away. She had to find him before his captors reached Cruachan. Fixing him in her mind, she focussed, but nothing happened. She tried again; nothing.

"For fuck's sake!" she swore, gesturing angrily.

"What is it?" Seamus asked quickly.

"It won't work. Why won't it work?" Already she was trying again. Still nothing. Afraid, she turned on Seamus. "It's you, isn't it? You're stopping me!"

He grabbed her hand, squeezed it tight between his fingers. "Stop, Jas, just stop. I'm not doing anything." She glanced at Drendas and he caught her look. "He's not doing anything either. Trust me, if he was, I'd know. No, it's not working because yer panicking. You need to calm down."

"But–!"

"This won't help Malachy. Yer need to calm down. Breathe slowly. That's it. Slow." He watched her for a moment. "Better?"

It was helping. "Better." She nodded.

"Whatever we do, we'll do it together. The last thing we need is for you to go running off on your own and getting yerself captured along with Malachy. Don't worry; whatever happens, we'll be going after him. They're taking him to Ellyllon, aren't they, and he's at Cruachan. Just remember Ellyllon has no reason to hurt him; he needs him alive. He's only taken him to get to you."

Jasmine lowered her head. It was impossible to argue with him; she knew he was right, but she couldn't bear it. The voices were back, whispering quietly on the edges of her consciousness. She couldn't hear what they were saying, the words too indistinct. But in the meantime, anything could be happening to Malachy. Ellyllon might want him alive, but it didn't mean he wouldn't hurt him. Breathing deeply, she tried again.

Ferdia had reached Drendas. "Cathbad took Daire."

"Yes," Drendas agreed calmly. "They travel to Cruachan."

"Cruachan is well-defended. We must rescue them before they reach it."

"We will follow them to Cruachan, as the prophecy foretold."

"What do I care for the prophecy? I am not druid!" Ferdia spat. "Ride fast and we will catch them." He turned towards the water, looked as if he would plunge headfirst into it.

"You will not go far without a boat," Ronan interjected mildly.

"Ferdia." Drendas touched his arm. "Is Daire not my son, as well as your husband? We must trust to the Goddess, to her light and her wisdom."

"Ferdia, be at peace, for our fight is the same," Ronan joined, with an uneasy glance at Jasmine. "Cathbad travels to Cruachan, and so, by the Goddess, must we. But we must ride carefully, for Cathbad knows we follow him. He has no honour. Even before the dark one, he had little care for our ways and our lore and would rather kill us on the road than meet with honour in open battle. Worse, we are few and he has warriors and druids enough for all Erin."

"Ferdia," Drendas pleaded, "Ronan is wise, and does not the Goddess see all?" Listening, Ferdia's shoulders drooped. The fight seemed to go out of him and he gave one slow nod.

Ronan looked at Maine. "Where are your boatmen?"

"On the island – there." He pointed. "I will use my horn to call them."

*

Jasmine breathed out. Nothing worked. She kept digging down, trying to find Iomlan, but it wasn't there. There was just this hole, a dark, empty space, where Iomlan should be. And as for Seamus and the others, they made her want to scream. All this talk, this debating, was just wasting time. And why were they waiting for Maine to call his boat? They were druid; surely they could just walk across the bloody water. She rubbed at her forehead. In the gap Iomlan had left, the voices were getting stronger, more insistent. She could hear what they were saying; just one word, over and over, like some crazed litany. *Cruachan, Cruachan, Cruachan.* Instinctively she knew they wouldn't leave her alone, wouldn't stop until they'd worn her down with their incessant chant.

"No, wait." Ronan put one hand on Maine's arm. "It comes, see."

They turned to see a boat crossing the water, coming from the direction of the north shore.

"No." Maine shook his head. "That is not my men."

The boat contained two figures. The first was sat in the middle, the hood of its cloak pulled down low, obscuring its face. The second was stood in the prow of the boat, wearing a long blue cloak. Black hair, streaked with grey, hung loose almost to her knees and her face was lifted proudly to the sun. The druids looked at one another; no one seemed to recognise her and then, in a low voice, Seamus said her name.

"Cethern."

Chapter Eighteen

Sandwiched between the riders, the chariot rattled and bumped as it sped across the uneven ground. Gripping the side, Malachy wished they'd slow, even for a few minutes. The hard, wooden floor made a saddle seem like a soft, fluffy duvet.

They'd left the high hills behind ages ago and returned to the flat land in the centre of Connacht. He couldn't be sure where he was; the forest looked so different from the bare rolling hills he was used to, but they were definitely going east. Not for the first time, Malachy twisted his wrists against the leather cord, hoping it might snap, but it was too strong. With all the bouncing, there was no chance of untying the knots, even if he could let go long enough to try. He looked at Daire. Still unconscious, he wished he would wake. With his power, they might have some chance of escaping. His body rolled with the movement of the chariot, only the cords binding his hands and feet stopped it from rolling off. Why didn't he wake? Malachy wondered. He didn't look injured. The wheels hit a tree root and the chariot lifted, coming back down to earth with a huge bump that shook every bone in Malachy's body. Daire's body rolled again, the cords straining. Cathbad must've given him something, some sort of potion, like the one Ellyllon had given Jasmine. He was going to a lot of trouble for someone Ellyllon hadn't wanted. Malachy frowned. It was obvious Ellyllon wanted him to get to Jasmine, but why did Cathbad want Daire? Was it something to do with what Cathbad had said he'd seen? His big surprise for Ellyllon? The riders and the chariot slowed. Turning, Malachy craned his neck to see. Up ahead, the path split, the left fork going what looked like upland, while the right continued on straight east. The riders and driver looked at Cathbad and each other. Almost there and lifting up his hand, Cathbad pointed. Veering wildly, the chariot swung, pulling Malachy with it as it shot into the left-hand fork.

*

Stood on the Sacred Isle, the druids watched as the boat moved closer.

To their left, Maine's men had left their island and were rowing towards them.

"Cethern?!" Drendas growled. "My old friend and brother is dead. What right has this woman to take his name? She is not welcome here."

"My brother, I would welcome anyone who comes to our aid," Ronan retorted, looking at the other druids for support. "And, look, see her power; she is druid."

A few nodded, Maine included.

"Ronan, a woman cannot be druid," Drendas scoffed angrily. "And yet, even as you speak, I remember you did not raise your voice with ours when the time came."

"I did not speak for I did not wish to stand against my brothers. I was young, barely a man, but it is to my shame I did not, for how can man take away what the Gods have given? Women are druid because the Gods make them so." Ronan sighed. "The time for difference is past. Men, women; all druid must unite if we are to defeat such a powerful enemy."

Drendas glared at him. "We have power enough; we have no need for one such as her."

"How do you know her?" Ronan asked Seamus.

"Malachy described her to me. She saved him and Daire."

"No she did not! My son would have spoken of it."

"He spoke of it to me," Ferdia countered quickly.

"Liar!" Drendas spat, his face livid. "My son is a powerful druid. What need has he for the false power of a woman?!"

He turned away. Shocked, no one spoke. Behind Drendas' back, Ferdia looked at him with something approaching contempt. The boat was only metres away.

"Druids, I am called Cethern," she called. "I would land."

"Come, Cethern," Maine replied with a glance at Drendas' back. "You are welcome."

Cethern waved her hand and the boat slowed. It hit the sand with a bump, threatened to tip her headfirst into the lake, but she jumped out with a natural agility. Another wave of her hand and using Iomlan, she danced lightly across the top of the water.

"Druids," she greeted them, grinning broadly as she touched sand.

She was enjoying herself, Jasmine realised, enjoying the effect she was having on them. Even at a time like this, she had to admire her for such an entrance. Cethern glanced at Seamus then gave Jasmine an appraising look, as if she were different to what she'd been expecting but she was willing to give her a go. The other figure remained where it was.

"Our thanks, Cethern," Ronan said, darting forward, the two of them clasping hands. "I am Ronan. Will you take us to the north shore? For we must ride for Cruachan."

"We came to ride with you, if you will it." She glanced at Drendas, who was looking fixedly at a far point of the lake.

Ronan examined the bent head. "Who do you ride with? Will he not show his face?"

"He will if you ask it," Cethern replied, her tone ironic.

Giving her a suspicious look, Ronan lifted his voice, out across the water. "Come, show us your face."

No answer.

Cocking his head, Ferdia took a step forward. "Do I know you?"

Still the figure hesitated. And then, slowly, carefully, it stood up. Long, delicate fingers grabbed the edges of the hood and pulled and it fell back, revealing loose, black hair.

"Emer?!" Ferdia shouted.

With a cry, Drendas whirled. Calling her name, Ferdia dashed towards her. Water splashed, soaking him, but he didn't slow. Reaching into the boat, he scooped her into his thick, strong arms and carried her out.

"What evil is this?!" Drendas demanded angrily, turning to Cethern. "What right have you to speak to my daughter and bring her here!"

His hand twisting around his staff, he looked as if he might throw himself at her. Then with a small cry, he fell back. His face paled. "Ele?"

Cethern drew herself up. "When Daire left, I knelt before the ancestors, that they might show me the way. They spoke to me through my heart, told me I should fight. But first, I should seek out Emer."

"To what end?" Ronan asked, frowning as he looked between her and Drendas.

Cethern raised her chin. "That she might know her true birth."

"You were dead, gone! Buried in your shame! I am her father!" Drendas shouted, one finger jabbing furiously at his chest. "Me, me."

"No, father, you are not. Emer is *my* daughter."

There was a stunned silence. Letting Emer down, Ferdia stared at her, as if seeing her for the first time.

"Ele?" Ronan asked. Stunned, he peered into Cethern's face as if searching for a feature he could recognise.

"Ele is dead," Drendas snapped. "Killed by her own hand."

Cethern's eyes flashed, but her voice remained calm. "No, father, not dead, but banished, my daughter stolen from me."

"Banished by the word of Noisiu, you were dead to your mother and father." Drendas drew himself up, his anger easily matching hers. "You lay with Ardan, husband to Fedelm, daughter of Noisiu. In your shame, your dishonour, you left your child and fled with him to the lands of Munster."

"Not shame, father, love. Noisiu's warriors followed us. Ardan was killed, struck by an arrow in the back as we tried to flee. He died in my arms."

"Why, then, did they spare you?"

"They did not spare me, I spared them, for I vowed I would not lift my hand to Ardan's people. But I was foolish to trust them. They attacked me and left me to die."

"Noisiu sent word you were dead and I thanked for the Goddess for her mercy, for your daughter would be spared your shame, the shame that killed your mother and sent us from our home. For how could I stay as druid to Noisiu?"

"Have I not paid for my love? Exiled, the man I loved killed and my daughter lost to me? Daire, my own brother, ate with me and he did not know me."

"Did we not suffer, even though the fault was not ours? As a child you were wilful, disobedient, lacked honour, the rightful respect to your father. Women cannot be druid. You hold neither the wisdom or the strength to wield such power. A druid must stand apart and even noble women, a queen, cannot rule without the guiding hand of men."

"And yet you bow to your Goddess," Cethern sneered. "Brid."

"I bow to her for she is God, even as she bows her head and her will to the father, Dagda."

"And Emer?"

"I have given her a father's love, a father's protection. She is free of the stain of your shame, free from the vice of her own nature."

"And what of your nature, Drendas?" Seamus asked suddenly, and they all turned to look at him. "It is true that you have suffered, but in your bitterness and your resentment, you have allowed your suffering to blind you. Women cannot be druid? They do not have the nature? Who kidnapped Daire and Malachy? Who follows the evil that is Ellyllon? None of them are women." He looked as if he was going to say something more, but thought better of it.

*

Behind them, Maine's boat came towards them, the splash of the oars loud against the sudden silence.

"The day lengthens," Ronan said with a shake of his head. "I say again, the time for difference has passed. We must ride." He looked at Cethern, "Ele?"

"Cethern. My father is right; Ele is dead. She died with Ardan."

"Then, Cethern, we have need of you. Your brother has need for you. Will you ride with us?"

Cethern studied the side of Drendas' face, for once again he refused to look at her. "I will."

"Drendas, my friend, my brother, our numbers are few and, without you, would be fewer. Your son has need of you. Will you accept this?"

Drendas' eyes slid away. "I will," he agreed reluctantly.

Emer stepped away from Ferdia. "I would come."

"No!" Drendas cried, his eyes horrified. "I forbid it."

She held his gaze. "Father – grandfather, it is my wish."

Darting to her, he took her hand. "Emer, you are young; you cannot know the battle that lies ahead."

"But Daire needs me."

"No." Shaking his head, he rubbed and patted her hand. Watching, Jasmine was shocked to see how distressed he was. "How can you aid us? You are not druid. I have lost one daughter and five sons. Even if the Goddess herself willed it, I will not lose another."

"But I am not your daughter." Gently withdrawing her hand, she looked at Ronan. "If you do not allow it, I will follow you."

Maine's boat was landing. Maine and two other druids went to help.

Ronan rolled his eyes impatiently. "Emer, daughter of Cethern and Ardan, if you will not obey your grandfather, will you obey me?"

She nodded.

"Then, come, ride with us. But when the call comes to battle at Cruachan, you must wait and watch, as is the way of women, for you are neither warrior or druid."

She nodded.

"Your oath on it."

"I vow as a woman who is neither warrior or druid, I will wait and watch."

Ronan relaxed. "It is agreed. Come, we must leave."

*

As dusk approached, exhausted, Malachy's head bobbed. They'd only stopped once, by a river, to let the horses drink. The men had passed beer between them but no one had bothered with him. Ellyllon might have said unharmed, but he hadn't mentioned food or water, although, of course, they couldn't actually let him starve. Gone beyond hunger, his stomach had stopped growling hours ago, as if realising there was little point. Cathbad said something to Anle, who turned and called to the riders at the back to join him. The chariot stopped and, blinking, Malachy rubbed his eyes awkwardly on the side of his arm.

Anle was giving orders. Surreptitiously, so as not to alert the driver, Malachy's fingers worked at the knots tying the cord to the chariot. The knot was tight, intricate; it was hard to find something to grip. A quick look at the driver and Malachy shifted, trying for a different angle. Horses galloped away. Malachy looked up and saw two riders disappearing through the trees. The chariot moved off and his fingers slipped from the cord. He hadn't even loosened it. Rinnach and the second druid watched the chariot pass then slipped in behind it, leaving Cathbad and Anle at front.

*

Night was drawing in, the path ahead of them darkening. Soon it would be too dark to see. Malachy sniffed. He could smell smoke and something else. His stomach growled, responding a split second after his nose; it smelt meat, delicious, aromatic meat, roasting. They turned a corner, the path widening into a glade. Sat in front of a fire, the two warriors cooked two skinned rabbits over a rough, wooden spit. The group stopped and as the riders and driver dismounted, Malachy's stomach growled again. Ignoring it, he twisted his wrists and pulled, but the cord was still too strong. Pulling a small clay pot from a sack tied to his saddle, Cathbad approached the chariot, Ilech following. Moving to the front of the chariot, Ilech took Daire's head, tilted it up and back and while Cathbad took the lid of the pot, then forced his mouth open. Together they poured the potion down Daire's throat, Ilech pinching his nose to ensure that even in his sleep, he swallowed it. He choked once, twice, but didn't wake.

"He will not wake until Cruachan," Cathbad said, his voice thick with satisfaction.

He glanced at Malachy, as if considering whether to give the potion to him, and then, with a shrug, replaced the lid. Returning the pot to the bag tied to his saddle, he and Ilech joined the warriors next to the fire. Knowing now that any chance of escape was down to him, Malachy turned his attention back to the cords.

The group ate in a circle around the fire, tearing the rabbit with

149

their bare hands then washing it down with mouthfuls of beer. Malachy had given up trying to get loose and was resting his head on his hands. "Cathbad, what of him?" Anle asked suddenly, jerking his head towards him.

He shrugged. "I care not; do as you wish."

There was a pause and then, tearing off a rabbit leg, Anle got to his feet and took it over to him.

"Eat," he said, thrusting it towards Malachy's hands.

His own face, flushed from the heat of the fire and the warmth of the beer, had the look of someone who'd drunk just enough to feel at one with the world.

"Thank you." Malachy took it.

Anle watched in silence as he bent his head to his hands and tore at it like a bird of prey. Grease dribbled down his chin, but he didn't slow. He was so hungry.

"Is it true? What the dark one said?"

Lowering his head, Malachy wiped his mouth awkwardly on the arm of his tunic. "What?"

With a quick, surreptitious look at the other men, Anle leant over him. "He put his hand in you?"

"Yes." With a slight thrill of shock, he realised he almost forgotten what Ellyllon had done to him. Less than a week ago, it seemed like far longer.

Anle was waiting, wanting to know more, but Malachy wasn't about to satisfy his curiosity. He continued to eat. Straightening, Anle paused, looked for a moment as if he was going to say something more, then changing his mind, went back to join the others.

Finishing the leg, Malachy let the bone fall over the side of the chariot and into the undergrowth. He wasn't anywhere near full, but his belly felt better with something inside it and his mind was clearer. He smacked his lips, feeling his tongue stick. Now all he needed was a cool, crisp drink of water. Over by the fire, with the rabbits eaten, the men were concentrating on the beer. If ever there was a time… revitalised, Malachy turned back to the cords. Slick with rabbit grease, his fingers slipped, refusing to grip, so he licked them and tried again. That was better. He pulled at a knot. He didn't have to untie the whole thing, just loosen it enough to slip his hands out. He moved to another, his fingers probing, trying to find the weakest point. Behind him, things were beginning to get rowdy; Rinnach had the beer, but he wasn't passing it on quickly enough. Protesting loudly, the warrior next to him made a grab for it, but Rinnach pushed him away. A third glance back; for a moment, Malachy thought there was going to be fight, but Anle was there, pulling them apart. A thread in a knot loosened ever so slightly. Trying to contain his excitement, Malachy pinched it between two fingers and, frowning with concentration, began, slowly, painfully, to ease it out.

Chapter Nineteen

Heading east, the druids rode steadily, following the path as it weaved through the forest. Light dappled the ground and kissed the bright green leaves. Travelling adjacent to the lake, the shore was never far away; sometimes Jasmine caught glimpses of it, traces of dark blue through the gaps in the trees. The lake was massive, bigger even than it had looked from the mountainside. With a cry of alarm, a pheasant shot out of the undergrowth, crashing through the leaves as it flew up and away. Led by Ronan, who seemed to have become their leader through natural authority more than anything else, Jasmine rode between Seamus and Drendas. Behind them came Cethern and Emer, then the rest of the druids. The path was too narrow, too overhung with branches for the group to do anything but concentrate on the way ahead. Ferdia and Maine had ridden on ahead to check for ambushes. Around them, the forest was quiet, the only sound the thunder of horse hooves. Behind them, the mountains receded as the rough, granite peaks softened into the velvet green of rolling, high hills.

Two riders appeared around a bend, riding swiftly. It was Ferdia and Maine. Immediately, Ronan called to the group to a stop.

"Cathbad's men lay to the west," Ferdia said as he and Maine joined them. "At the Waters of the Salmon. The druids, Redg and Cass, stand with them."

Ronan frowned. "Can we pass?"

"Only if we fight." Ferdia shared a look with Maine. "The river is wide and deep and flows fast. It is not easily crossed. But not far to the north lies Ath Killimor. We can cross there, but there is no path through the forest and the way is slow."

"And Cathbad?" Cethern asked, nudging her horse forward.

With Emer just behind her, the similarity between them was striking. The same features that were interesting in Cethern were beautiful in her daughter. Ferdia shook his head.

"We won't catch him either way," Seamus offered grimly. "Going west or north."

"His wish is not to stop us, only to slow," Drendas said suddenly, the first he'd spoken for some time. Since Emer's arrival, he'd withdrawn deep into himself. "Believing himself to be a son of the Gods, he will obey the prophecy."

"If I were Cathbad, I would have warriors wait at both," Ronan mused, ignoring him.

"Yes," Ferdia agreed. "If he knows of it. It is not a way known to many."

Ronan looked at Jasmine, as if asking her which way they should go.

"North," she heard herself say.

Even though it hurt her to admit it, Seamus was right. With the obstacles in their way, north or west, it didn't really matter. They couldn't catch them now, not unless they flew.

Seamus' head swivelled. His hazel eyes examined her for a moment and then, without a word, he turned back. For the first time she could remember, she didn't care what he thought of her, or the decision she'd made, or why Ronan had asked her to make it. All that mattered was they kept moving. Her earlier impatience and frustration had melted away, along with the voices, the flashes of memory and self-doubt, leaving behind one single burning purpose; to get to Cruachan and rescue Malachy.

"North," Ronan agreed, nodding.

*

It wasn't far, maybe a mile or so, but, pushing through the forest in single file, the going was slow. Still not daring to use Iomlan other than to shield themselves, the forest was so dense they had to dismount and lead the horses. Once again, Ferdia and Maine had moved ahead, searching for signs of Cathbad's men. Out of nowhere, Drendas gave a cry and the group stopped and turned. Fallen; he was on his knees, his staff lost somewhere in the undergrowth. In an instant, Emer was there, helping him to his feet then going back for his staff. She found it and, without a word, handed it to him.

"Emer," he whispered softly, taking her hand and kissing it.

"Emer?!" Cethern frowned, anger and worry mingling.

Emer looked at her mother, but her face was unreadable.

"Drendas," Ronan interrupted gently.

Drendas nodded and let go of Emer's hand. He watched her return to her horse, then retrieved his reins.

*

They continued. The sun was beginning to lower, sending long shadows behind them. In front of Jasmine, Seamus' horse nervously flicked his tail. No one spoke. The land beneath their feet was changing, moving from soft, forest soil to hard rock and stone. Abruptly the trees began to thin, revealing patches of open land and in the distance the edge of a line of trees. Water gurgled faintly. They were almost there. Ronan lifted his hand and one by one they stopped.

"What is it?" Jasmine hissed to Seamus.

"Ferdia and Maine; why aren't they back?"

They heard voices. Crouching low, Ronan crept forward. Her heart in her mouth, Jasmine watched as he carefully lowered a branch.

"Ronan!" a voice whispered.

Everyone jumped. Maine stepped out from behind a tree. Her hand on her heart, Jasmine saw even the battle-hardened druids grinning stupidly.

"Forgive me," Maine grinned.

Ronan let the branch drop and straightened. "Ferdia?"

"He waits at Ath Killimor. Cathbad's warriors watch in the forest across the river, but I sense no druid."

Ronan returned to his horse. "Show us," he ordered, taking the reins.

*

Ferdia was waiting for them on the edge of the trees. Crouching next to Seamus, Jasmine looked out across the river. Stone swept down from a nearby hill, scarring the land in one giant swathe. Grey, smooth, the surface was lined with fissures and pockmarked with holes, where rain had worn into the soft, porous rock. A river, flowing furiously, cut through the rock. Sitting wide and low, a rough line of white boulders, with gaps just small enough to step across, formed a dam or natural bridge across it. Water gushed, swirling and foaming as it rushed between them, sending drops of spray into the air. No sound came from the trees on the other side, no sign of movement.

The druids were debating the best way to cross, but Jasmine had stopped listening. Iomlan was back, swirling inside her, eager for use. She felt a thrill of excitement.

What are warriors to me?

Watching them talk, she took a step back, towards the river. No one seemed to notice. She took another, then another.

"Jasmine?" Cethern was watching her across the men, one eyebrow raised quizzically.

What are you doing? She screamed at herself, but too late. Whirling, she ducked under the branches and out onto the stone.

"Jasmine!" Seamus cried and she heard rather than saw the other druids leap forward to grab him.

Focussing Iomlan, she began to walk steadily across the stone towards the dam. Still no sign of them; she knew they were there, their eyes fixed on her.

Reaching the dam, she stepped sideways onto the first stone. On the other side, nothing moved. Three small steps across the stone and widening her stride, she stepped over the gushing water and onto the second stone. Still nothing. She glanced down. Water surged, the fury of it making her head float and quickly she looked up. An arrow shot out of the trees, whistling loudly through the air. Calmly watching, she let it come. A few feet from her, it bounced backwards, as if it had hit an invisible wall and fell uselessly into the water. Another came, then another, each bouncing harmlessly away as Jasmine continued across the dam. She reached the last stone and a man stepped out of the trees, his sling swinging. She sent out Iomlan just as he let the pebble fly. It caught him under the chin, the force of it snapping his head back with a loud crack and propelling his twisting body into the trees. The pebble hit the water and sank as more arrows came towards her. Another pulse and they fell away, dropping like rain into the river. Moving inside them, she clambered onto the stone bank and drawing herself up, faced the forest.

"Come," she shouted, seeing the figures moving amongst the green. "Or do brave, fierce warriors fear to face a girl?!"

There was a pause. She sensed more than heard the druids step out of the trees behind her and then slowly, hesitantly, the warriors emerged with their weapons raised. Only twenty in total; Cathbad had knowingly, carelessly, sent them to their deaths.

"Leave now and go in peace," she told them, trying to control the fury inside her. "For the dark one would not die for you, nor your king."

They looked at one another and for one moment she thought they might listen and return meekly home to their families, but then, their voices raised together in one, inhuman shriek, they charged.

There was no need to focus. Effortlessly, she pulled the power and the fury tight to her and slowly lifted her arms. Behind her, the river roared. Water surged, lifting up, up, past her hands and high into the air, its white surf curling into the tip of a giant wave. It towered over her. Jasmine blinked. In an instant, she was gone, in behind the warriors, facing the wave as it came crashing down towards them. They tried desperately to throw themselves out of its path, but it was too late. Reaching them in seconds, it cut their legs out from under them and tossed them headfirst into the spray. Water smothered their cries, turning them over and over as it surged towards her, seemingly unstoppable. Inches from her feet, it hit the wall of her protection and fell back, straight into the path of a second wave. Colliding, the two forces tussled, pulling at the bodies like some macabre tug of war. And then, its fury spent, the water began to recede; slipping away from the bank and back into the deep stone sides. Rolling lazily, the warriors' bodies went with it. The back of a head, a hand and the side of a leg bobbed as the river sent the bodies downstream. Slowly the surface calmed, settling back to its gentle roar. On the far bank, Seamus and the druids stared silently at her over the top of the water.

*

Malachy was almost there. The knots almost loosened enough to withdraw one hand. He twisted his wrist and pulled. Not quite. He began again, his fingers working against the edges of the cord. His fingers spasmed with cramp. Wincing, he flexed them against the pain, trying to stop them from stiffening. Next to the fire, having finished off the beer, the men were beginning to quieten. Curled up away from the group, Ilech had already fallen asleep, but of Cathbad there was no sign. The pain in Malachy's fingers eased and he started again. The men were moving about and shuffling as they settled for the night. Ignoring them, he concentrated all his energy. It had to be tonight. Tomorrow would be too late; another bone breaking journey ending at Cruachan and Ellyllon. Someone moved behind him and Malachy dropped the cord, but it was just Anle, carrying the beer jar in one hand.

"Here." He held it out to him and the last of the beer sloshed.

"I – thanks," Malachy said quickly, wanting to get rid of him as soon as possible. He gestured with his hands.

"Ah." Stepping forward, Anle placed the jar to Malachy's lips and he threw his head back.

It took a moment, and then tasting beer and herbs, he swallowed. Three more mouthfuls and he drained the jar.

"Thank you."

Anle nodded, putting the jar on the chariot beside him. And then, to Malachy's horror, he moved towards his bonds. A tug, a quick suspicious look and he began to tighten them again.

"Rinnach will guard tonight. Fear of Ellyllon has not stopped the vengeance in his heart. I would not try to run."

Tying the last knot, as if to emphasise, he jerked the cord, slicing it against Malachy's wrist. Malachy winced.

"Try, but these will not loosen. You would do better to sleep, for tomorrow, we must ride hard to reach Cruachan before night."

"Don't you want to know why Ellyllon's going to all this trouble, just for me?"

Anle gave him an even look. "By his oath, a warrior must follow his king. He will fight by his oath and he will die by his king. He does not ask."

Picking up the jar, he returned to the fire. Anle muttered something to Rinnach and then picking up a woven blanket, he laid down and pulled it over him. Malachy tugged at the cord. The knots were even tighter, and worse, Anle had tied them so that his wrists were pressed tight to the stick. He had no chance of loosening them now. All he could do was to wait and hope that Jasmine and Seamus found him before they reached Cruachan. Next to the fire, Rinnach shifted around so that he could see the chariot and, sitting back, settled down to watch him.

*

No one said anything as they'd joined her on the other side of the river. Even Seamus handed her the reins of her horse in silence. Confused, and a little hurt, she waited for Ferdia to lead them into the forest before tucking in on the end. At first, she thought they were angry with her, disgusted by what she'd done to the men. But then she realised it was more than that. They were afraid of her, or afraid to be with her, afraid of what she might do.

You scared them, the voice agreed softly.

Hearing it, her heart sank. With the return of the main voice, the others usually followed soon after.

They're just jealous, rejoined the older voice, right on cue. *Of your power*.

No, not hers, ours, came the third, chirruping with youth, like a bird.

Shut up, shut up! She shouted back at them, wanting to put her hands over her ears. She wished they'd go away and leave her alone. She'd never asked for them. She'd never asked for any of it, but especially not a power so strong it would cause her mind to crack and splinter.

*

Early evening and finally reaching the path, they travelled on, going west until the light began to fade. Ferdia had found a clearing away from the path and stopping, they'd made camp for the night.

Sat close to the fire, Jasmine listened to the wind catching the top of the trees. Seamus and Cethern had slipped away from the group and into the night. As soon as they left, Drendas had beckoned to Emer. She stared at him for a moment, then getting quickly to her feet, went over to join him. Placing his hand over hers, he talked softly to her. Nodding, she listened in silence to him. And then, suddenly, she lifted her head and looked straight at Jasmine.

I see you.

Startled, Jasmine looked away. Ronan was studying her over the top of the fire. Not him too. She shifted uncomfortably. She felt like an animal in an experiment with the druids as the scientists, waiting to see how she would react. Sat the other side of Ferdia, Maine said something and Ronan turned to answer. Almost immediately, as if he'd been waiting for a chance to escape, Ferdia scrambled to his feet and went off in the direction of the horses.

He knows too, the voice inside her whispered.

Jasmine waited a few seconds, then got to her feet and followed him. Ferdia was checking the horses, although to Jasmine they looked fine.

"Ferdia."

He looked up and almost immediately looked down again. Stop it! She wanted to shout at him. *I won't hurt you. I'm struggling, but I can control it.* But, she didn't. Instead, she joined him, standing the opposite side of Drendas' horse's head.

"Is he alright?"

Ferdia nodded.

"I'm sorry about Daire."

He moved away."Ferdia, what's happening to me?!" Her voice cracked and immediately he turned back.

"I gave my word."

"Then you know?! Tell me, I have to know."

He looked away. "I cannot."

"But I thought we were friends. I thought you cared."

"I do."

"Then tell me!"

"I cannot. When the time is right, you will know."

"What does that mean?" she demanded, flapping her arms at him in frustration. "It doesn't even make sense!"

She wheeled and moving between two trees, stomped back the way she'd come.

*

Light from the fire appeared through the trees, followed by the murmur of voices. Not ready to face Ronan and the rest of the druids, Jasmine veered left. Her pace quickened, her feet crashing through ferns and around tall, late summer nettle, as if by running she could leave it all behind. She was such an idiot. Why was she asking a question when she already knew the answer? She knew what was happening to her. How many times did she need to say it to herself before she accepted it was real? The voices were just another symptom. She was disintegrating, the person she once was being consumed by the power within her. Like a high sandstone cliff eroded by waves, whole sections of her were crumbling slowly away, before finally, with a loud roar, toppling into the sea.

Jasmine slowed, hearing more voices straight ahead. The deeper one she recognised instantly: Seamus. Trying not to make a sound, she moved closer, slipping from tree to tree. He and Cethern came into view, leaning against opposite trees.

"I know what it means, your father's prophecy." Breaking off a twig, Seamus rolled it between thumb and finger.

Cethern laughed. "Then you are wiser than me."

Seamus shook his head. "Not really. I should've seen it before. I let my prejudice blind me, my certainty that I knew how the world worked. Even now I'm not sure I believe it. But I could've helped Jasmine, made it easier for her, but I preferred to blame Drendas."

"You speak strangely. Malachy spoke strangely."

He laughed softly at that, the sound sad. "I suppose, to you, we do." He threw the twig away. "I've spoken to your father and finally understand what I must do. This time I don't expect Jasmine will forgive me, but you, will you forgive your father for what he did?"

Leaning back, Cethern regarded the sky through the trees. "I cannot. I fear for my daughter, for Emer loves him and her heart is soft, generous. She will forgive him, I think."

"But how much can one person forgive? I promised Jasmine no more secrets, but I've been thinking maybe I'm too used to them. My whole life's been a secret. Hiding Iomlan, my power. Always having to take care, to mind who's there, who could be watching, who might see. I've spent my life pretending to be something I'm not and now I'm afraid to be what I am." He sighed heavily. "I've had enough of 'em. Jasmine's right; secrets are like a disease, a cancer. They eat away at you. After tomorrow, this is my last one. Cethern, you're a mother. There's something you should know."

Her eyes narrowing, she straightened. "Malachy told me," Seamus continued, "It's about–"

But at that moment, Maine came crashing through the undergrowth. He nodded to Jasmine and continued on, going, she guessed, to find a private spot to go to toilet. She looked back, but it was too late; hearing him, Cethern and Seamus had moved off. Feeling her bladder twinge, Jasmine let them go and wandered off to find her own spot.

*

Later that night, turning over, Jasmine pulled her cloak tighter to her. Everyone was asleep, apart from her and the druid keeping watch. She didn't know his name and he was quiet; she hadn't even heard him speak. She thought of tomorrow, of reaching Cruachan and the battle that would take place. People would probably die on both sides. It was possible he could be one of them and indirectly she'd have caused the death of someone else she didn't know and hadn't even spoken to.

Yes, but it will be a glorious death, the voice reassured her.

She turned again, trying to shut it out.

But a waste of a body, the older voice laughed, cackling lasciviously. *Those fine, strong hips.*

Something shuffled noisily through the undergrowth. Jasmine focussed on the sound, tried to use it to distract herself. A tree creaked, and there, a rustle of leaves. It was strange, she thought desperately, when you'd never slept in a forest before, you tended to imagine it would be silent. The druid keeping watch reached over to put wood on the fire. The flames whooshed; light flickered across the glade, casting shadows that made the branches of the trees dance. Jasmine closed her eyes, willing sleep to come, but still the voices whispered.

Chapter Twenty

Cathbad's group set off at first light. Just before dawn, Anle woke Malachy and untying him from the chariot, helped him clamber stiffly down. He gave him a small piece of dry bread and cheese, then led him behind a tree and waited for him to urinate. Luckily, Malachy thought bleakly, he hadn't eaten enough to do anything else. He didn't think he could face crouching down in front of Anle, although he suspected that he wouldn't really take much notice. Since they'd been travelling, it wasn't the first time he'd had to go in a wood, it was just he'd never had an audience.

They continued east. The sky was grey through the trees and, although dry, there was a dampness in the air. The first sign that summer was beginning to turn and autumn was on its way. Resting his head on his hands, Malachy dozed. He'd slept badly last night, despite his exhaustion. It seemed he'd only just got to sleep when Anle had woken him.

His mind wandered, lulled by the sounds of the forest and the noise of the chariot with all its thuds, creaks and rattles. Half-asleep, daydreaming more than dreaming, he saw Jasmine and Seamus coming to rescue him. The former charged her horse straight through the group, knocking them to the ground with Iomlan, her eyes swirling with green. Rain began to fall softly through the trees, murmuring gently. Cold drops fell on Malachy's head; he opened his eyes and the rescue vanished. A pace or two behind, Rinnach watched him from his horse, his eyes dark and hooded. Malachy looked away. A few minutes later, he glanced surreptitiously back. Rinnach was still watching him.

Abruptly, the forest ended. The riders and chariot rode out onto a wide, grassy plain and into a light, misty rain. Across the plain was a hill; long, wide, the flat land around it made it look taller, more impressive. Sat on one end of it, covering the highest part, was a huge hill fort. A series of earthworks had been built around it, moving inwards in ever decreasing circles. The first, a ditch, had been cut deep into the hill and the soil banked high behind it then topped by a thick, wooden wall. A second, smaller earthwork sat inside it, topped by another wooden wall and crossed by four entrances. And inside that, towering above the rest, was an enormous roundhouse. A hall, or maybe a temple, standing higher than anything else around it. This then, was Cruachan, the fabled city of Queen Medb. Malachy swivelled, trying to get a better look. Three smaller forts lay to the north of the hill, possibly some sort of religious or ritual centres. Below the hill, a few even smaller forts dotted the plain, small farmsteads or village communities, built like satellite towns to a city. Malachy knew this land; it wasn't very far from his home. It was Rathcroghan, where he went on a school field trip. First, they'd gone to the museum in the village of Tulsk and then they'd drudged out, into the cold and wet and across damp, muddy fields to all that was left; vaguely circular lumps in the ground. But even then, when he'd mimicked the boredom of his friends, there had been an atmosphere about the place, the tiniest sense of what had been. But now… he gazed at it, for a moment forgetting he was on his way to Ellyllon, if only they could've seen it as he saw it now, in all its magnificence.

The chariot bounced over tufts of thick grass. As the group rode towards the settlement, Ilech took out a horn from his belt and blew. Higher in tone than Ferdia's, it soared over the plain, towards the hill. Silence. And then, from the hill came an answering call, the sound the twin of the first. Cathbad sped up and the rest followed.

They were almost to the hill when the rain turned heavier. Within minutes, Malachy's hair was plastered to his head. Curling into the side of the chariot, Malachy tried to use his legs to kick his cloak out over his body. It didn't really work. He glanced at Daire. Still on his side, at least his cloak covered most of him. Hunched miserably against the elements, raindrops dripped off Malachy's hair and down the back of his neck.

At the base of the hill, they followed a narrow road upwards. The chariot rattled and shook as the wheels rolled over a stone surface so regular it had to be man-made. The horses slowed, their heads nodding. Malachy gazed up at the ditch and the wall and wondered at the work they had taken. By the time they reached the top of the hill, the rain had slowed and settled again into a light, hazy mist. The road crossed the ditch and entered the settlement through a huge wooden gate built into a gap in the bank. Moving away from the others, Cathbad urged his horse forward and approached the gate. He called once and immediately one of the doors swung open and four warriors appeared, laden with weapons. They stepped back as soon as they saw Cathbad, and the group was admitted.

The chariot rolled inside. Looking eagerly past the driver, Malachy's jaw dropped. Made of wood and reeds cut into wattle and daub, with a thatched roof, the roundhouse towered over the whole settlement. Only this wasn't the settlement Malachy had been expecting; it wasn't a camp built for warriors, it was a city, where people lived out their normal, everyday lives.

"Queen Medb's hall," the driver muttered to no one in particular. "Home of Daithi, son of Cet and King of all Connacht."

The group followed the road through the centre of the city. Men, women and children dressed in a dazzling array of colours stopped what they were doing to watch them pass. They gazed curiously at the young man tied to the chariot as he gazed curiously back. Dressed in brown knee-length tunics, a group of children began running along the side of the chariot catcalling the driver, asking who Malachy was. With his hair short compared to theirs and still in the sixteenth century clothes, he guessed he must look very strange. A dog joined them, running and yapping excitedly, before falling away and toddling serenely home.

"Go," Anle growled, shooing them away with one hand. "Before the druid turns you into squealing piglets!" He made a ferocious face. "And I tell your mothers to cook you on a spit!"

The children laughed, delighted, only fleeing when Anle made as if to dismount. Laughing to himself, he caught Malachy's eye and sobered, but not before Malachy had glimpsed the man behind the warrior; the husband and the father. They passed more roundhouses and a young girl carrying a baby lifted him to watch. They passed the Iron Age equivalent of an allotment; saw a woman bent low in the earth, then a forge, the smoke thick and heavy, as the blacksmith worked his craft. So many sights, sounds and smells; it made Malachy's head spin. Reaching the second earthwork, they rode through the open gates and left the everyday city behind.

*

The hall, stood on the hill's peak and in the centre of the second earthwork, was huge, imposing, looking big enough to hold a hundred warriors. Around the side, thick wooden struts the size of trees held the lines of wattle and the roof in place. Painted a myriad of colours, Celtic symbols had been carved into the length of them then covered in thin, melted gold. The roof, made of reed and hardened with mud, hung low. Its edges sheltered the two warriors stood either side of the high, willow doors. Behind the hall, to the right, was a line of roundhouses, the medium-sized house flanked on both sides by four small ones and to the left, another large roundhouse, although this one had no walls. Inside, warriors fought with different weapons, their movements slow and practiced. They were practising, Malachy realised; the wall-less roundhouse was a kind of academy or gym for warriors. Around the outside, groups of warriors sat watching, talking or drinking. They were, in fact, everywhere; standing, walking, even lying. Too many to have come from one tribe; they were part of the army Ellyllon was amassing, ready for war. An army that would march only to his word. Daithi, King of Connacht, was nothing but a figurehead.

Cathbad dismounted.

"Bring him," he growled at Anle, with a nod towards Malachy. "Leave the druid."

Doing as he said, Anle dismounted and, slipping a knife from his belt, cut the cord binding Malachy's wrists to the chariot.

"Come." Grabbing his arm, he helped him off the chariot.

Trying to walk, Malachy's legs buckled, but Anle still had hold of him. Carefully, he walked him round in a small circle.

"Can you walk?" he grinned suddenly, nodding towards the hall. "Or must I carry you, as a mother carries her young?"

"I can walk," Malachy retorted. He looked at the chariot. "But what about Daire?"

Cathbad cocked his head impatiently. His eyes narrowed.

"He will be well," Anle reassured him quickly, tightening his grip.

Seeing them coming, the warrior to the left span and almost falling over in his haste, pushed the doors wide open. Without a word, Cathbad stopped and waited while Anle took Malachy inside. It was dark, the only light coming from the door behind them. Malachy blinked as his eyes adjusted to the dim light. In the centre of the room was a huge round fireplace, an iron spit next to it. Further back, sitting facing out into the centre of the room, were two tall wooden chairs, or thrones to be precise, their arms and backs intricately carved. A piece of ironwork sat between them, the metal ring at the top making it look like some kind of stand. Otherwise the hall was empty. A gentle pull guided Malachy to the fireplace.

"Sit," Anle ordered, letting him go.

Malachy did as he was told.

Cathbad gestured to the warrior. Leaving Anle with Malachy, the warrior rejoined Cathbad and turning, one by one, closed the doors behind them.

*

Unknown to them, Jasmine and the druids set off not long after Cathbad. Maybe thirty or so miles behind; just minutes away in the modern world, they would have been tantalising close.

Overcast, the grey morning sky and dim light felt more like winter than late summer, with its thick, oppressive air. But riding in silence, to Jasmine it seemed to match their mood. Grim. Taciturn. Beside her, Seamus was as distant as the moon.

As the land evened out and flattened, the forest path widened, allowing the group to speed up. Maine and Ferdia stayed ahead, checking the way, but Ronan was certain they wouldn't meet anyone else. Cathbad had already achieved what he wanted. They stopped briefly at midday to eat and rest the horses. According to Ronan, it would take them the rest of the day to reach Cruachan; they'd arrive late into the night. A few hours' sleep and they would be ready for battle.

*

The hall darkened further, the only light coming from the gaps around the door. A few seconds and once more their eyes adjusted. For a moment, Malachy and Anle looked at one another and then Anle moved away and began walking restlessly around the hall.

"Are you married?" Malachy asked.

"Yes," Anle answered, his voice coming from the back of the hall. "We have four sons and three daughters."

Slowly, awkwardly, Malachy shifted round so he could see him. Facing away from him, Anle seemed to be examining the thrones.

"Then you would kill to protect them?"

"I would die to protect them. Our last was born at the time of Samhain. His breath was short. Now he waits in the arms of the ancestors with his brother and sister."

"I'm sorry."

Silence.

"We had our time of mourning." Anle turned suddenly. "You are not druid; why does the dark one want you?"

Malachy hesitated. What he said next could be crucial. Something had changed between them; he could feel it. And as Anle said yesterday, he was a warrior, a member of a tribe; he was bound to follow his king, his chieftain, and yet here he was asking questions. Crossing his legs,

Malachy placed his bound hands on his shins.

"There's a girl; she's druid," he said, picking his words carefully. "She's very powerful, more powerful than Cathbad. Ellyllon wants her, wants to use her power."

Anle came towards him. "He has a great power, great magic."

"No." Malachy paused, trying to think of a way to say it that might make some sense to him. "He has only the power to speak and make others follow him."

"He put his hands in you, and he is there and then he is…" He closed and opened his hand, as if to say poof, "…gone."

"Yes, but that's all." He saw Anle's frown and sighing, rubbed at his forehead. "Ellyllon was druid once, but the druids of Brigantes took his power from him, but because he was so powerful, they couldn't–"

"Why?"

"Why?"

"Why did they steal his power?"

"It's not important. OK, wait, punishment. It was a punishment."

"Why?" Anle asked again, sitting opposite him.

"I don't know. But that's why he wants the war; revenge."

"He is dishonoured. Is it not his right to seek vengeance?"

"But if he breaks the law?"

"Yes." He nodded his understanding. "What law?"

"I don't know."

"You are no storyteller," Anle complained seriously.

"No." Malachy bit back a sigh.

"The girl you speak of, she has love for you?"

"Yes. And me her."

Anle stroked his beard. "I have not heard my Aoife laugh since before Samhain. I would hear her laugh and see her smile and dance." He looked away, and his voice hardened, like a man determined to just talk business. "It is a good plan. If I were the dark one, I would do the same."

"Thanks," Malachy said drily.

Anle gave him a puzzled look. "You speak strangely."

"Yeah, I know."

The doors rattled. Turning simultaneously, they watched them open. Stood in the entrance, his black cloak framed against the last of the daylight, was Ellyllon. In his right hand he carried a lit torch.

"Malachy," he greeted him, stepping inside.

Flames illuminated the area of the hall around him, cast the shadows up into the roof. Malachy didn't answer. Ellyllon's eyes slid to Anle then back. "Go," he ordered.

Anle got to his feet. He looked down at Malachy and for the first time, Malachy thought he saw regret in his face.

"I said, go."

Anle walked stiffly around Ellyllon, careful not to get too close, and then, with a last look, went out. The door closed behind him. Without a word, Ellyllon's dark eyes stared into his.

"Where's Daire?" Malachy asked when the silence had got too much.

"Still sleeping. Cathbad lacks finesse, the light touch." Ellyllon flicked his long, thin fingers irritably. "It's been too long, I'd forgotten what it's like here. Why kill someone neatly and quietly when you can bludgeon them to death?"

"Are you going to kill Daire?"

"Not if he does as I ask. And being the son of Drendas, he may prove useful." He looked up, as if studying the reeds in the roof. "So, Jasmine saved Seamus. I'm impressed. I didn't think he'd make it, not with the damage Cormac did. Tell me, how did she do it?"

"I don't know."

"Don't know?! Come, Malachy, you were there." He moved towards the thrones, the light in his hand scattering the darkness back towards Malachy. "What harm to satisfy my idle curiosity?"

Malachy squinted. With Ellyllon, there was no such thing as idle curiosity. He always had a reason, but other than to confirm Jasmine's growing power, Malachy couldn't see what it could be. Placing the torch in the iron stand next to the thrones, Ellyllon disappeared behind them.

"Perhaps I should call Cathbad, or Rinnach?" His black cloak lost in the darkness, his disembodied voice purred.

Malachy frowned. As if threats could work. Something moved behind the thrones, the sway of his cloak, maybe.

"And what of Cormac?"

"What do you care?"

"She killed him. I knew she would."

"No she didn't!" Malachy snapped, biting finally. "She aged him."

"Aged him?" Ellyllon appeared around one of the thrones, his white face gleaming in the torchlight. "How did she do that, I wonder?"

"How d'ya think!"

He pressed his hands into thighs. He had to calm down; getting angry wouldn't help. In fact, with Ellyllon's manipulations, it was probably playing right into his hands.

"Hmm, and Seamus?"

"I told you, I don't know."

"She healed him, didn't she? I told her, her power was growing, but she didn't believe me."

"If you knew, why did you ask?"

Ellyllon laughed, one hand caressing the arm of the throne. "Just testing, Malachy, just testing."

Slipping around the front of the throne, he lowered his body delicately into the seat. Flames from the torch flickered, sent light rippling across his face, catching the bones beneath his white, paper-thin skin, making it look like a skull. The hair on the back of Malachy's neck lifted.

"Power, Malachy," the skull breathed, watching its fingers play with the carved wood. "In Britain, lone druids are held in check by a strict hierarchy, with a few, those deemed the wisest, holding the power. The young are well-versed in the accepted ways and those that question are judged unworthy and ostracised, or worse. From early on I was marked, for I had my own ideas. I disagreed with my mentor, used my power, my gift of persuasion in ways he did not approve of. Like the druids here, he followed the old ways, the word, the law, but even then I knew it for what is was. Fear. Fear to use our full power: to be who we should be."

He sat back, and to Malachy's relief the skull disappeared.

"Seamus has done it to Jasmine. He's made her weak, paralysed her by a fear of doing harm. Yes, I want her," he said, his black eyes glowing. "I want to use her power, but I want to see her as she truly is, to bask in the glory that is Iomlan."

He stopped, as if sensing he'd given something away. Malachy looked at the floor, scared of showing what he'd seen in his face. Ellyllon's weakness. He should've seen it when Seamus had told him what Jasmine had said. It was obvious, when you knew it. What she'd seen and what, now, inadvertently, Ellyllon had shown him, was that in the centuries of consuming Iomlan, he'd become addicted to it. He didn't just need it to stay alive: he needed to know and feel its power, needed it to live, just as an addict needed their fix.

Frowning slightly, Ellyllon continued. "The druids argue their way is the way of nature, but does nature stop the lion or the tiger?"

"No, but nature balances it out," Malachy replied eagerly, keen now to talk, to discuss, if only it would keep Ellyllon from realising that he knew. "The lion doesn't always get the kill."

"True. But still the lion uses all its skill, its cunning, its power."

He had a point, but it wasn't the same. He was twisting it.

"It's not the same. A lion kills to live. And it's not just about what's right and what's wrong. What happens when you use your power, and something happens you didn't mean?"

Ellyllon smiled. "Ah, I hear Seamus talking. How do you know you didn't mean it? How do you know that in some deep, dark place it wasn't exactly what you wanted?"

"But you could say that about anything. Accidents happen, things you don't mean. Look at Killaspugbrone; it wasn't her fault, she didn't mean for–" He stopped.

Ellyllon's fingers froze. He went very still. Watching him, Malachy's stomach sank. In his eagerness, he'd given something away, something important. But, then, incredibly, Ellyllon changed the subject.

"Do you know what the Druid Council did to me?"

Malachy breathed out. Maybe he'd got it wrong. Maybe he hadn't given anything away. Maybe Ellyllon was just playing mind games with him, deliberately trying to unnerve him, and it was working. He took another breath, telling himself to calm, calm.

"Yes, Seamus told me."

"Did he tell you what is does to you, to have someone reach inside you and rip out the centre of you?! They took my Iomlan, cut it out of me while I still lived. You can't conceive of the pain."

"No, how could I?!" Malachy retorted sarcastically.

Ellyllon smiled sadly. "I was sorry for that. I bear you no ill will, Malachy, I just need you. You're the chink in Jasmine's armour, my best hope in persuading her to join me."

He sounded so sincere. If he didn't know better, Malachy would've believed him.

"And what about people like Jasmine, how many of them have you killed? Taken their Iomlan when they're still alive?"

"You think I want it, that I enjoy it?!" Ellyllon spat. His black eyes were livid and he sat bolt upright. "I do it to survive. If I could, I would have what was taken from me."

"What do you expect? Me to feel sorry for you?"

Ellyllon's anger faded as quickly as it had come. "No. I'm trying to make you understand. I am not what I was born to be, but what the Druid Council made me; a freak, an aberration."

He paused, and in the silence, Malachy heard the sticks in the walls creak in the cooling evening air. Night was drawing in. Even inside, he could feel it.

"I know what you're trying to do. You're trying to manipulate me, to—"

Ellyllon laughed, the sound surprisingly soft, affectionate almost. "Of course I'm trying to manipulate you, Malachy. I ache, I burn with the need to use, to feel my power, and manipulation is all I have left." He sighed sadly. "Why wouldn't I use it? Is there nothing you love, Malachy, apart from Jasmine, nothing you would give anything to have, to do?"

"I – the farm." The words were out before he could stop them. Suddenly, Jasmine and Seamus, Ellyllon and his thirst for power, none of it made any sense. He wished he was back on his father's farm, driving the tractor, or feeding the cattle, feeling the familiar soil beneath his feet.

Ellyllon's smile was like the sun coming out. "Yes, you do understand."

Slipping out of the throne, he began to slowly walk around the hall.

"This hall is the king of Connacht's seat of power," he said, his voice light, musing. He sounded just like a teacher Malachy had once: Ms Greene, young, with thick black curly hair and rosebud lips, standing looking out of the window as she'd talked, as if they were incidental. She loved history, enthused them with her passion, and all the boys had been half in love with her. "It holds not just a symbolic power, but a real, practical power. Within these walls, deals are done, wars are decided and judgements passed. And yet, is it the king that holds that power, or the men that advise him? The men that smile and creep and flatter him. The men that draw him quietly to one side and whisper gently into his ear."

Away from the torch, Ellyllon stopped, half in shadow. With the darkness behind him, the light played across his face, giving it a strange, ethereal glow. He fixed his eyes on Malachy, who couldn't help but stare into their deep, dark depths. "We all want power to some extent, Malachy. Even you. Power to do what we like, power to make others like us, to want to sleep with us or to do as we wish. Drendas is no exception."

"Drendas?" What did he know about Drendas?

"More than I like."

It was as if he'd read his mind. A voice rose up inside him, telling him to stop, look away now, before he lost himself inside that terrible darkness, but it was already too late. He couldn't do it.

"Jasmine is safer with me," Ellyllon continued, unblinking. "If she will only let me, I will give her everything she's ever wanted. And Malachy, you too, whatever you desire, name it and it will be yours. I don't want to hurt you or Jasmine. If she would but join me, I will help her control Iomlan and you can be together, just as you were meant to be."

It wasn't so unreasonable, Malachy thought dreamily. At least Ellyllon was honest, unlike Drendas. It was strange, he, Malachy, had never been alone with him before and he was so different to what he expected. More human somehow. Even his face seemed softer, his dark eyes shining now with a bright, warm glow.

"Drendas is a liar. He's using Jasmine for his own ends and Seamus can't see it."

He threw Malachy a look, a look that said he didn't want to interfere, didn't want to cast aspersions but he had to, for Jasmine's sake.

"But he does. He knows Drendas is up to something," Malachy replied eagerly. Suddenly, it seemed very important to explain it to Ellyllon, to have him understand.

Ellyllon cocked his head. "But does he?"

"Yeah, he told me."

"But what is it? What does Drendas want?"

"Her power."

One eyebrow lifted. "Nothing else?"

"No. What else is there?" He thought for a moment. "Other than the prophecy."

"Ah, yes, the prophecy." Shining, Ellyllon's black eyes slid away. Suddenly free of them, Malachy fell back against the wall.

"Shit, what did you do to me?!" he gasped.

Ellyllon smiled. "I showed you my power."

"Power?!" Guilt made him furious. "A few easy words and I'll forget everything you've done, everything you're planning?"

"No, Malachy, not easy words." Ellyllon's anger matched his own. "Every word is picked carefully. Every tone, every nuance picked to persuade just you. And each one I say costs me."

Quick as a striking snake, he leapt across the hall. Crouching in front of Malachy, his white face loomed. "You did forget, Malachy. You forgot because I made you, and a little while longer, and you would've forgotten completely. You would've followed me as the King of Connacht follows me; happily, fervently, like a dog crawling on his belly to his master." Leaning in, he pressed his face close. "But I don't want that. I want her to believe she can save you. Why else would she come willingly? Why else will she do as I say? And keep doing it. But then, Malachy, when she has felt the perfect pleasure of real power, she will get a taste for it and she will do it for its own sake. She will do it because she can." He stood up, and the eyes that looked at Malachy were empty, "Then she will turn on you, and all your love, your soft words and your loyalty will be nothing. She will consume you while I sit and watch. It's not me that'll be her undoing, Malachy. It's you."

He moved away, back towards the doors.

"I wouldn't try to run if I were you; there's a new guard outside the door. I don't think I need to tell you his name."

The doors opened and, without another word, Ellyllon went out. Immediately the doors began to close, but not before Rinnach looked in. He saw Malachy and gave him a smile, a nasty one, and then he was gone. The doors closed and a few seconds later the torch went out, leaving him in darkness.

Chapter Twenty-One

An hour after dusk, Jasmine, Seamus and the druids turned off the main path and heading north, went deeper into the forest.

"Owennaforeesha River lies northeast of Cruachan," Ronan had explained earlier. "We will rest there, for Cathbad will watch the road and not think we will come from the north."

Still mounted, they pressed slowly through an undergrowth grown tall in the dark, rich soil. It was dark by the time they finally reached the edge of the forest. The sky was clear, and shining brightly, the moon illuminated the thin ribbon of water that was the start of the Owennaforeesha River. As the other druids paused, Jasmine wheeled her horse and rode around them. Across the plain, the fires of Cruachan burned bright, lightening up the sky above and turning it a paler blue. Huge, the sky covered the plain, filled with millions of stars. Twinkling silently, there were too many to be real, and too brilliant. The land seemed to fade away before them. A thrill of contentment slipped through her, like a person returning home after a long absence.

"Come," Ronan said, nudging his horse forward. "We must rest."

*

His back against the far wall of the hall, Malachy stared into darkness. As night descended the last of the room's light had faded, leaving a room filled with shades of dark grey. All was quiet. Malachy shifted awkwardly, his bottom stiff after too long sat on the hard ground. He'd shuffled to the wall in the hope of digging his way out. With nothing to use but his bound hands, he'd tried to unpick the wattle, to prise apart the woven sticks, but it was too secure, and the rough edges had made his fingers bleed. He rubbed his eyes with the bottom of his thumbs, wishing for the umpteenth time that sleep would come. He was so tired. He'd gone through things in his mind, turning them over and over, and it was getting so he couldn't think straight. Around him, the darkness felt as if it were closing in on him, the unseen walls sliding slowly, silently, closer.

Come on, Malachy, he told himself quickly, trying to rouse his spirits.

Sitting up, he pulled up his legs and hugged them close. He had to keep his focus, to stay strong. Jasmine and Seamus were bound to try and rescue him and he needed to be ready. Ellyllon wanted him to feel helpless; that's why he'd done what he did. It was mind games, like leaving him here, alone in the darkness, waiting, dreading. Psychological warfare. He pulled his knees in tighter. If he was honest, the power of Ellyllon's manipulation had shaken him. He still couldn't believe how easily his mind had been changed. No wonder Ellyllon had managed to unite the chieftains behind him so quickly, and the druids. No, inwardly he shook his head. Not the druids; they had Iomlan to protect them. If they didn't, Ellyllon wouldn't need him to control Jasmine. The druids followed him because they wanted to. Anger rose up inside him. Frustrated, he bumped the back of his head into the wall. He never should've listened to Grainne. He should've stayed where he was and waited for them to return. Seamus had warned him, but he'd been too stubborn, too certain that Jasmine needed him, to listen, and now look at him. Ellyllon was right, he decided angrily; if Jasmine gave herself over to him, it would be all his fault.

*

The bark of a fox carried high into the night sky, its cry sharp, unearthly. It woke Malachy from his doze. Opening his eyes, he rubbed at them. It was still dark. He probably hadn't slept very long, but he felt better for it, his mind clearer. He'd let Ellyllon's words get inside his head, but he was stronger than that, more determined. If Ellyllon was devious and manipulative, then he'd have to be even more devious. Starting with what Ellyllon had himself given away.

Wait a minute. Malachy took one mental step back. "*Nothing else?*" Ellyllon had asked, and he'd answered him. "*—the prophecy.*"

And then he'd stopped, for Ellyllon had got the answer he'd wanted. The prophecy. What did he know, that Malachy, or Seamus, didn't?

The fox cried again, louder this time. Only it didn't sound quite right. It came again and Malachy's stomach dropped. That sound was no fox, it was a man screaming in pain. It came again, then again, the sound sharp with agony as he screamed over and over. There was only one person it could be: Daire. Flinching, Malachy turned his head away and put his hands up to his face, near one ear, as if to try and block out the sound. Unable to influence him, Ellyllon was torturing him, trying to get from Drendas' son what he knew Malachy couldn't give. Unable to bear it, he clambered to his feet and began to move along the wall.

If only he could find a way out, he could go find Seamus and Jasmine and they could… abruptly, it stopped. Malachy waited, ears straining. Nothing. Pressing his back to the wall, he sank back down and put his head in his hands.

*

He woke for a second time, blinking against the sudden light. The doors were open. Holding Daire under his arms, two men were carrying him into the hall, his feet dragging. Rinnach watched from the door, a lit torch in his hand, and behind him waited Ellyllon. The men dropped Daire in front of the fireplace, then retreated back out and away. Behind them, the sky was beginning to brighten, dawn not far away.

"Rinnach," Ellyllon said.

With a nod, Rinnach walked over to the spent torch and, taking it from the stand, threw it on the ground. He replaced it with the lit one and then, returning to the doorway, pulled the doors to.

Getting to his feet, Malachy dashed over to Daire and awkwardly turned his body over. In the flickering light of the torch his face was pale and his eyes heavy.

"Daire, are you alright?"

He didn't look alright. A gash on his right temple swelled the skin around it. Dried blood had been smeared down one side of his face where someone had tried roughly to wipe it away. "Malachy," Daire whispered, his voice dry and husky. "I can't move."

"I think it's Ellyllon's potion. He gave it to Jasmine to stop her using Iomlan. She couldn't move either."

Daire looked down his body. "Our power lies within."

"What did they do to you? Did they hurt you?"

"They tried to make me speak, to tell them of my father, but I would not."

"Here." Sitting down, Malachy pulled at his shoulders, trying to lever him up.

It was difficult; his body was a dead weight. Puffing, Malachy managed to lift his shoulders up and slip his legs under them. Daire's head fell back into his lap.

"I wish I had something to wash away the blood."

Daire's eyes watched him wearily. "It is nothing."

Malachy looked away. "I heard them torturing you."

"Cathbad."

"I'm sorry." He swallowed, close to tears. "There was nothing I could do. But you're only here because of me. Without me, you'd be home with Ferdia."

"No, Malachy. It is the prophecy."

"I don't understand."

"My father spoke of it."

"You mean he knew what would happen?!"

"Yes. He follows the words of the Goddess. As do I."

It took him a moment. "You knew?! And you let it happen!"

"Yes." The look in Daire's eyes was intense.

Malachy tried to get his head around it. It was Drendas' prophecy. Why would he want him to be captured by Ellyllon? He could see why he might want to get rid of him, in the same way that'd he probably wanted to get rid of Seamus, but not to Ellyllon, surely? And why Daire, his own son? A thought occurred to him.

"If you knew, why didn't you just let us be captured when we were in Sligo?"

"My father did not speak of it until I returned home."

"But why? I don't get it. All he's done is to make Jasmine vulnerable."

No answer. Daire's eyes flicked away.

Malachy frowned. "Daire, what is it? What aren't you telling me?"

"Yes, tell him, Daire."

It was Ellyllon; stood in the open doorway, with Cathbad behind him.

*

Something touched Jasmine's face. Instantly awake, she sat up, blinking. There was nothing there. Beyond the horizon was a slither of light. It was almost dawn. Pulling back her cloak, she got to her feet and, stepping quietly so as not to disturb the others, left the shelter of the forest and walked towards the river. The druid Cet had been left on guard, but had fallen asleep and she didn't have the heart to wake him. There was no point in worrying about Cathbad. He'd know they were somewhere close. The voices had told her, and her instinct told her they were right. For reasons of his own, he'd given up trying to ambush them and was preparing to meet them in battle. Narrow, the river cut deep into the riverbank, but finding a lower spot, she knelt and began to wash her face.

"Jasmine."

It was Emer, coming up behind her. She rocked back onto her heels.

"You woke me." It wasn't a question.

Emer nodded. "I would speak with you."

She joined her on the bank, sitting with her legs tucked under her.

For a moment, neither of them spoke.

"I am druid," Emer said finally.

"What?" Jasmine spluttered. And then she realised, she already knew. Those voices again, or rather, she corrected herself, Iomlan. "Does anyone else know?"

"My grandfather, and – Malachy."

"Malachy?! Why Malachy?"

"He fought with Badb for my honour."

"He fought with Badb?" She felt a sudden twinge of jealousy. *Why would Malachy fight for Emer's honour?*

Emer smiled. "He is kind. Badb used his power, but–"

"You had to use yours to save him." She saw it all clearly. Malachy's bravery had forced Emer to reveal her secret to him, but he'd kept it. He hadn't even told her. Her eyes pricked. It was so like him.

"Why are you telling me this?"

"My grandfather speaks to me. I would you know what lies inside you."

"But I already know. My Iomlan too strong for me. It's corrupting me. Your fath – grandfather told me."

Emer stared deep into her eyes. "He lied. It is not druid power that corrupts you."

"Then what is it?"

"The Goddess, Brid."

"Goddess!" she laughed, a loud, explosive bark. "I don't think so."

"Jasmine?" Seamus came towards them. Behind him, Drendas was using his staff to clamber to his feet.

"Forgive me." Uncurling, Emer got to her feet.

"No, wait a minute, you can't just go." She stood up, but too late. Lifting her skirts, Emer scurried away.

"Jasmine, what's wrong?" Seamus asked. "What did she say?"

"Nothing. It's stupid."

"Tell me."

"She said it's not Iomlan doing all this stuff to me, it's the Goddess, Brid."

"What? Why would she tell you that?"

Jasmine froze. Not, why would she say something like that, but why would she tell you. "Seamus?"

"She shouldn't have told you. Drendas agreed I would be the one to tell you." He looked down. "I'm sorry, I only realised at the Sacred Isle and even then, I didn't want to believe it. Gods aren't real; they don't exist. But seeing what was happening to you, it all made too much sense. I couldn't deny it. Only now, I realised it was too late and there was nothing I could do; she was already inside you. I had to trust Drendas and follow his guidance and when the time was right…" Breathless, he tailed off.

"I don't understand. Are you saying it's true?!"

"She needed you to be ready. She needs you to accept her. She was afraid that if she was too quick, too eager, you'd become scared and reject her."

"Seamus!" she cried, exasperation mixing with fear.

"If I'd realised sooner, maybe I could've stopped it," Seamus continued miserably. "But somehow, she got in and there's nothing I can do. Those voices inside you are her, but it's not enough. She needs more than that. She needs you to choose."

"Seamus–?" She stopped. "What did you say?"

"She needs you to choose. Accept or reject her. Either way she won't leave until you do." *Choose. Rogha. Oh, My God!*

Her mind flew. She was back on the slopes of Knocknarea, seeing an old woman inside Queen Mebh's tomb. Then, half-drowning in the tarn sat in the mountains above Ballintubber Abbey and the lost memory; falling into Drendas' beacon, her flesh burning and the middle-aged woman. The one with the voice. Three women; all giving the same warning. Or so she'd thought.

"Brid, of the Tuatha de Danann. The triple aspect Goddess, or the three ages of woman. The girl; young and passionate, the mother; strong and tender and the hag; old and wise, yet mischievous."

She took a step back. The three women; it was them. One by one they'd kissed her, and one by one she'd unknowingly accepted them inside. *Rogha.* It had nothing to do with Seamus, Cormac or even Ellyllon. It was about Brid, and her.

"Then all these things I did–?"

"It was Brid, not you. Or rather, her influence on you."

But that wasn't strictly true, her instinct told her. Brid couldn't make her do anything she didn't want. Part of her must have wanted it, or at least, been enough happy to relinquish control. She pushed the thought away. Too close, at the moment, it was more than she could bear.

"But if she's inside me, what do I have to choose?"

"Whether to join fully with her. You're disjointed, fighting each other for dominance. As each part of her joined you, so her power over you grew. Mostly you've been in control, but in times of stress, when you've been afraid or confused, or in shock, she's taken over. That's why you've done all those things. Even back in Sligo Abbey, it was Brid who showed you how to heal me, not Iomlan. And Cormac was Brid's judgement, not yours."

"So she's bad?"

Seamus shook his head. "No, I don't think so. Else why would she have saved me? Look around you. I think she's just part of her time, part of this time. And, maybe, of having been worshipped for hundreds of years."

"To join with Brid is an honour beyond all," Drendas said, appearing behind Seamus. "She is Erin's true mother, for she gives her lifeblood in water, earth and fire."

"But why didn't you tell me? I thought I was losing my mind. I could've chosen before now."

"No, you could not, for she did not wish it." Drendas shook his head. "We are but children to the Goddess. Without my care, her power would have scattered your wits as the wind scatters the seeds of a dandelion. As I prepared you, so you will accept her."

"And if I don't?"

"Ellyllon will prevail. With the Tuatha de Danann, the last of the Gods, gone, there is no power in Erin to stop him."

Jasmine looked at Seamus. "So she really is a Goddess?"

"I don't know. I'm still not sure I believe in Gods and Goddesses. Maybe she's just like us, only her Iomlan is far more powerful. Maybe that's all any of the Gods were."

Jasmine, time is short. The prophecy comes to its fruition. Accept us.

But it wasn't that simple.

Yes, it is. Come, let us show you.

Memories blasted her, sights and sounds flooding her mind. She had just enough time to think Drendas was right after all. That up until now, Brid had spared her the full force, and then the wave hit her and she fell to her knees.

A voice sounded through the others, faint but familiar, and she felt a hand. Fingers closed in around hers, grabbing her and holding her, like a lifeline against the tide. It was Seamus, talking softly but urgently, bringing her back to herself.

"Jas, stop fighting it. She won't hurt yer, and it'll stop soon. Just let it flow over you."

His grip tightened. Brid was there too, listening, and to Jasmine's relief the tide of images began to ease, then lessen. And then, through the last of them, she saw a boy, looking out across the harbour. Small, his auburn hair blown by the wind, she knew instantly it was the harbour at Aughris Head, and the boy was Seamus. As she watched, his whole life began to unfold before her and she was seeing, witnessing things, she knew she shouldn't. But now so many things began to make sense.

"Join with Brid," Drendas' voice whispered, close to her ear. "Become one with her and bathe in her glory."

*

Inside the hall, Ellyllon stepped towards Malachy and Daire.

"Tell them," he repeated.

Following, Cathbad shot Rinnach a look and he closed the doors behind them.

"You were listening!" Malachy spat.

Ellyllon laughed. "Of course I was listening. Why do you think I had him brought here? I want to know what he knows."

"Don't tell him, Daire," Malachy countered quickly, changing tack.

Ellyllon's eyes glittered. "But don't you want to know? Don't you want to know why Drendas wanted rid of you so badly? What he and his son have planned for Jasmine?"

Malachy went cold. So, Drendas didn't care what happened to him, he just wanted him as far away from Jasmine as possible. But there was still Seamus, he told himself desperately. Unless he'd done something to him too?

"Forgive me," Daire whispered, his eyes shining.

"Tell him," Ellyllon's voice sharpened. "Or do I have to tear it out of you?"

"Do it," Daire retorted, his eyes never leaving Malachy's.

Ellyllon smiled. "I have no need, for I know your secret, druid. To tear it from you would ravage your mind and for the moment I would like it intact. Unless Malachy wishes to see you suffer. And after what I tell him, he just might."

He cocked his head and Cathbad stepped forward. In the torchlight, his hair, gold lying on top of a burnt orange cloak, made Malachy think of the tip of a flame.

"I saw her on the Sacred Isle. I saw her eyes as she burned with Godfire; the Child of Erin and Brigantes."

Eyes? Malachy thought, remembering the green he'd seen swirl through them. *Godfire?*

"Drendas' prophecy," Cathbad continued. "The return of the

Goddess, Brid. *Only through the Child of Erin and Brigantes can the Goddess be brought forth.* Her sacrifice. When my ancestors, the Tuatha de Danann, travelled for the Otherworld, it is said that one stayed, guarding the entrance that lies in the place between."

"What are you saying?" Malachy looked from Cathbad to Ellyllon.

He knew well what they were saying, but it was stupid, ridiculous. Goddesses weren't real, they didn't guard entrances to the Otherworld. Ellyllon leant forward, his black eyes fixed on Malachy's face. "If the Goddess exists in a place between worlds, she'll need a body, a host, to allow her to return."

"A body? Oh, my God, you think the Goddess is inside her?!"

It couldn't be true and yet, incredibly, it made a strange kind of sense. Jasmine's growing power, the dreams she complained about that were so obviously memories, her inexplicable behaviour, so unlike her it was as if she were someone else.

"The place between worlds lies to the west, on the outer edges of Cruachan," Cathbad continued. "Beneath the temple of Oweynagat."

Ellyllon's face was suffused with excitement. "The power I felt is just the beginning. A Goddess' magic, the power to move mountains." He glanced at Daire. "With your father sitting beside it."

"In the place that it is rightfully mine," Cathbad scowled.

"My father cares for nothing but the glory of the Goddess."

Ellyllon laughed, the sound lifting up into the ceiling and reverberating round, loud and mocking. "Your father is a true priest, a cardinal of faith. Pleading piety and all the time grubbing and grasping for power. If he cares nothing for power, then why does he steal it?"

"Steal it?! My father has no need to steal; he is the most powerful druid in Connacht."

Ellyllon ignored that. He turned to Malachy. "I'll give you this one thing, even though it would cost me. After what he and his father have done, if you want, I'll tear his mind apart for you. Ask it, and it is yours."

Malachy stared into Daire's face. He didn't look repentant and yet his eyes were sad. "No, I won't."

"But, Malachy," Ellyllon hissed, "You heard him. Jasmine is being sacrificed on the altar of Drendas' Goddess, her mind obliterated. Why should I not do the same to him?"

"Because – I don't know!" Malachy retorted, angrily. "Because it's wrong, because he saved my life, because he doesn't know any better. Because I don't care what he's done, I don't want you to torture him to death."

"Malachy, I give you my oath the Goddess will not harm her. She seeks only to join with her." Daire urged, willing him to understand.

"But she thinks it's Iomlan growing inside her. Your father tricked her. He never gave her any choice."

"Brid has chosen and lies within her, but to join, Jasmine, too, must choose." Daire stopped, his horrified eyes sliding towards Ellyllon.

"She hasn't chosen yet?" Ellyllon breathed. "How can that be?"

His black eyes were bright with triumph, their darkness bleaching his skin an even starker white.

"It isn't set. This changes everything." He whirled. "Cathbad, tell ten of the most loyal druids to make ready. You will stay to lead the rest into battle. When the time is right, release him to his father." He leant over them. "You see, druid, you told me after all. Malachy, you will come with me to Oweynagat. And, druid, I have spared your life, so you owe me. Return to your father, to Seamus and Jasmine, and tell them where we've gone. Tell Jasmine not to doubt me; I will kill him if she doesn't come."

Chapter Twenty-Two

With Ellyllon and Cathbad gone, Malachy and Daire stared at one another.

"Forgive me," Daire repeated.

Malachy shook his head, resisting the urge to move his legs away. To drop his head, let it smack. He hadn't wanted Ellyllon to torture him, but it didn't mean he could forgive him. After all they'd been through together and he'd done this to him, and to Jasmine. And then he thought of what Cethern had told him, *a son must follow his father*. How could he expect him to choose complete strangers over his father, his beliefs? He sighed, wishing he could believe it was simple. Then, maybe, it would feel OK to hate.

"Do you really think your Goddess won't hurt her?"

"Brid is just. Our healers follow her; her words, her teachings. She will not harm her."

There was a pause. Inwardly, Malachy shook his head. All the things Jasmine had done; if that was Brid, he didn't think he'd like that kind of justice.

"What will happen, when they join? What will happen to Jasmine?"

"My father believes they will become whole."

Whole — Iomlan. The word was the same. Jasmine had described their joining as a bringing together of two equals, only Iomlan wasn't conscious, sentient, but Brid was. Would she become some kind of hybrid, a Brid/Jasmine? Or a Jasmine/Brid? Either way, the person he'd fallen in love with would be gone, the two of them subsumed into another personality entirely.

Daire's eyes searched his face. "She has not chosen."

"Yeah." He nodded. But she would, and he knew exactly what she'd choose. Drendas had seen to it. That was why he'd done what he did. A thought occurred to him.

"But will she know? Will she know that what she chooses is forever?" he asked urgently.

"Brid will speak the truth. She will hide nothing."

"But will she? If Brid doesn't tell her, will your father?"

Daire's eyes darkened, but when he didn't respond, Malachy knew he had his answer.

Abruptly, the doors swung open.

"Up," Rinnach growled at Malachy.

He lowered Daire gently to the ground. "Please don't tell her where we've gone."

Daire eyes were shining. Unable to use his hands, he tried to blink away the tears. "She will know, for Brid will feel it."

Rinnach gestured impatiently, but Malachy ignored him. "Then tell her not to come."

"But he will kill you."

"No, he won't. He doesn't have anything without me."

"Up," Rinnach repeated. Slowly, deliberately, he took out his sword.

"What are you going to do? Kill me!" Malachy sneered.

Suddenly he didn't care. He was fed up with people threatening him and pushing him around and deciding his life for him.

Rinnach pointed the blade at him. "No, I will cut you. My blade is sharp and it will hurt."

He would too; and itching to avenge his brother, he'd enjoy it. And ultimately, it wouldn't make any difference. Determined not to give him the satisfaction, Malachy climbed to his feet.

"I saved your life, not Ellyllon, so it's me you owe," he said to Daire. "Tell her not to come."

*

Outside, he blinked in the morning sunshine. The city lay beneath him; filled with the noise, sights and smells of people going about their daily lives. Beyond them, the land was quiet; in the distance a river meandered lazily through thick, green grass, framed by miles upon miles of forest, and there, on the horizon, was the pale outline of Croagh Patrick's peak. Mounted, a group of druids waited at the bottom of the slope, a chariot positioned in between them. There was no sign of Ellyllon or Cathbad.

"Move," Rinnach ordered, pushing him down the slope.

They reached the chariot. Another push, this one harder, and Malachy climbed awkwardly onto the back. His head bent and his hood up, the driver didn't even bother to look. Without a word, the druids moved off and then, with a click of the driver's tongue, the chariot went with them.

Leaving the city, they followed the road down the hill. At the bottom they turned right, off the road and onto the grassy plain. Following the road, but veering increasingly to the right they moved towards a circle of small, narrow trees. Leafless even in late summer, they looked almost black against the white, fluffy clouds. They moved closer. Malachy swivelled awkwardly, trying to see the entrance of the place they called Oweynagat, but apart from the trees he could see nothing but grass. The first druid reined in his horse and as the others followed, the chariot driver pulled back his hood and turned to look at Malachy. It was Anle. Seeing his surprise, he gave him a wink and Malachy's heart leapt. He didn't know what Anle had planned, but he was pretty sure Ellyllon hadn't intended for him to be there. Somehow, incredibly, what he'd said to him had gotten through.

Suddenly Ellyllon appeared, stepping out of the circle of trees. Immediately the druids moved forward, but Anle held back, waiting as they streamed past him. His shoulders tense, he glanced back. *Be ready*. Malachy swallowed and tightened his grip on the chariot's side. Still, Anle waited. One metre, two, three. He lifted the reins, his body angled, as if preparing to turn. Malachy stiffened. Just another metre… and then, to his dismay, the first druid looked back. Immediately, Anle raised his hand, as if to apologise, and nudged the horses on. But his body was still angled, the horses already moving slightly to the right as Anle prepared to turn and run. A flick of his arm, and the druid's horse wheeled and turned, as he rode back towards them.

"Anle, don't!" Malachy cried, afraid for him.

They stared at one another, and then, with a nod, Anle straightened, the horses straightening with him. They joined the druid. Giving them a suspicious look, he turned again and, with his hand still raised, rode alongside them.

Reaching Ellyllon, the other druids had already dismounted. With the circle of trees to their left, to their right lay a large stone slab. Flat, the edges splitting into thin, brittle shards, it seemed to rise up out of the ground. They moved closer, and now Malachy could see the two stone slabs that held it upright and the darkness between them. Made into a rough doorway, this, then, was the entrance to Oweynagat, the underground temple of the Cave of the Cats. The chariot bounced left as Anle steered around two large boulders, then shuddered to a stop just in front of it.

"Taur, bring him," Ellyllon ordered.

The first druid dismounted and grabbing Malachy's arm, pulled him out and around the chariot.

Sat low in the ground, the soil in front of the doorway had been cut away and more stones laid to create steps down. Inside it was black. Malachy shivered. He knew the stories from his childhood. If Cathbad was right, then this was the entrance to the Otherworld. The place from which the Tuatha de Danann left this world and the place from where the Sidhe (the Shee), or the fairy folk, came creeping.

Ellyllon went first. Ducking his head, he twisted sideways, slipping through the entrance and into the ground. Taur came next, propelling Malachy in front of him. He had time for one quick glance back at Anle sat watching, and then he was pushed through the doorway and down, into the black. His feet slipped on smooth, invisible stone and then, bound arms outstretched, he was scrambling, half-sliding down a loose soil slope. Part of the way down he fell, his body bouncing. He cried out as his elbow hit stone. Another bounce, and he came to rest on his side. Shocked, he lay in darkness, panting.

"Taur?" Ellyllon's voice cut through darkness.

Light flooded the cave. Ignoring the pain in his arm, Malachy sat up. It was enormous. Formed on a slope, the end furthest from the entrance was a good metre lower. Rounded, the roof and sides looked as if they'd been cut and chiselled to make the space bigger. Symbols, written in bold, colourful ink, covered almost every surface. Most were Celtic, but others belonged to no culture Malachy recognised. Nearest the entrance, they were carefully and evenly spaced, the artists' design evident, but as the cave deepened they became more frenzied, drawn like a nest of spiders crawling over one another.

Frozen, his back towards them, Ellyllon was stood in a gap in the far wall. Behind him were the outlines of more frenzied drawings. Hand raised, Taur was coming lightly down the slope. The light, Malachy realised, wasn't coming from him, or rather, not directly. High in the wall opposite, a round alcove had been chiselled and inside that lay a large, round stone. Smooth, brown and yellow veins glowed brightly, sending off warm rays of light. Acting like a bulb towards electricity, it was soaking up Taur's Iomlan and converting it into light. One by one, the other druids were coming through the entrance. Ellyllon had already gone through the gap and disappeared. Taur reached Malachy and with his free hand, helped him up. Seeing Malachy wincing in pain, he placed his hand on his elbow and focussed. Iomlan caressed the bone; soft and warming. Malachy's arm tingled. And then, abruptly, Taur let him go. He flexed his elbow. The pain had gone; Taur had healed him.

"Thank – my thanks."

Taur bowed his head, and then, grabbing Malachy's bound arms, pushed him towards the gap.

Thinking that he'd never understand these people and their strange codes of honour, that healing him was like healing an opponent in order to run him through with a sword, Malachy stepped through the gap and into a second chamber.

Narrower than the first, but with the same chiselled ceiling, the chamber was empty apart from a huge rectangular stone table sat in the centre. Made of granite, etched into the top of its smoothed, sculptured surface, were three interlocking spirals or triskelion. Inside each swirl had been placed a shallow wooden bowl, their sides touching as if deliberately placed there to create a second, three-dimensional triskelion. More shapes covered the table's sides, etched deep with thick, blunt lines. Stood behind it was Ellyllon. And behind him, a small doorway, just big enough for a person to squeeze through. Inside was dark, as if the doorway contained an invisible barrier that not even light could penetrate.

"What is this?" Ellyllon asked Taur, indicating the table.

Bringing Malachy with him, Taur moved closer.

"The triple Goddess," Taur explained. "Brid."

"No, this." Ellyllon jabbed impatiently at the bowl nearest him.

Malachy leant forward. Inside the bowl was a piece of wood the size of a finger. Blackened, and the tip flecked with ash, it looked as if it had been taken from the bottom of a fire. In the second bowl three perfectly round balls of stone nestled together, and in the last was sat a small pool of water.

"It is sacred," Taur said quietly.

Ellyllon's black eyes flashed. Reaching out, he picked up the piece of wood, and held it just above the bowl.

"Warm."

Letting the piece of wood roll into the centre of his palm, Ellyllon closed his fingers. The other druids fell back. Silence. Then Ellyllon yelled. Ear-piercing, it reverberated around the chamber. He dropped it and it fell neatly back into the bowl. Holding his wrist, Ellyllon took a step back, his face twisted in pain. Red, the skin on his fingers and palm was already beginning to blister.

"Taur!"

But he was already there. Placing his hand over Ellyllon's, he closed his eyes and focussed. Watching, Malachy could hardly believe what he was seeing; Ellyllon injured. Not even Jasmine's Iomlan had inflicted that kind of pain on him. Finishing, Taur lowered his hand and took a step back. If Ellyllon had been shaken by what had happened, he showed no sign.

"Malachy," he said, with another look at Taur.

Taur waved his hand and the cord binding Malachy's hand slowly unwound. It dropped to the ground and Malachy rubbed his wrists, trying to ease the chafing.

"Your turn," Ellyllon smiled, his eyes gleaming.

For one brief moment, Malachy considered trying to run, but with the druids crowding in behind him, there was nowhere to go. He studied the two bowls left; the one containing the water and the other, the stones. And then, bending over the bowl nearest him, he touched one of the stones with the tip of his finger. Smooth, slightly warm, it reminded him of an egg. He looked at Ellyllon.

"Pick it up."

Not knowing what else to do, Malachy did as he said. Letting the stone roll into the centre of his palm, he arched his hand, so that it touched as little skin as possible. For a moment nothing happened, and then, coming from deep inside, he saw a light. Growing stronger, it began to pulsate gently, illuminating the stone's grain, thin strands of yellow and brown, from the inside out. Intensifying, the pulse settled into a regular beat. It was, Malachy realised, with a small thrill of shock, following his heartbeat. He pulled back, his hand jerking and the stone fell. It hit the bowl with an audible crack and two, perfectly symmetrical, pieces rolled to a stop. Quartz, milk-white in colour, twinkled.

"A Godstone," a voice behind Malachy hissed.

Ellyllon's dark eyes swivelled towards the speaker then down towards the third bowl. "And the next."

Reluctantly, Malachy turned his attention toward the third bowl. Still, its surface shining silver, the water looked fresh, as if it had just been put there.

"Again." Ellyllon's voice was thick with menace.

Flexing his first two fingers, Malachy dipped them gingerly into the water. Cold tickled his skin. He pressed down, expecting to feel the bottom of the bowl, but it wasn't there. Water rose up his hand, circled his wrist then moved up his arm. With a yell, he tried to pull back, but it was as if the water were alive and refusing to let him go. It reached his elbow and then, the floor of the cave seemed to flip and, impossibly, he was flung headlong into the wet.

Gasping against the cold, he struggled upwards. Water hit the back of his throat and slid down into his lungs. Choking, unable to stop his desperate grasp for air, he broke the surface. Above him, a grey winter's sky was framed by thick green branches. A figure appeared, leaning over him, its face blurred by shadow. He knew it was Jasmine and she was talking to him, saying something he couldn't hear. She reached down towards him, their fingers met through the water and the shadow cleared. Faces covered hers, the lines and features of other women transposed onto hers, but somehow her features and bright green eyes shone through. He gave a shout of surprise and then the water was pulling him back. His hand slipped from hers and as his head fell back, water surged over his face, obscuring her.

Malachy opened his eyes. Stood next to the table, he was back in the cave, his body perfectly dry.

"What happened?" Ellyllon demanded.

He shook his head. "I don't know. I thought I was in a lake."

"The power of Brid," Taur breathed.

Behind him, the druids looked doubtfully at one another, and Ellyllon, as if sensing he was losing them to an older, more established power, shot Taur a venomous look.

"There are no Gods or Goddesses. Only the universe, the laws of nature and power. This Brid has power certainly, and greater than most. She uses our superstitions against us, the limitations of our minds. But whatever she is, inside Jasmine she is flesh and blood, with all its vulnerability and weaknesses."

Frowning, he stared at the side of the table, tracing the shapes with his eyes, as if seeing them for the first time.

"Ah," he murmured, looking up at Malachy and smiling. "Clever."

"Taur, remove this, now," he demanded, cocking his head towards the table.

*

Something shifted beneath her, like the air shimmering under a hot sun. Jasmine stirred, conscious suddenly of her surroundings. She was still sat on the riverbank, with the early morning sun shining on the water. Ellyllon, she knew, was inside Oweynagat, searching for the entrance to the Otherworld.

Jasmine, you must choose now, three voices said in unison, their tone urgent.

She turned. Seamus was watching her, his face twisted with anxiety.

How long she'd been sat there, lost in Brid's mind, she had no idea, but it only felt like minutes. Yet the sun told her differently. The other druids had gathered behind Seamus, but were facing away, back towards Cruachan. She knew Cathbad was coming. She turned back. Brid, Ellyllon; it didn't matter, they were both using Malachy to get what they wanted. She glanced down into the water, and Malachy stared back at her. Shocked, it took her a moment to realise that it was actually him. In a mirror image, he was reaching down, dipping his fingers into the same water. Only he couldn't be, for he was in Oweynagat with Ellyllon, stood next to the stone table, his hand in the sacred bowl. Knowing instantly the fluidity and malleability of all things, if only you knew what to do, she reacted before she'd realised. Iomlan flew from her and reaching down into the water, her fingers touched his. She grabbed him and using Iomlan, began pulling him through the water to her. Her heart sang. He was coming, coming back to her and to safety. His head broke free of the surface and gasping for air, his blue eyes gazed at her. But the Brids were talking again, all at once, trying to tell her something. She tried to stay focussed, but they were too distracting and Iomlan stuttered and failed. Malachy's face lowered, his eyes widening as he felt himself falling backwards. Furious, desperate to keep him with her, she pulled at him with all her strength, but it wasn't enough. His hand slipped from hers; his face disappearing back into the water. Platinum smoothed as the surface settled behind him.

Shouting for him, Jasmine scrambled to her feet. She would've launched herself into the water after him, if it hadn't been for Ferdia encircling her arms and holding her to him. On the edge of her control, Iomlan swirled. It took all her effort not knock him from her and send him spinning to the ground.

Rogha.

"Jasmine! Stop. Stop!"

Seamus was there, his hands on her shoulders as he tried desperately to calm her.

"It was Malachy. I had him, but they stopped me."

"Who? Jasmine, tell me, what happened?"

From deep inside the earth came a roar. Low, it rumbled across from the west and upwards. She felt a tremor and then the ground beneath her feet shook.

The entrance is open.

The tremor faded, disappearing as quickly as it had come. If Seamus had heard or felt its rumble, he showed no sign.

"She used our knowledge to pull him to her."

Horrified, Jasmine stared at Seamus. It wasn't her. Her lips had moved, but it wasn't her that had spoken.

Seamus' face paled. "Brid?"

"Time is brief. He has found the entrance. She must choose."

"Can't you do something?"

"She must choose. The dark one knows weakness, as water knows cracks in a stone. Her love weakens her; she cannot be trusted. We dare not face him until we are as one."

They let her go.

"Seamus?"

He leant in close. "Jas, I'm sorry, but it's the only way. Brid's right. You can't face Ellyllon like this. He'll use Malachy to manipulate you. You don't have to do this, but if you do, you and Brid have to be united."

"I can't."

Suddenly she remembered saying this to him before. At home, on her bed, when Ellyllon had pulled Malachy through the void and Seamus had asked her to go with him. She was such a coward. Malachy would do it for her in a heartbeat, but she was so scared. Scared of being subsumed into a whole and losing herself so completely, it would be as if she'd died. And yet what she'd just done had proved Brid right; she couldn't be trusted. She'd do anything for Malachy, and Ellyllon knew it. Anything. The three faces of Brid smiled. There really was no choice. She took a deep breath.

I...

"Daire!" Ferdia shouted, his voice ripping the air.

Hooves thundered. A sole rider shot towards the group, the body of a man lying astride the horse's neck. Daire. The rider slowed. Pushing at Daire's shoulders, he threw him to the ground before turning his horse and galloping back the way he came. The druids rushed towards him, Ferdia, Emer and Cethern leading.

Hands pulled gently at Daire, turning him onto his back. Faces pressed into his.

Cethern stood up. "Jasmine. Jasmine. Come, he would speak with you."

Getting to her feet, she and Seamus went over to them.

Avoiding Drendas' eyes, Jasmine looked down. Daire's face was ravaged. Iomlan had been used to torture him not once, but twice.

He will not live beyond the night.

Brid's anger flooded through her. Across the grass plain, at the foot of the hill, was Cathbad. Surrounded by druids and warriors, he was stood on the back of a red chariot edged with gold. Dressed in yellow leggings and a long, brown cloak, his hair had been pulled into a tight, high ponytail then draped across his shoulders and chest in thick golden waves. He wore no tunic, but instead had painted his skin with gold and smeared it across his lips. Around his neck, he wore a large, flat golden torc. With his head high, she could feel the arrogance emanating from him, born from the certainty that the the knowledge and power of the Tuatha de Danann was his for the taking. His birthright. As if he were the Golden One, the special one of legends.

I know you, usurper. False God.

Her eyes met Emer's as Daire struggled upwards.

"Ellyllon waits for you in the temple of Oweynagat," he gasped, his bloodshot eyes fixed on hers. "If you do not go, he will kill Malachy."

He fell back, into Ferdia's waiting arms. Letting the anger settle in the pit of her stomach, she straightened.

Come. It is time. Choose.

Pulling up her hood, she lowered her head and closed her eyes.

Chapter Twenty-Three

When she opened them again, she was inside the temple of Oweynagat. In the room behind the second chamber, facing the doorway. Stood behind the stone table, Ellyllon was talking, his back to her. Above the ground, voices roared as Cathbad's warriors hurtled towards Seamus and the druids. The battle had begun. She felt their power, the strength sending ripples through the air. Ignoring it, she took a step forward, and immediately Ellyllon turned.

"She's here," he cried, staring into the doorway.

Hidden by the darkness, he might sense her, but she knew he couldn't see her. She moved to the doorway.

"Brid?! Is it you?" He fell back, around the table and for the first time she saw the damage that had been done. "Come, see what I have found."

Slipping through the doorway, she stepped out of the darkness and into the light. A huge crack had rendered the table in two, shattering the triskelion and sending the wooden bowls rolling. The two sides thrown back, the table had been ripped open like the disembowelled carcass of an animal, revealing the steps beneath. Anger at the desecration swirled in the pit of her stomach and carefully, deliberately, she let it build.

"Brid, see the entrance to the Otherworld," Ellyllon breathed, his eyes glowing.

"I think not."

He shrugged, though she sensed his displeasure. "Then to the place between worlds. I have forced open one entrance, I can do another."

"Do you really think it is so easy? The entrance is guarded."

He laughed at that. "Yes, by you, Brid, by you. And yet here you are, *outside*. And afraid to show me your face."

In answer to him, she pulled back her hood. The druids stared at her, their eyes wide. One gasped and another swore. Enjoying their shock, she felt their urge to fall to their knees before her, and for a moment she was tempted to wave her hand and assist them, but she resisted. Instead, reaching the table, she slipped around it, letting her hand trail. She traced what was left of the symbols lovingly, and despite the damage, felt the soft warmth of the stone. Its energy tingled as it moved up her arm and down into her chest. Malachy too was staring at her, and she sensed his fear, not for himself, but for Jasmine.

"Ellyllon," she greeted him, gliding past Malachy and positioning herself carefully between them.

Seeing the movement, Ellyllon smiled. "Brid," he greeted her, bowing low.

Elegant, she thought to herself, impressed with how quickly he'd recovered. The part of her that had once been Jasmine stirred warningly, but she ignored it, knowing that his mind games and manipulations wouldn't work on her.

"Not Brid, not Jasmine."

"A union?" He understood her meaning instantly. Once more, she was impressed by his quickness. "How does it feel?" He leant towards her, his dark eyes intent, and she knew his curiosity was genuine.

"It's strange how significant the adding of one part can be to the whole. All these new thoughts, words and memories. How different we are."

"I thought you were trapped in the place between worlds. How did you escape?"

"You have forgotten much. I had no need to flee, only to will it."

"Only to will it." He took a deep breath, as if savouring fresh, sweet air. "Such power. Even the laws of physics cannot contain you."

"Physics?" Her pause was barely perceptible. "Ah, yes, Science. 'The universe is not only stranger than we imagine, it is stranger than we can imagine.'"

Ellyllon laughed, delighted, "Einstein! You learn quickly, Brid."

"All her knowledge is ours. And more, for we see what she has forgotten. And we understand, for we have been here for some time." She pointed to her chest. "Waiting for her to be ready."

"Then the power I felt was yours." He took a step towards her. "Such power, such beauty. Once tasted, never forgotten. I would I had such power. Even before, my power was as a child's compared to yours." Lowering his eyes, he slowly lifted them again, like a proud man chastened by rejection, still daring to hope. Black pupils, stark against the white, burnt into hers. "Have you thought that there might be others to join with? Someone who can give you more. Someone worthier?"

"And who might that someone be?" she teased, but the green swirl in her eyes quickened.

"I too have lived for centuries." He took another step. "But unlike you, I have lived in the world, among people, not apart. I have the knowledge of eons, of all the civilisations that have risen and fallen. All I lack is the power. But I had that once too. Besides, you have enough for both of us."

Her nostrils flared. "And you, who have lived for so many centuries and know so much, would you truly sacrifice everything you have, everything you are, to have that power again?"

He took a third step. "Perhaps not, but your power is so much the greater. And what of myself would I sacrifice? You said yourself the significance of one to the whole. My mind, my will is stronger, my design and my desire limitless. How much more of me to the whole would I give? Our union would be a meeting of giants, two burning suns that would shake the very universe. How can a girl, little more than a child, compare to that?"

He was close enough that if he reached out, he could touch her. Behind her, Malachy shifted nervously. Ignoring him, she lifted her face to Ellyllon as, smiling gently, he took the last step.

"I cannot die nor age," he murmured softly. "Even with Iomlan, this girl's body, this vessel will crumble and die. Even with your power, it cannot be sustained forever. And then what will you do? Return to your world, while you wait for another? I offer you a body that will last forever."

"You?"

Bending, he lowered his lips towards hers. "Leave her, join with me. Together we can do anything."

She laughed, still resisting. "Do you think there is anything you can give me that I can't do already?"

"I know that you long to feel the sensation of the sun on your face, water slipping across your skin, to taste the juice of an apple, the touch of a lover."

His fingers were on her arm, his touch light and caressing. In answer to him, she lifted her hand and placed it lightly over his heart.

"You forget. I know you and I've seen what you do. Your heart is empty. Dead, lifeless. Your hunger for power, your desire for what once was, has consumed you."

"But you are Brid, the triple Goddess and healer. Surely you have heart enough for the both of us? And maybe, with you, I can be redeemed and the heart of not one woman, but three, will save me. Undo all the might of the druids of Brigantes and bring this living corpse back to life."

His eyes darted right, giving Taur a meaningful look so brief she almost missed it. She sensed the other druids ready themselves as Taur prepared to pull their powers to him and unify, crystallise them into one pure pulse. It was a rare power. An aberration, a throwback to earlier times, and she wondered how Ellyllon had managed to teach it to him. Or why he hadn't taught it to Cathbad. Unless…

Thinking of Cathbad was a mistake. Separated by centuries but still kin, his blood was her blood and his pain pulled her to him. Dragged her out of the temple and through the soil, into the sunshine. The air was thick with Iomlan as druid fought against druid. Warriors dotted the grass, their bruised and bloodied bodies twisted into grotesque shapes. Most were dead or had fled the carnage. There were druid dead on both sides, but most were too evenly matched. Seamus and Drendas were stood fighting together. Stepping forward, Drendas swung his staff around in a wide arc, sending those around them scattering. Seamus followed him, using his Iomlan to keep their struggling bodies pressed to the ground. Drawing himself up, Drendas twisted his staff, holding it like a spear, and shuffled towards them.

Bent over the side of his chariot, Cathbad shouted with pain as Ronan's pulse pummelled his back. Across his right cheek was a livid red welt where Cethern's Iomlan had caught him. Cursing loudly, Cathbad focussed. Iomlan burst out of him, sending Ronan's pulse scattering. Another pulse sent him tumbling to the ground. Slowly, Cathbad straightened.

"Ronan!" Cethern screamed, slowing her horse and wheeling.

His golden hair gleaming in the sun, Cathbad turned to face her. With a wild shout, she charged at him, sending streaks of Iomlan out before her. Cathbad parried furiously, deflecting each pulse harmlessly away. Her long hair flying, she was almost on him when a slingshot smashed into her shoulder and bounced upwards. It caught the side of her head and she fell, crumpling. Smiling, Ilech lowered his hand and turned just in time to see Maine's hammer coming towards him. With Iomlan behind it, it smashed into his face, shattering the bone and knocking him, spinning and screaming, to the ground. Maine swung again and the screaming stopped. Righting himself, he hefted his hammer and turning away from Ilech's body, looked around for his next opponent.

Cathbad moved towards Cethern. Back on his feet, Ronan's Iomlan flew. It hit Cathbad's defence, the shock of it tipping him forward. As quick as cat, he was on his toes, spinning and sending a pulse back at Ronan. It caught him in the chest, pinning him as if to an invisible wall. Ronan groaned; Iomlan flew all ways as, arms flailing, he tried to free himself. Keeping his hand raised against him, Cathbad turned back to Cethern.

Lifting her head, Cethern saw him come. Her eyes glazed from the wound on the side of the head, she pointed her hand at him, but nothing happened. And then, he was beside her. Looking down, he smiled and raised his other hand.

"Cathbad!" a voice screamed. Loud, shrill and full of fury, it was barely human.

Emer appeared the other of side of his chariot. He whirled, but too late; her Iomlan cut the legs from under him, sending him reeling. Rolling over, he leapt to his feet and sending out a pulse, knocked her spinning. A stone whistled through the air. Cathbad raised his hand and it sailed away, missing him by inches. He turned back to Emer, but not quick enough; her Iomlan swept over him, the force of it knocking him flat on his back. Winded, his face twisted as he tried to push his power up and outwards, but she was too strong. He fell back, gasping for air as Ronan raced towards them. Stood in front of the trees, Anle lowered his sling.

"What are you?" Cathbad croaked, staring at Emer.

"Vengeance."

With her Iomlan pressing him tight to the ground, she bent and gently slipped his knife from his belt. Lifting it high into the air, she gazed at it as if it were the most beautiful thing in the world. And then, turning it slowly in her hand, she griped the hilt. Her fingers tightened. Suddenly her eyes swivelled, she turned her head and looking past the battlefield, stared directly at Brid.

I see you.

Brid flinched. There was a knowledge in those eyes, an understanding Emer shouldn't have. Turning back, Emer's arm jerked as she plunged the knife down. The connection to Cathbad severed, Brid was wrenched back, through the grass and the earth and down into the rock below.

"Brid? Brid?" Ellyllon's black eyes were wide, feigning concern.

His hands were on her waist, but his fingers curled downwards, itching to caress her stomach. As if it were a sign he'd been waiting for, Taur struck with the full force of the druids' combined power. Disorientated, she managed to parry and hold him at bay. But the pressure was immense, the weight of their power like a juggernaut, and her defences strained against him.

"But what if there's no other choice?" Ellyllon asked.

She felt his fingers splay, felt the part of herself that had once been Jasmine screaming at her, and suddenly she saw what he was doing. But Taur's power was too strong; it was taking all her energy just to defend herself. The air around her stomach shimmered. She tried to pull away but fast as a striking snake, he plunged his hand inside her.

The pain was excruciating. Doubled over, she heard Malachy cry out, felt him launch himself at Ellyllon. But Taur was too quick. Sending out a second pulse, he caught Malachy across the face and threw him violently away. He hit the cave wall, his body sliding to the floor. For a moment, Taur's power lessened. She pushed against it, trying to take advantage and fight back, but Ellyllon's hand had moved into the centre of her. His fingers touched Iomlan, sending shockwaves through her body. Convulsing with agony, her focus slipped. Taur blasted through the last of her defences, pinning and holding her there as Ellyllon's fingers closed on Iomlan. His grip tightened; then, with a low moan, he began to pull. Her scream ripped the air. It was like being ripped in two. Ellyllon's arm jerked. She screamed again, and as he pulled Iomlan from her, her body collapsed. But for Taur's power holding her upright, she would have fallen.

Taking a step back, Ellyllon lifted his hand. Light leaked between his fingers, staining his skin a deep, forest green tinged with brown. She tried to straighten, but her body wouldn't respond. Without Iomlan, it couldn't sustain them. Already, she could feel the Jasmine part of her slipping away.

"My," Ellyllon breathed, his eyes wide. He looked down at her. "How is this possible? How can it still be alive?"

She didn't answer. She was too busy trying to hold herself together and keep the part of her that was Jasmine alive.

"What matters," he murmured, returning his gaze to his hand, to the light that seemed almost to dazzle him.

He closed his eyes, concentrating. She sensed the effort in him and then Taur's power faded and she slid to her knees.

"Jas."

It was Malachy. Kneeling next to her, he pulled her to him, cradled her in his arms. Her head flopped back onto his shoulder. And as she gazed into his horrified eyes, she saw the understanding and wanted desperately to tell him that it was alright, but she couldn't seem to get her mouth to work.

Ellyllon opened his eyes. Smiling dreamily, as if he were savouring something very special, he opened his hand. It was empty.

"I don't know how you did that, but thank you. I waited a long time for that. Even without you, Jasmine's Iomlan was very powerful. But nothing compared to yours. I think, after all, you do need me. I would never have fallen for so simple a trick." He grinned, showing his bone-white teeth, his eyes savage. "A flattery so obviously false. Brid, I welcome you to me. Come."

Silence.

"Come, Brid." he repeated.

His eyes widened, threatened to pull her into their black, bottomless depths. She stared back at him, still not answering, and his face twitched with irritation.

"That body's dying. It's over. Unless you want to be trapped again, you have no choice. Come, I am waiting."

Ignoring him, she turned to Malachy instead.

"I'm sorry," she whispered, finding her voice at last.

There was so much more the Jasmine part of her wanted to say, but there wasn't time. She saw it hit him. He bit back a sob, his body jerking, and pressed his face into hers, feeling her breath tickle his cheek. She breathed out, her chest rose, then stopped.

Chapter Twenty-Five

She lay limp in his arms. Sensing the finality of her stillness, but unable to comprehend it, he looked into her face. Brid's eyes were open, her three faces looking past him towards Ellyllon. Beneath them, Jasmine's skin was white, her face still. His grip tightened, as if he could hold her there through pure will, but it was too late; she'd already gone.

"Brid, time is short." Ellyllon's voice was tight with impatience. "She's dead. This is your only chance. Or will I have to enter the place between worlds and come find you?!"

Too stunned to cry, Malachy glanced at Taur. To his surprise, he looked shocked, strangely bereft, as if he'd witnessed something beyond him. The other druids too; his expression mirrored on their faces.

"Brid, come to me. I have waited too long for this. It is my right!" Ellyllon shouted.

Malachy cocked his head. Something was wrong, an edge to his voice, a touch of panic that didn't quite fit. He dragged his eyes from Jasmine's face. Ellyllon's white skin glistened, as if he'd begun to sweat, and his right hand was trembling.

"Ellyllon?" Taur asked.

"Use your power, make her leave!" Ellyllon cried.

"I cannot. I do not have the power."

"Then what use are you to me?!"

The trembling in his hands was getting worse.

"Brid, come," he cried, squeezing and twisting his wrist, as if trying to force it stop. "Or do I have to force you out?"

"Then do it, if you think you can," she replied, her voice high and clear.

Everyone froze. Jasmine's body twitched in Malachy's arms. With a cry, Malachy looked down and saw four faces gazing up at Ellyllon, not three. The white, still cast to Jasmine's face was gone. Her body felt soft in his arms, but more importantly, it felt like her.

"What is this?" Ellyllon demanded angrily. His hand was shaking violently now, the tremor moving through his wrist and up into his arm.

"Did you not wonder how I, Brid, could be so easily tricked?" she asked, her voice hard and mocking. "To allow you to destroy so thoroughly what I spent so much time creating?"

Gently extricating herself, she stood up.

Ellyllon took a step back. "But I killed her. I took Iomlan from her and watched her die."

"No." She shook her head. "You did not. It is still here, as we all are still here. Do you think you are the only one who can manipulate? Show the heart what it wants to see?"

"Why would you – lie?" Clutching his arm, he took another step back.

He was sweating profusely, the sheen on his face giving his skin a yellow, sickly glow.

"Even my power cannot take the life from one who does not possess it. But your hunger, your desire for power and what you once had, was your weakness. If–"

"You've poisoned me!" Ellyllon interrupted hoarsely.

"Not poison, but power. With it I will destroy you from the inside out. If you had tried to kill this body in any other way, it would be dead. But you forget I know you." She smiled, her eyes hard. "You wanted power; I gave it you. As you kill to appease your appetite, so are you killed."

"But it can be driven out – Taur?!" Ellyllon cried, with a wild look.

Taur glanced at Brid then lowered his eyes.

"See how easily they switch their loyalty?" Brid sneered.

Taur's eyes met Malachy's. He didn't look repentant, Malachy thought, scrambling quickly to his feet. He looked calculating, as if he were thinking of a way out.

Ellyllon's face twisted as his body spasmed with pain. He staggered, somehow managed to remain upright. "Why are you doing this? What matters to you what I do to the Druid Council?"

Brid drew herself up. "You are a curse. A wound fouling the air with the stench of rotting flesh, and must be cut out. You crow, say you have the knowledge of centuries, and yet you have learnt nothing."

Across the chamber, Taur nodded to the druid on his right and, closing his eyes, began, once again, to gather the druids' power to him.

"You know our ways, our lore, you were born to them. To speak the words of your science: everything is connected. The universe must have balance, and by your death, so will it be restored. It was written I should leave my place guarding the Otherworld, not for life, but for you."

Leaping forward, Taur's druid threw out a hand towards Malachy.

"Don't you dare!" Brid spat, the green in her eyes bright with sudden, ferocious anger.

With a quick flick of wrist, she dipped her hand then raised it again and tiny specks of green light appeared on the ground in front of him. Lifting, like rain falling upwards, they slipped around him, swirling and twinkling as they closed in on him. His Iomlan faded. Moving as one, like a voile curtain, the lights inched closer. They touched his outstretched hand and he shrieked in pain, the skin blistering instantly. Behind him, Taur twisted away and then, flinging out both arms, threw everything he could at her.

Brid's hand shot out. It hit her defences, the force of it making her body rock, but she held firm. Taur pressed harder, pulling more and more power to him, and turning it on her in one, perfect pulse. The air crackled with energy, the pressure even greater than before, but still she held him. Malachy backed away to the far wall. Taur groaned, his face twisting with effort. A low rumble, the floor shook and behind Malachy a crack appeared. He jumped sideways as shards of stone dropped, missing him by centimetres. They hit the floor, shattering and splintering into thin, jagged pieces.

Inside the lights, the druid sobbed as he pulled his hand in towards his chest. Around him, unnoticed, the lights began to throb. Once again they shifted, growing larger and stronger, as if feeding on his pain. He turned towards Taur just as the lights touched the edge of his cloak. It caught instantly, the fire bursting upwards with a loud whoosh. Engulfed, the druid screamed in pain, the sound piercing over the roar of the flames. Malachy covered his face with his arm, unable to bear the sounds as they echoed through the chamber and up towards the surface. And then, mercifully, it was over. The screams stopped. Malachy lowered his arm. There was nothing there. No body, no bones, no ash; nothing but a scorched and blackened stain and green, throbbing lights.

Brid pulled back her head and shouted, a loud, guttural sound that made the hair on the back of Malachy's neck lift, and the lights scattered. They hurtled across the chamber, blasting into stone and through bodies. They hit Taur first and he burst into flames, his body incinerated before he'd realised, then the other druids. Tearing through skin and flesh, setting them alight before bursting into the first chamber and up and out, into daylight and across the grass to the battlefield.

"Brid, finish me!" Ellyllon croaked, his voice weak.

He'd crawled to the end wall and half-sitting, half-lying, was curled into the stone. Joining him, Brid crouched low so she could look directly into his eyes. Flinching with each new spasm of pain, he stared back at her.

"It will not be long. But first," she cocked her head, "I want him to see it. He has earned the right."

Footsteps sounded, moving quickly across the first chamber, then Seamus' head appeared.

"Seamus," Brid greeted him, straightening.

Stepping inside, Seamus' eyes widened as he took in the chamber's emptiness. Behind him followed Cethern, a livid bruise spreading across one temple from the side of her face. Then came Ronan, and Ferdia leading Drendas.

"It is finished. The balance will soon be restored. Come, Seamus, see."

Spotting Ellyllon, he stopped.

"He's dying," Malachy explained.

Seamus glanced at him, but his eyes didn't seem to want to focus. Skirting the table, he crossed the chamber to where Ellyllon lay.

"Ellyllon," Seamus said softly, kneeling next to him.

Black eyes fixed wearily on him. "Seamus."

"I'm sorry."

Ellyllon laughed, then grunted in pain. "Spare me your pity. I should've waited. Watched Cormac gut you before I came through the portal."

Another spasm, more violent than the last, and his body began to shake uncontrollably. His head rolled back, he gave a small, helpless cry of exhaustion and then, with a final shudder, his body lay still.

*

"Is he…?" Malachy asked, coming closer.

Seamus nodded, unable to speak. Malachy looked at Brid, but her whole attention was fixed on Ellyllon. Wide open, his eyes and mouth were black against his white face, reminding Malachy of the necklace Ellyllon had given Jasmine. Only… he leant forward. In the centre of the black was a tiny pinpoint of light. Increasing, it radiated outwards, covering his eyes and mouth until they were green and glowing.

"By the Gods, what is it?" Cethern cried.

As if in answer, Seamus scrambled hastily to his feet. Still increasing, the light spilled onto Ellyllon's face. Spread across his skin to his hair and then down his neck towards his torso. They watched helplessly, as slowly, inexorably, it swallowed his body. But it didn't stop there. Its glow intensifying, it began to creep outwards, across the floor and walls towards them. They fell back. It reached the stone table, exploding with a sudden burst of energy, and green light shot across the room, dazzling them. Malachy shut his eyes, but the light was still there, burning its way into his brain. He gritted his teeth, trying to resist the urge to scream; then, abruptly, it was gone.

Tentatively, Malachy opened his eyes. The chamber was back to how it was before they'd entered; the stone table fixed and the three wooden bowls neatly in place. Ellyllon was dead, his head fallen forward onto his chest. Only it wasn't the Ellyllon, Malachy knew. It was his human self, how he'd once been, with strong features, long black hair and deep brown eyes.

"You made him human again," Seamus said.

Brid shook her head. "Not human. Half-God."

"Half-God?!"

She nodded. "Half-God, but still my kind, my kin."

"But I thought he was druid!"

"As did he. He had forgotten much."

"That's why the Druid Council couldn't take all his power. Why he retained more of himself than the others."

She nodded again. "His was the severest of punishments, but his crimes were great."

"But why didn't the other… Gods intervene?"

"His birth was a crime. A God's power is too great for a half-God/ half-druid to wield wisely."

So, in the end, it came down to something as simple as that, Malachy thought grimly, sharing a look at Seamus. *The very first thing Seamus warned Jasmine about when she discovered Iomlan: power corrupts.*

Seamus nodded, seeming to read his mind. "And absolute power corrupts absolutely."

Brid lifted her hand and the Godstones inside the wooden bowl began to glow with a soft white light. Immediately the lines around it illuminated, the light following them across the table, like power through a circuit. The symbols glowed.

Seamus joined Malachy.

"What about Jasmine?"

No answer. One hand snaked sinuously across the back of his

shoulders.

"Seamus?" Malachy cried in alarm. "You can't be serious? You can't let her; she only did it to save me!"

He tried to break free, but Seamus' other arm was around him, holding him tight.

"Malachy, you can't. It was her choice."

"I don't care!" Malachy strained against him, but using Iomlan to help him, he was too strong.

Brid had finished. Turning from the symbols, she looked straight at him. For one brief moment, there was no Brid, only Jasmine, and then she turned away. He blinked. She was gone. Just like that. No power, no ceremony. One moment she was there and the next, gone; lost to him forever. He shut his eyes.

*

When he opened them again, they were outside, the entrance to Oweynagat in front of them. Emer was sat on Cathbad's chariot, cradling Daire's head in her hands. Drendas, Cethern, Ferdia and Ronan appeared next to them. Emer looked up, but she didn't speak. Incredibly, Anle was there too, watching him sadly. Rousing, Malachy pushed against Seamus and he let him go.

"Why didn't you do something?" he demanded, rounding on him.

Seamus' eyes were sad. "It was too late. Once Jasmine joined with Brid there was nothing anyone could do."

"So why did you let her?" Malachy shouted.

Seamus just looked at him, and for a moment he was so angry, angrier than he'd ever been in his life, and all he wanted to do was to punch him. But he couldn't; he knew all too well why she'd done it.

"Malachy," Seamus said softly. "I've lost her too. And we're not the only ones to have lost someone." He gazed at Emer's head bent over Daire. "You know, I think it's time we went home."

Chapter Twenty-Six

The bus pulled away and Malachy began walking up the hill towards his house. They'd been back almost five weeks. Five weeks. Long enough to make it all seem like a dream, although sometimes, in the middle of the night, it was coming home that felt like a dream. A magpie flew across the hedgerow, shouting. Malachy turned away. She was gone, as finally as if she'd died, and he had no choice but to accept it. Time, Seamus had said knowingly, but not for the first time he wondered how much time it was going to take for him to wake up and not think of her. Maybe he'd never get over it. He'd be like John pining after Jasmine's mum, only without the second chance.

His mother was home when he got there, hovering in the background as he dumped his schoolbag and changed his clothes. She was trying not to fuss, knowing that it irritated him. Appreciating the effort, even as her quiet, anxious look set his teeth on edge, he gave her a quick kiss. And then he was outside, breathing deeply in the cold, fresh January air. It wasn't their fault. Returning as inexplicably as he'd left, there were too many unanswered questions and he'd changed too much. Become old before his time, so that even his friends irritated him; obsessing over the smallest, most trivial of things. Life was short as it was precious. Why couldn't they just get on with it? At the road, Malachy turned right, heading inevitably for Seamus' house and the only person who understood.

Jasmine's house came into view. This was the worst part. There were too many memories and he dreaded seeing her mum. He wouldn't know what to say to her. Especially now she knew everything. Seamus and John had told her not long after they'd returned, and from what Seamus had said he'd half-expected to see John gone and the house on the market. But against all the odds, they were still here, still together, clinging on.

Seamus was in his side garden, bent double as he covered the last of a newly planted row of garlic. He'd extended his vegetable patch a few weeks ago, cut and sliced the grass away and dug the soil like a man possessed.

"I can't taste the stuff they sell in the shops." He'd explained to Malachy when he found him raking the earth. "It's full of chemicals."

Malachy knew exactly what he meant. As soon as they'd arrived back, he'd smelt the difference in the air, the toxins and the pollution. And the land wasn't much better. Even now, he could still feel the chemicals covering everything like a translucent film.

"Isn't it a bit early to plant?" he asked, looking at the neat row of bumps.

"It's garlic, it likes the frost."

He flapped his hand towards the back yard. "Come and have a look at this."

Malachy followed him across the yard to the front of the stone barn. Sat nestled into the wall was a greenhouse.

"I'm getting a heater for it. So I can plant early."

"What will you do with it all? The vegetables, I mean."

"Sell them, give them away. It doesn't matter. What matters is the growing."

It was better than feeling sorry for yourself, or waiting endlessly, hopelessly, for her to return.

"What do you need me to do?" Malachy asked, metaphorically rolling up his sleeves.

*

Winter slipped into spring. Keen to grow his vegetables organically, Seamus had visited an Organic Centre in the nearby county of Leitrim and come back with all sorts of ideas. So different to farming, it had piqued Malachy's interest and he'd thrown himself into Seamus' plans with gusto. And slowly, tentatively, like the first of the seeds that were germinating, an idea began to take shape in Malachy's head. Easter came and went. The end of March and, with his exams looming, he knew exactly what he wanted to do. He didn't just want to farm the land, he wanted to protect it.

*

The first Saturday in April, and Seamus was in the greenhouse when Malachy came around the side of the house. Stood with his back to him, one hand frozen in midair, he seemed lost in thought. He didn't even notice when Malachy crossed the yard and peered in through the glass.

"Seamus, are yer OK?" Malachy asked, tapping lightly.

Stirring, Seamus turned to look at him, but his eyes didn't seem to want to focus.

"Seamus?" He tapped again.

With a visible effort, Seamus opened the door and came out. "I'm grand."

"Are you sure?"

His eyes focussed. "Of course. Time for a break. Tea?"

*

They sat drinking tea on the bench in front of the house.

"I was thinking," Seamus said suddenly.

"Of Jasmine?"

"No, Grainne. Wondering what she's up to."

"You miss her?"

Seamus laughed. "Who wouldn't! Me and Granuaile, the pirate queen. Ya couldn't make it up!" Sobering, he took another drink. "But even more, I miss Iomlan. I'm tired of hiding it. Of not being who I should be."

"Like Cethern."

Seamus nodded. "Like Cethern."

Malachy took a gulp and swirled it around his mouth before swallowing. He could understand his restlessness and the lure of someone like Grainne, but he'd lost Jasmine and didn't think he could bear to lose him as well.

"You know, Grainne is a pirate. She kills people."

"And she's ruthless, and manipulative. And there's no proper medicine or toilets."

"Or toilet paper."

"True," Seamus agreed, smiling. But his eyes were sad.

"C'mon, we've weeds to pull," Seamus said suddenly, changing the subject. Downing the rest of his tea, he stood up.

*

Friday, a week later and coming in from school, Malachy's mother called him from the kitchen.

"Yeah?" Letting his bag slide off his shoulder, he dropped it in the middle of the hall.

She appeared in the doorway, a small, white envelope in one hand. "I found this on the doormat." She held it out to him. "It's for you. I think it's from Seamus."

He took it from her and ripping open the envelope, read the first two lines.

"Shite!"

"Malachy, Malachy," she called after him as he ran down the hall. "Yer bag – don't leave it there."

But it was too late. He was already out of the house and running down the drive.

*

Breathing heavily, Malachy reached Seamus' house and slowed. John was on the bench, waiting for him.

"Where is he?" Malachy demanding, flying up the path.

"You're too late. He's already gone."

Malachy stopped. "But he wouldn't go without saying goodbye."

"Did you read it?" John asked, eyeing the letter.

"No, not all of it."

"Then I think you should." He moved along the bench, giving Malachy room to sit. "It's his goodbye."

Reluctant, Malachy sat. Slipping the letter from the envelope, he unfolded it.

Malachy,

You'll be off to college soon, doing new things, meeting new people, and that's as it should be. With Jasmine gone, and now myself, you're the last of us. You and John are the closest thing I have to a family, and he won't take it, so I've signed the house and farm over to you. John will look after it until you've finished college and then it's up to you. Live on it or sell it, I'll have no need for it, for I won't be back. I'm sorry for the way things turned out. Maybe its for the best. The time for magic's passed. There's no place for it, or me, in the modern world.

Seamus.

Malachy refolded the letter.

"What about Bran?" he asked John, sliding it back into the envelope.

"We'll take him back. He's used to us anyway."

"Do you know what it says?"

"Yeah, Seamus told me."

"What do you think?" John cocked his head quizzically. "What should I do?"

"What do you want to do?"

"I don't know," Malachy admitted, shaking his head. "Go to college."

"Then why don't you keep it. Decide after. I can look after it while you're away."

"Yeah." Malachy looked down at the envelope. "Do you think he believes there's no place for him here?"

"I think," John replied slowly, carefully, "he was tired. What happened to Jasmine was the last straw. I think he blamed himself."

"Do you blame him?"

John sighed. "I'd like to. It would make everything so much easier, but I can't."

"No, me neither."

They didn't speak after that, but still, Malachy felt better.

*

April moved into May. The days flew by as Malachy juggled revision with helping his father on the farm and tending Seamus' garden. Saturday evening. His mum was out and his dad moving the cattle. Coming back from checking the vegetables, Malachy turned into the driveway. He stopped. A horse was stood by the side of the house, its back to him.

"What the—?!"

There was something familiar about it. Malachy's heart began to pound. The horse turned its head as if sensing his presence.

"Eoin?"

Feeling strange, he moved towards him. He touched the horse's rump, let his hand slide along his back and onto his neck. Turning, the horse nuzzled into his neck, saying hello.

"Eoin, it *is* you!"

Malachy rubbed around his ears. "How did you get here?"

It must've been Seamus. He'd found him with Grainne and had brought him to him. But why hadn't he stayed, even for a few minutes, to say hello, or was it goodbye?

"Mal."

It was her. She came around the side of the house as if she'd never been away. He took a step back, into Eoin's side.

"Oh, shit, sorry Mal. Are you OK?" She reached out her hand, but he pulled away.

"Why are you here?" he croaked.

He swallowed noisily, trying to lubricate his throat.

"I've come home."

"But you can't. You're—" He stopped, unable to say her name.

"What?" The penny dropped. "Oh, no, it's me, Jasmine. Brid's gone."

Her eyes were their normal brown, but he still couldn't be sure. Just when he thought he was getting used to things without her, here she was.

"But you could change that, pretend."

Don't be stupid, he told himself crossly, *why would she do that?*

"I know, but I'm not. It really is me: Jas."

She smiled, trying to show him everything was alright and he knew she wasn't lying. But now he knew it was really her, he became angry.

"But you chose Brid. I saw you joined and – she said it couldn't be undone. And it's been months."

"I know. I'm sorry Mal, but it's a bit complicated. There were things she wanted to show me."

"So now you're telling me you didn't choose her?!"

"I thought I had, but I hadn't." She flapped one hand impatiently. "It's hard to explain, but when I chose, I didn't really want it, so it wasn't a real choice. And Brid didn't really want me if I didn't truly want her."

There were too many wants. They made Malachy's head spin.

"I don't understand. Why do all that if she didn't want you?" he asked irritably.

"Because of Ellyllon and what he'd do to – everything. At the start all she wanted was to defeat him, but then she got a taste for living again. I don't think me and Brid were very compatible. I'm too different. Too modern. Or maybe I'm too mouthy." She grinned, just like her old self, and his treacherous heart skipped a beat. "But I am from London. Like I said, she just needed me to defeat Ellyllon."

"So what happened to her?"

She grinned, managing to look unbearably smug. "I'll tell you later."

Infuriated, he found himself bristling. "Later?!"

"I have to go home. I haven't seen mum or – John."

"So that's it?! You come back, dump Eoin on me then feck off again!"

She reached out and for a moment, Malachy thought she was going to try and touch him again, but she rubbed Eoin's nose instead. "I'm not sure how you'll explain him, but he's kinda my way of saying sorry."

"Sorry?! But it's been months! I thought you were gone for good!"

"I know, I'm sorry, but there was nothing I could do."

Slipping past him, she moved towards the drive. He watched her go, open-mouthed. She kept saying it, but she didn't sound the slightest bit sorry.

"I've got a new girlfriend, you're too late!" he shouted angrily.

He winced; he'd wanted to puncture her smugness, but had only managed to sound petulant, childish.

Stopping at the gate, she swivelled and, with a mischievous grin, cocked her hip at him. "No, you haven't. You forget, Brid sees everything. Come round about eight."

Stepping through the gateway, she was out, onto the road and away.

"Well, she didn't see that, because I won't be there," he muttered, absentmindedly stroking Eoin's head.

Eoin's ears twitched. He bobbed his nose and pulled away.

Malachy tutted. "Don't even think of taking her side. Not if yer want to be fed."

The house came into view through the trees. It looked good, better than when she'd last seen it. The outside had been painted, the guttering repaired, and smoke curled out of one of the chimneys despite the day's warmth. Her stomach fluttered. She felt sick. Seeing Malachy had been hard enough, but her mum and John… The confidence she'd shown Malachy was a lie. A show Brid had taught her. Inside, she felt like a little girl; quivering with excitement and fear. Of course, Brid couldn't see everything, and even if she could, she, Jasmine, couldn't.

*

The car was on the driveway. She opened the gate and to her surprise it didn't catch and scrape on the concrete. They'd fixed it. They'd fixed the garden too. The lawn was short and neat and its edges widened into borders and filled with tall, late spring flowers. Slipping around the house, Jasmine couldn't resist a peek through the back window, but the kitchen was empty. She reached the door, pressed down on the handle and taking a deep breath, pushed it open. The smell of home cooking wafted over her. The oven hummed, as if full of pride at the deliciousness being created inside it. Just the thought of it made her stomach gurgle. Real, tasty food. A voice called from upstairs, following the footsteps that were thudding down the stairs. Blinking back tears, Jasmine turned to face them.

It was John. He stopped when he saw her; one hand clutched at the side of the staircase.

"I thought I felt – but I thought I was wrong."

"Hello, Dad." She smiled weakly, feeling foolish. She'd rehearsed the words so many times, but they still sounded awkward.

His eyes widened. "You know?! Seamus told you?"

"No, I sort of guessed."

"And what do you–" He stopped, unable to continue.

"It's OK. Actually, it's better than OK."

Rushing to her, he threw his arms around her.

"You know he's gone," he said softly, holding her tight.

"Yeah."

His grip tightened, threatened to cut off her breath.

"John? John?"

Letting her go, he stepped to one side. Stood in the doorway, she looked older than Jasmine remembered, the grey in her hair devouring the brown.

"Jas?!" Her mum cried, her eyes filling with tears.

Something inside her broke. Sobbing, they fell into each other's arms.

*

Stood at her bedroom window, Jasmine looked at her watch. Twenty past eight and still no sign of Malachy. Maybe she'd got it wrong and his feelings had changed. Six months was a long time. But more than that, maybe he wanted a normal life. One that didn't involve being pulled into a void by a power crazed demigod. Sighing, she moved back to her bed and threw herself down. She'd give him an hour and then she'd go back downstairs with her mum and John (no, not John; dad!). Turning, she pulled up her pillow and used it as a bolster against the headboard. They'd talked for hours, through dinner and beyond. There had been so much they'd wanted to know, so much to explain, although Jasmine had skipped over the worst parts, or simply missed them out altogether. Some things would have to wait until she and John were on their own. Seamus would have told him some things; the bits he'd known, anyway. She checked her watch again. Twenty-eight minutes past.

"Jas, Jas." It was her mum calling her from downstairs. Her heartbeat quickened. He'd come.

Closing the bedroom door, she turned to look at him. He was stood with his back to the window.

"I wasn't sure you'd come."

He folded his arms. "I thought you saw everything."

"I wish." She smiled crookedly at him. "I was joking."

"Very funny." Unfolding his arms again, he made as if to leave. "If there's nothing else, I've revision to do."

"But you've only just got here!"

"Yeah, well, I shouldn't've come."

"So, why did you then?"

"I don't know. I wish I hadn't." He sighed impatiently. "Look, you can't just come back and expect everything to be the same. I thought it was my fault, that you'd sacrificed yerself for me. All these months I've been blaming myself… you could've let me know, sent a message through Seamus, anything."

"I know it's hard, but I couldn't. I thought it was forever. I didn't know until later, and by then it was too late. We had to finish."

He frowned. *Finish what?* She could almost see the words running through his head. She waited for him to say them out loud, but he didn't.

"So, what happened to her? Brid?" he asked eventually.

"She joined with Emer."

"Emer!"

She smiled. "Yeah, I know."

Stunned, he sank down onto the edge of her bed. She shifted, fighting the urge to join him. It was too soon. He was still angry with her; one wrong move and he'd be gone.

"I can't believe it. Why Emer?"

Slipping around the bed, she moved to the window and looked out. That way he couldn't see her face. "Actually, it's perfect, or was perfect. Emer was from that time, that culture, and her power was much greater than anyone guessed, even Drendas. I think. Some of his power was actually hers; that's why he was so powerful."

"But how? Surely he'd know?"

"I don't understand it meself, but Emer was born with Brid's knowledge and skill. She knew how to do things no other druid could. But she also knew what would happen and understood that no one could know. In a way, she was waiting for it her whole life."

"That doesn't make sense. She was born before any of this happened. If anything, you'd be the one born with the knowledge."

"Oh, I had some of it too. Seamus said I was a fast learner, remember."

He smiled at her. "Apart from almost dropping me on my arse."

"Yeah, but I didn't."

Trying to look casual, she joined him on the bed. He looked, but he didn't say anything. More importantly, he stayed where he was.

"What happened to Drendas?"

"Brid changed under Emer's influence. She was always a healer, but she became less of a Goddess and more a druid. But she was different to the other druids; she had her own teachings, her own ways. I suppose, like, I dunno, Buddha. I can see why the Christians adopted her as Saint Bridget, her influence was so strong. Drendas became her right-hand man, her helper."

"Ironic."

"Totally. Of course, he changed his attitude to women druid pretty quick, but I think, in the end, it was genuine."

"What about Cethern?"

"That was hard. She was just beginning to build a relationship with her daughter and she lost her all over again. Of course, they saw each other, but it wasn't the same. But I think it helped when she and Ronan got together."

"Ronan?"

"One of the druids."

"And Ferdia?"

Her smile faded. "Brid healed Daire as much as she could. Enough for Ferdia, although he could never be the same."

"So Drendas' children suffered more than he did."

"Yeah. I guess life still isn't fair."

"So what now?" He gazed into her eyes.

Her stomach fluttered. "Haven't you got revision?"

"Oh, I can stay for a bit," he replied lightly, leaning forward.

They kissed. And again; harder this time, their bodies pressing into one another. Malachy's right hand traced the line of her waist and moved upwards.

"I've got something – it's in the drawer," she murmured, her mouth wet against his.

"So have I. It's in me pocket." He laughed, falling backwards on the bed and pulling her with him.

*

Malachy was fast asleep. Taking care not to wake him, she got out of bed and putting on her dressing gown, went downstairs. John was in the kitchen making a drink of hot chocolate for him and her mum.

"D'ya want one?" he asked, lifting the tin at her.

"No, thanks." She paused. "No, wait, yes please. I haven't had one for ages."

She watched him in silence.

"Is mum OK? She's not freaked?"

John stirred her cup furiously. "Of course she is. I'm freaked, let alone her." He paused. "Things OK with Malachy?!"

She flushed. "Yeah. You don't mind, do you? I know mum doesn't."

"Of course not. I'm not that old or that hypocritical. Yer old enough; almost an adult. As long as you're sensible."

They shared an awkward look. Now the lines had been established, they both wanted to change the subject.

"Anyway, here's yer chocolate." He handed her the cup and, after a quick blow, she took a tentative sip.

"Lovely. Thanks."

"Let me give this to ya mum, and I'll be back."

She waited, blowing and sipping alternatively.

"What did you want to tell me?" John asked, coming back into the kitchen.

Pulling the door to behind him, he grabbed his hot chocolate and joined her at the table.

"How do you know I've got something to tell you?"

He gave her a pained look. "Jas, please."

"Sorry." She took another sip. "With Seamus gone, I need someone to help me. I can't do this on my own."

John lowered his mug. "Do what?"

"I said Brid didn't want me, but that's not totally true. She showed me all that stuff because she wanted me to do something for her. By now Brid's gone, but not before she saw what was coming. Climate change, what we're doing to the planet; it's like Ellyllon all over again. The earth's lost its balance and it's all our fault. Seamus was right; we can't just take and take, we have to give back. We are druid, or the descendants of druid. I promised Brid, if there's a way to stop it, I have to try."

"What about Malachy?"

"I'll tell him, eventually, but it's too soon. It's not fair on him." Playing with the rim of her mug, she smeared the chocolate with her finger.

"I think you should talk to him. Have you seen Seamus' garden?"

She shook her head. "No. Why?"

"It's incredible what he and Malachy achieved working with nature instead of trying to suppress it. Maybe what happened has affected Malachy as profoundly as you. Maybe you should trust him." He paused, letting it sink in. "What will you do?"

"The first thing is to find other druid. We're stronger together."

He leant forward. "Tell me, was Brid really a Goddess?"

She laughed. "I suppose it depends what you think a Goddess is. I prefer to think of her as like druid, only far more powerful. Her DNA is human; well, sort of. Our connection wasn't perfect and there was a lot she didn't want me to know, but I saw flashes of things, snippets."

She stopped, thinking she was making it all sound so easy, as if her time with Brid had been so natural and so painless. But not even Brid could have forseen the depth of their incompatibility. The difference that over time seemed to get bigger not smaller, until it threatened to pull their joined minds apart. But to separate hadn't been easy either, and it wasn't the clean break she was letting Malachy and John think it was. But how could she explain it without freaking them out? Opposite her, John was speaking.

"So, with this plan of yours, what do you want me to do?"

She grinned. "Just what you're doing. I can't do this alone; no one can."

He shook his head. "Seventeen; and I was wrong, you're already an adult. When did you get so mature, so grown-up?"

Her grin widened. "I forget, but I think it was about two thousand years ago."

*

Back in her room, she slipped into bed next to Malachy, gently pulling on the duvet to cover herself without waking him. He was warm and she pressed her body into his to get the heat.

"Jas?" he asked sleepily, the cold of her waking him.

"Sorry, go back to sleep," she whispered, brushing his face with her lips.

"You're freezing!" he exclaimed, properly awake. "Where have yer been?"

She looked at him, wondering if she should tell him her conversation with John, but almost immediately decided against it. There was plenty of time later. Now she just wanted to sleep in the arms of the person she loved more than anyone else in the world.

"You're going to miss him?" he asked, misreading her silence.

"Yeah."

"Maybe we'll see him again," he said hopefully, putting his arm around her, and pulling her to him. "We could always go back to see him and Grainne."

"Yeah, maybe."

But she knew they wouldn't. Moving through time was serious; it wasn't for holidays or visits. If it hadn't been for Brid, who knew what damage they could have done? But at least she'd been able to say goodbye, and seen Seamus happy with Grainne. And more, importantly, knew exactly who he was. It was Brid's last gift to her. Showing her how, one day, against all the odds, Seamus and Grainne would have a daughter. Deliberately obscuring her to hide her power, she would marry and have children of her own, and the family strands would narrow down the centuries into a single line. Culminating into a family of eight, where the youngest, a boy, would gain a power only to lose it, before moving to England and falling in love with the girlfriend of his best friend. Faint, the bloodline diluted almost to the point of nothingness, and yet, it was still there, still strong enough to count. She sighed, for a moment back in Grainne's castle with Seamus, listening as he gave her his last bit of advice. A trace of green swirled across her eyes; faint, it was gone as quickly as it came. No more secrets. She'd tell them tomorrow. She snuggled down, finding the spot in his shoulder that fitted her head so perfectly it seemed to belong to her, and closed her eyes.